BOUND BY BLOOD

Shawn David Brink

Bound by Blood, by Shawn David Brink

© 2024, Shawn David Brink

Tell-Tale Publishing, LLC

Wise Words Publishing, a subsidiary of Tell-Tale Publishing Group

Swartz Creek, MI 48473

Tell-Tale Publishing Group supports the right to free expression and the value of copyright. The purpose of copyright is to encourage writers and artists to produce the creative works that enrich our culture. The scanning, uploading, and distribution of this book without permission is a theft of the author's intellectual property. If you would like permission to use material from the book (other than for review purposes), please contact: permissions@tell-talepublishing.com. Thank you for your support of the author's rights.

Printed in the United States of America

ACKNOWLEDGMENTS

Bound by Blood would have never been possible without help from others. I appreciate you all.

Special thanks to Elizabeth Fortin and her staff at Tell-Tale Publishing. Your editing skills and eye for detail elevated this book to new heights.

To my literary agent, Christopher Liverman, I appreciate your support, expertise, and perpetual upbeat attitude.

To my wife Katie and my children Zoe, Joshua, Elijah, and Paige; thanks for your patience, honest feedback, and for allowing me to constantly bombard you with nutty story ideas.

To my readers, thank you for being you and for reading my books. You're the best!

To all the book reviewers who have reviewed or will review this work, I appreciate your opinions and feedback.

To all those who helped me, but who are not listed here – You're awesome. Thanks for the help.

Finally, to God: Thank you for everything. I don't always understand your ways, but I know you love me and take care of me. I will follow you always. Thank you, Jesus.

Seth waited on the sidewalk. Even there he could hear his mother's hateful voice and venomous language. It passed easily through the dilapidated walls of the clapboard house. Her boyfriend took the brunt of the onslaught. Seth didn't really care though. This man was only his mother's flavor of the week.

He heard the unmistakable sound of breaking glass. That was usually his queue to leave and come back later.

This time though, he would not be coming back. He turned from the house and walked away.

CHAPTER 1

The high priest's dark gaze sent a chill down Seth's back.

He withstood the pressure of that stare, but it wasn't easy. He wondered how it affected Jason, his identical twin. He stood so close that their shoulders touched – two blond-haired, blue-eyes men. Around them, the Kinship gathered with obvious interest.

This room was dark except for the twinkling light of many tiny flames. They flickered from candles held by every member of the Kinship. Each one held a candle with the exception of the high priest, Jason, and Seth.

The Kinship were uttering various mantras and incantations, an offering of noise to their benevolent spirits, spirits that Seth wasn't sure even existed. When the priest raised his hands, the sudden silence felt ominous.

The stillness beckoned. Seth could feel it. *Yes, something existed. Maybe not spirits, but something.*

He wondered if Jason felt it. He was sure his brother believed the idea of spirits here. Jason hade a two-year head-start in the Kinship. No doubt he believed it all.

The priest wore only a black leather kilt and unbuttoned matching vest that exposed his bare chest. Scattered across his skin, pagan symbols emphasized his devotion. Some were tattoos. Others appeared to be carved or even burned into his flesh.

Of the carvings, some were old and scared, raised and pale. Others were fresher. One still glistened with fresh blood.

The priest looked like a psychotic biker, the sort that even bad girls didn't date. His blond beard was long and unkept as was the matted tangle of hair on his head. His tanned skin was weathered rather than a healthy glow.

This was all new to Seth, new and terrifying.

Part of him wanted to run away. He wasn't sure anymore that this was where he belonged.

He wanted it to be where he belonged. Jason had certainly talked the Kinship up – told him how they'd rescued him from the streets two years earlier and how they could do the same for him, if he only bought into their beliefs hook, line, and sinker.

In the end, he didn't run. How far could he get? And even if nobody stopped him, could he outrun the Spirits, if indeed that's what they were?

Why am I here? he wondered. *What did the Kinship want with him? What was in it for them?*

There's always a quid pro quo. He'd learned that from his mother.

He could only say why he was here. *Because of my brother.*

Unlike Seth, Jason seemed certain that the Kinship was where he belonged. He'd spent most of the last few hours trying to convince Seth about why he should feel the same.

All Seth saw was the power of two years of indoctrination. He'd almost ran away with him back then. Staying with Mom wasn't an easy decision, and Seth never blamed Jason for running away. What kept him from leaving was his suspicion that something might happen to their mom.

He should have cared more about Jason. Their mom, Amanda, was Seth and Jason's flesh and blood mother, but that was where the relationship ended.

Because of her life choices, her sons suffered deplorable living conditions. In fact, the only thing that prevented them from being homeless was Amanda's ability to keep men around. These men secured a roof over their heads and supplied Amanda with what she needed to feed her addictions, but they provided little else.

Quid pro quo arrangements abounded between Amanda and her men, and the brothers were rarely part of the negotiations. The boys were allowed to live in the house, Amanda always made sure of that, but the boys needed more than a roof over their heads. They needed a father.

Seth used to fantasize that their real father would come home, kick all the other men out, and get Mom cleaned up. Then, they would all be just one big happy family, eating dinner at the table and playing catch down at the park.

Seth's fantasy was a pipe dream. Neither he nor Jason had ever met their real father. He'd left before they were born, which probably meant that he was no less a loser than their mother.

What hurt Seth most was the fact that Amanda didn't seem to mind the presence of all these strange men. All that mattered was that she got what she needed from them.

None of Amanda's men ever laid a hand on the boys. These types always looked for the easiest targets. The boys stuck together to ensure they would not be easy targets.

The decision to run away was a hard one for Seth to make. He'd always hoped that somehow, he could save his mom. Eventually though, he understood that she was beyond saving.

When Seth ran away, he searched the streets for his brother. Unfortunately, Jason wasn't easy to find. After a few days, he became desperate. By this time, he had no food, friends, or protection.

Finally, Jason heard his brother was searching the city for him. They reunited on 42nd Street. From 42nd Street, Jason took Seth directly to the Kinship and introduced him to the high priest.

The high priest's name was Cain. He seemed happy to meet Seth – almost too happy. Immediately, he called for an official Kinship gathering and required all to bring initiation candles.

While the Kinship gathered, Cain spoke to the brothers in private about a prophecy which the Spirits foretold. "Two identical brothers would come separately and when they joined forces, their power would be greater than the sum of their parts." Cain believed that this prophecy was about to be fulfilled in Seth and Jason – it had been revealed to him through the rolling of bones.

Jason nodded vigorously throughout Cain's monolog.

But Seth remained skeptical.

***

The Kinship crowded in close, their faces reflecting the candlelight in ghoulish fashion. They appeared enthralled with Cain's story.

Cain finished telling of the prophecy and how he'd been given knowledge regarding Seth and Jason and how they were the chosen instruments of the Spirits. Through them, the prophecy would be fulfilled, and the Kinship would rule the city.

Somewhere above, Seth thought he heard a soft murmur. Evidence of the Spirits? He wasn't sure if he'd heard anything at all, and now all was silent. Seth's confusion shifted toward fear, and he once more felt an urge to flee.

What prevented him from bolting was the knowledge that he had nowhere to run. Plus, there were obvious advantages to affiliating oneself with the Kinship. They offered protection from the streets. They offered reputation. They offered a home. His only requirement was to pledge loyalty and join the ranks.

And do whatever I'm told, no matter what it is, or how ghastly.

But was this any different from the world he'd just ran from? Certainly, he felt the same pressure of quid pro quo here that always existed in his mother's home. Was Cain just like the men in Mom's life? Was Cain's real motive simply to exploit him and Jason for his own benefit? For his own power?

Seth felt torn. He didn't think he wanted anything to do with this cult, but he finally found his brother and his brother was all he had in the world. And the Kinship was his brother's world.

BOUND BY BLOOD

Cain's voice boomed. "Now, let the ceremony begin!"

The Kinship moved closer. Seth felt the weight of their anticipation pressing down upon him.

Cain continued. "The Spirits among us are pleased. They revealed to me that the prophecy will soon be fulfilled. Jason has brought to us his dear brother, his own flesh and blood."

A sense of foreboding came over Seth. He didn't know what the Spirits were exactly, but there was something here – something powerful.

The light of the candles flickered as an unseen presence moved through the room. In that light, Cain looked diabolical.

"Spirits don't give power without blood-sacrifice."

"There must be blood," the Kinship chanted in unison.

"Power is in the blood," Cain shouted.

"Power is in the blood," the Kinship replied.

Power is in the blood. Those words compounded Seth's fear.

Cain moaned, low and guttural. The Kinship joined one by one. Even Jason joined, leaving Seth the only silent one.

Don't resist, Came a disembodied whisper.

Seth trembled.

Surrender to us. Confess your loyalties.

Seth tasted blood as he bit down on his lip in fear.

Join your brother, receive great power. Fulfill the prophecy.

Seth opened his eyes. He hadn't noticed closing them. All moaning ceased. The resulting silence was akin to standing in the eye of a hurricane, knowing the tempest would soon resume.

"Blood is demanded," Cain's voice shattered the silence. "It must be spilled."

Cain drew a knife with an evil curved blade and Seth's skin instantly goose-fleshed. "Blood will spill," the priest shouted.

"There must be sacrifice."

"There must be sacrifice," the Kinship agreed.

Seth yelped. Pain hit. It was over in less than a second.

Cain's knife sliced deep into Seth's flesh. Blood spilled.

***

Maxine sat in the first row of Zion's Hill's sanctuary. She was one of about a dozen worshipers – average attendance for the Sunday evening prayer service.

She focused on the pastor as he led worship. He wasn't standing at the pulpit. For this small service, he chose to preach from a folding chair.

The Pastor's name was Pete Jones. He was of average height, small-boned without an ounce of fat on his frame. His face, always clean-shaven, was just starting to show the wrinkles of time. His hair was dark, thick, and always combed straight back without a part. His near-constant smile either conveyed pure contentment, or one hiding discontent. Maxine could never decide which.

Maxine, was saved about a year ago, accepting Christ and receiving baptism at Zion's Hill shortly after arriving in the city. She came to find a job that utilized her degree and was still looking. But her newly found faith and church family was a definite plus for a young Black American college graduate such as herself.

Maxine lived in a small apartment only a block or so from the church. She took advantage of grocery store sales. She paid her bills, and anything extra went to the collection plate at Zion's Hill which she gave gladly. Adulting was tricky, but she was determined to succeed.

The Sunday evening service was always informal. Zion's Hill was in the middle of a blue-collar neighborhood where jeans were preferable to slacks, t-shirts were chosen over blouses and open collars won out to ties and sports jackets. People simply came as they were.

The evening service began with a few hymns, sung acapella. Then, pastor read some chosen scriptures followed by the message. Lastly, the prayers would start when someone had some to say.

There was no set time to end the service. "When the praying's done, we're done," pastor always said.

Maxine loved Sunday evening service, especially the prayers. They'd just started that portion when something odd occurred.

A darkness fell over her. It was so intense, it pulled her from her prayers.

She had never experienced anything like it. Maxine opened her eyes, but nobody else seemed affected.

It felt like a wet wool blanket had been placed on her face, making it hard to breathe. Just then, a voice called out.

"Something's coming against this church!" The voice was Jasmine's.

All eyes turned to the old prophetess. Ms. Jasmine's wrinkled face was stone-cold serious. Her snow-white hair, which was usually kept in a neat little bun on top of her head, looked frazzled, complimenting the agitation in her eyes. She leaned her 90-pound frame against her cane and looked fiery enough to take on an elephant, and win.

She glared through glasses thick as binoculars. "Something's coming against this church!" she declared again.

The spiritual darkness over Maxine pressed harder as the old woman spoke.

Jasmine raised her fist and uttered for the third time, "Something's coming against this church!" She added, "It's ugly. It's dark, and it's powerful!"

"What's coming, Ms. Jasmine?" asked Marcus, a tall man seated behind Maxine with early-onset male-pattern-baldness.

"Marcus," she retorted. "How long have you been saved? How mature is your faith? Can't you answer your own questions by now?"

Marcus looked down, his bald head reflecting the light.

"We know what's coming," she said to everyone. "We know who it is. Who's the ugliest? Who's the darkest?" she paused. "I tell you, it's the fallen one himself. It's Satan who's preparing an attack." Her cane bowed with the strain she put on it as Jasmine's eyes roamed the crowd.

This passion was one of the reasons Maxine became part of Zion's Hill. It wasn't just Jasmine, or Pastor Pete, or any of the others. It was all of them. Zion's Hill was a family of believers who loved God and held to Biblical truth. Nothing was watered down, especially when it came to every Christian's enemy – the one who has many names: Satan, Lucifer, the Devil, Beelzebub, Prince of Darkness, etc.

There's a war raging, Pastor Pete always said. *The day you become a Christian, is the day Satan puts a target on your back. Mark my words, the Devil wants to destroy you in this world, but take heart, Christ has overcome the world.*

"We must prepare for onslaught!" Ms. Jasmine shouted. "The battle lines are drawn. Jesus have mercy!"

Pastor Pete stood tall. "Put on your armor. Wear the belt of truth. Don the breastplate of righteousness. Shod your feet in the gospel of peace. Grab your shield of faith and helmet of salvation. Take up the sword of God's word."

"The armor is best donned through prayer," Ms. Jasmine added.

"Oh, we'll pray," Pete answered. "God is good. We are under his protection."

That said, the prayers began and Maxine's darkness retreated. Still, it existed and could return, so she prayed in earnest and prepared for the battle to come.

***

Seth groaned against the pain as Cain's blade cut into his hand. Blood pooled in Seth's palm.

Seth pulled against Cain's grip, splattering blood onto the floor, himself, Cain – everything, but Cain refused to relinquish his hold.

Cain's eyes were dark as night. Seth sensed a presence within the priest – a spiritual presence. Identical darkness rested upon Jason as well.

"Come to your brother." Cain said to Seth. Then to Jason, "Hold out your hand."

Jason grinned. He held out his hand.

"There's power in blood," said the priest as he sliced deep into Jason's palm.

Jason's grin remained as his blood overflowed his hand, trickling along his arm and falling in great drops to the floor.

Cain dropped the knife and pressed both men's wounds together. That's when Seth's senses heightened. The darkness felt stronger, the silence – deeper.

Seth shut his eyes tight, hoping to push it all away – wanting to push it all away. But this was reality – his reality and it could not be discounted so easily.

Blood oozed between their clasped fingers. It ran down their arms. It dripped to the floor.

Jason's pulse pounded strong through Seth's lacerated palm. But with the pulse – something else. The presence made itself known.

Seth opened his eyes and looked up. The shadows above felt alive. From that point on, he couldn't discount the existence of the spirits because he beheld them with his own eyes. He looked away – repulsed.

"You are flesh of the same flesh and bone of the same bone, separated before birth and yet connected." Cain's voice boomed.

The priest's voice felt so close, almost within him. He looked up once more, sensing the presence in the shadows.

"Do you sense them, Seth? Do you sense them, Jason?" Cain pointed up. "The Spirits approve of your union!"

The shadows descended. Seth wanted to run, but his legs wouldn't move. Plus, his brother remained tightly gripping his hand.

If Jason felt the same repulsion, he hid it well. Jason's grin grew to absurd levels, like the Cheshire cat's toothy smile.

Cain shouted, "Flesh of same flesh. Bone of same bone. Bound by blood, you are connected. Together, you will do great things for the Kinship and the ruling spirits."

Their heartbeats synced and boomed loudly in Seth's head. He felt their shared blood pulse through the circulatory system they now shared.

"The Spirits have spoken," Cain said. "Now, a test."

Seth didn't want to be tested.

"There is an unwanted presence upon our turf," Cain continued. "A poisonous enemy stronghold that must be eradicated."

"We will kill for the Kinship and for the Spirits." Jason answered for them both.

No! Seth thought. *I can't. I won't.*

"Who is this enemy?"

"The Spirits have revealed the stronghold's name." Cain paused. "Zion's Hill!"

That name boomed like a thunderclap, causing Seth's blood to chill within his veins. He knew of Zion's Hill. It was a church located just a few blocks away, over on 42nd Street, very close in fact to where Jason had found him earlier that day.

Cain drew near. "I see it in your eyes. You know the place."

"It's nothing – just a small church," Seth managed a small, insignificant voice.

"They are deceptive," Cain shot back. "Bigger than they appear. To us, they're a venomous cancer that must be eliminated.

I can't. I mustn't.

"Their prayers are poison. The Kinship Spirits hate it. Zion's Hill must be destroyed."

Seth cringed. He didn't want to destroy anybody. But this was the test on the table, and he saw no way out. *What would happen if I decline?*

Cain moved within an inch of Seth's ear. He whispered, "The prayerful of Zion's Hill must die." And then almost as an afterthought. "Or, you can take their place instead."

And that last statement said it all.

***

Maxine shivered. *The prayerful of Zion's Hill must die.* Where had that thought come from?

She opened her eyes. Pastor Pete stopped his prayer mid-sentence. Had he heard the same words, *The prayerful of Zion's Hill must die.*

He resumed praying. Maxine closed her eyes. The voice didn't speak again. However, what it said stuck in her mind: *The prayerful of Zion's Hill must die.*

"Dear God," came Pastor's voice. "We come to you, needing your strength and wisdom. There is a darkness coming against us, and within the darkness, an enemy hides. Please give us strength. Please overcome our fears. We know that you are far greater than anything this enemy can muster. Jesus, you overcame death itself for us. Protect us."

Jasmine put in her two cents. "Lord, cover us with the blood of Jesus," she yelled. "Because that roaring lion, the Devil, is on the prowl looking for somebody to devour!"

Pete's voice. "Lord, protect us from that prowling lion, the one who comes only to destroy, only to steel. Lord protect us, your faithful servants."

Maxine nodded. Yet, a shiver escaped. Her chill remained deep in her bones.

Pete was right. God was mighty to save. The God of Zion's Hill was far greater than anything Satan could throw against them. Yet, her chill persisted.

What if I'm not strong enough? A disturbing thought.

"Jesus, help me overcome my doubts," she whispered.

She shivered again.

***

What exactly was coming against God's church? Pete knew it was satanic, but what form would that take? *Would it be spiritual or physical? And when would it show itself?*

What he did know was that if God wanted him to have specifics, then they would have been provided in Jasmine's prophecy.

A test of faith? He thought. *I'll pass the test!*

Despite his resolution, he shivered in fear.

***

The setting sun might be beautiful, but Seth didn't notice. He led Jason toward Zion's Hill. Only thirteen hours ago, he'd nearly entered that place. It felt much longer since he'd read that sign. Zion's Hill Church: Call on Jesus – He alone can save.

The mission's weight pressured him. This was the point of no return.

The prayerful of Zion's Hill must die. Or, you can take their place. Cain's words haunted him.

Both brothers carried a black cinch bag. Cain instructed them not to investigate them until at Zion's Hill. He'd added, "And remember, completing this test will verify prophecy fulfillment."

Or, you can take their place instead.

"Are we almost there?" Jason hissed.

Seth nodded. They continued down Jackson Street, toward 42nd.

No cars drove by. No pedestrians walked on the sidewalk. *Odd,* thought Seth. But welcome. Absence of people meant absence of witnesses.

"How near?" Jason inquired.

"Just around the corner."

"Let's open our bags."

Seth paused, then nodded. Cain had made it clear that Jason was the lead on this mission. He made the calls. Seth obeyed the order and looked into his bag. The contents confirmed he'd passed the point of no return.

The nearest streetlight's lamp revealed the bag's contents: a black ski mask, a pair of form-fitting black gloves, a compact handgun along with enough clips to get the job done.

"Beretta, nine-millimeter, the perfect choice for tonight, wouldn't you say?"

Jason's joy made Seth's gut wrench. *When did you learn so much about guns, brother? The last two years must have been quite an education.*

Seth had no idea if it was a good choice. He's never held a gun in his life and had certainly never fired one. His expression must have given away this fact.

"It's easy," Jason said. "Just flick the safety switch, snap in the clip, point the dangerous end in the right direction, and pull the trigger."

I can't. Seth told himself. At the same time though, he remembered, *"The prayerful of Zion's Hill must die. Or, you can take their place instead."*

They put on masks and gloves. Then, they each slid a clip into their weapon and chambered a round.

Seth looked around once more. No witnesses. The street remained deserted.

"Looks like hunting season is open," Jason said as his lips curved into a grin through the mouth-hole of his mask.

Seth nodded and tried to keep his hand from trembling. *Could he kill for the Kinship?* He'd know the answer very soon.

You have no choice, Seth thought.

He watched Jason sling his bag of clips over his shoulder and did likewise with his own.

"Just like old times." Jason said through a grin.

Seth shook his head, "We've never done this before."

"Here's to doing new things then." Jason nodded. "We've got to fix your jacket."

Seth looked down at the jacket he wore. It was one of the few things his mother gave him on a rare day when she'd been sober enough to take on some semblance of motherhood. Getting it was one of his few good childhood memories. He wore it everywhere.

It was an old olive-green Vietnam-era Army jacket with many pockets. The insignia and rank stripes had been removed before he'd received it from the thrift store. However, for some reason the name patch remained. *Jacobson.* It hung lose on him back when he first received it, but he'd grown into it over the years. Now, it fit him like a glove.

Jason said, "That jacket is far too recognizable. You've got to lose it."

"No."

"No?" Jason asked. "I'm in charge here remember?"

"You're in charge, but you know what this jacket means to me. I won't throw it away."

"You must. It's too easy to identify."

"If the Spirits are as powerful as you say, it won't matter now will it?" Seth retorted.

The stare-down continued. Finally, Jason looked away. "Well, do something about it. I'm not going to prison because you can't part with your security blanket."

Seth removed his cinch bag and tried to stuff it in, but it wouldn't fit with all those full clips in there. So, he put on the jacket inside out. "This will have to do."

Jason shook his head but didn't argue.

They rounded the corner, with guns drawn, held low and close to avoid attention, but the street remained empty. "The Spirits are working in our favor," Jason said.

The church appeared out of the endless line of downtown storefronts. Its only identification was that sign which hung out front.

They drew near. The street remained still. The silence felt unnatural and conflicted with Seth's inner screams.

He didn't know what to think about the Spirits. Could he kill for them? That was the real question – one that would soon be answered.

Seth closed his eyes and drew a deep breath. His hands trembled. He held the gun in both hands, trying to steady his grip. His knuckles bulged through the gloves from the pressure of grasping that gun's handle.

He glanced at Jason. That ever-present grin was plastered on his face. His hands were steady as a rock.

Light illuminated the sidewalk outside Zion's Hill's store-front window. Seth' frown deepened. The church wasn't empty. *There's no going back.*

They entered the light from that window and looked through the glass. Jason, cool as a cucumber, pressed his ski-masked face right up against the glass. Reluctantly, Seth joined him.

The reflection of Seth's face nauseated him – a masked man with a gun and an agenda for murder. Looking past his reflection, he saw that the church was actually an old, repurposed movie theatre.

The lobby was from a bygone era and had seen better days. Still, the tarnished brass and chipped wood of the space held a certain charm.

Seth's eyes followed the light. The lobby itself wasn't lit. Beyond the old candy display, and a sign on an easel angled toward the front windows that mentioned worship service and Sunday school times, was the entrance to the theatre. This was where the light came from.

Seth heard a knock and jumped a foot back. Somebody was staring out at him through the glass!

Jason stood there looking out at Seth. He motioned for Seth to join him. Seth nodded. He reached out, with his still-trembling hand, and opened the door to Zion's Hill.

***

Pastor Pete continued to lead prayer. Maxine closed her eyes and bowed her head, but the chill in her bones was distracting.

What did Jasmine's prophecy mean? Maxine wondered.

Boom!

Maxine's eyes shot open, her ears ringing. Her head jolted toward the sound.

Two masked men stood in the sanctuary's entrance at the back of the sanctuary. Both wielded handguns. A thin wisp of white smoke came from one of the guns.

Maxine's eyes widened and her pulse-speed doubled.

***

Seth knew now that Jason was 100% committed to the Kinship. Also, there was no going back for either of them.

Jason's bullet embedded itself into the far wall's molding, missing the pastor's head by inches.

That round would have met it's intended target if not for Seth's last-second reaction. Now, judging by the rage in his brother's face, he wondered if deflecting Jason's aim had been wise.

Jason shoved him hard. "What's wrong with you!"

Seth stumbled back, using the doorframe to stay upright. *I can't live with murder on my hands, no matter what the cost.*

The hatred in Jason's eyes forced Seth to look down. "There has to be another way." Seth finally said. "No amount of power can be worth shedding innocent…"

"Shut up!" Jason hissed. "I take you in! I offer you protection! And this is how you thank me?"

Cain's words rang in Seth's mind. *"The prayerful of Zion's Hill must die. Or, you can take their place instead."*

It doesn't matter, he told himself. "These are innocent people," he said to Jason, his voice wavering with fear.

Jason scoffed. "Innocent? Innocent!"

"Yes," Seth countered. He looked at those seated in the rows. Not one of them moved a muscle.

"These are those who pray to the enemy. THESE ARE THE ENEMY!"

"It's not right."

"You don't know what a world of trouble you've just opened for yourself – for us both! We're bound by blood oath to do the Spirits' bidding – to fulfill the prophecy! But now…!"

Seth mustered his courage. "I don't care about any of that! I won't kill for it!"

Seth looked up from the floor as Jason took aim at his brother. "We're at war," Jason spat. "This is your last chance. Choose your allegiance."

"Don't do this," Seth begged, his breaths coming in fearful gasps.

Other than the brother's dialog, all was silent. Nobody in the congregation moved.

"We have no choice." Jason retorted. "We're bound by blood to do the Spirits bidding. We're bound by blood to the Kinship."

"If you do this, then you're no better than all those men mom took in."

Jason's aim teetered. His hands shook. "Don't say that!"

"It's true," Seth dared say.

"Shut up," Jason murmured. He now held the gun in both hands, steadying his aim.

"Don't do this." Seth pleaded.

"My loyalties are to the Kinship." Jason's voice was low and guttural. "And that makes you my enemy."

In the distance, a siren wailed, growing louder with every passing moment.

"Looks like we've been discovered," Seth said. "Probably wasn't wise to fire your gun."

Jason's rage couldn't be ignored. His face was venomous with it.

The sirens were very loud now. His trigger finger played against the trigger, on the cusp of discharging his weapon point blank into Seth's face.

Seth looked away, bracing himself against the doorframe, wondering if it would hurt much to die this way. But the bullet never came.

"Go ahead coward," Jason's voice hissed. "Run away, but don't go running back to the Kinship. And don't ever come crawling back to me."

Seth looked at Jason. There was no love in his brother's face – only hatred and rage.

Jason lowered his weapon. "Get going."

Seth turned and ran back out the way he came. The outside air chilled him; drying the rivers of perspiration which covered every inch of his skin.

He ran down the sidewalk. The street was still empty. The red/blue alternations of emergency lights flashed just around the block's corner. They'd be here in only a few seconds!

He crossed 42nd and entered the darkness of the nearest alley. His brain screamed *"Don't stop!"*

So, he didn't.

***

Jason watched his cowardly brother flee. Then, he turned his attention to those seated in the old theatre. The terror in their eyes verified why none of them dared run.

He still had a cinch bag full of ammo, but without his brother's help, and with time running out, killing them all would prove problematic.

He thought about Seth. *I should have killed him when I had the chance.*

"Lord, have mercy on us," he heard a voice. It came from one of the seat warmers.

Two years with the Kinship meant Jason hated it when Christians prayed. He'd been sent to silence prayers just like that.

"Oh Lord forgive him, he knows not what he's doing," the old woman's voice grated on his nerves.

"Shut up!" Jason screamed, waving his gun in the congregation's general direction.

"I tell you that if these keep quiet, the very stones will cry out!"

He saw who it was that spoke – an old lady with a cane. He aimed at her. "I said shut up!"

He considered shooting her, but time was nearly gone. With a grunt, he lowered his weapon and fled the scene.

By now the cops were probably out front. So he bolted past the congregants, beyond the old theatre screen, and exited the building via the back door.

The instant he exited, the emergency alarm sounded. He sprinted the length of the dark alley, bolted across the street, and into the next alley.

He heard shouting. The cops must have reached the back of the theatre.

He kept running and the shouts grew fainter. Soon after, they could no longer be heard.

He kept running.

CHAPTER 2

Everything went down so fast. Maxine was in a fog.

She remembered the masked men entering and firing. *Dear God,* she'd thought when the bullet barely missed her pastor.

And she remembered the gunmen's eyes, but didn't know why. One of them held a deep sadness.

Something's coming against this church! It's ugly. It's dark, and it comes with great power!" Jasmine's prophecy rang over and over in her mind.

Now that the danger was past, the numbness was beginning to wear off. *It's like waking up from a nightmare only to discover it really occurred.*

"Take this." One of the first responders handed Maxine a blanket. "You're shivering."

She took the blanket and began to cry in short bursting sobs, but nobody noticed. The one who'd handed her the blanket was already onto his next task.

She looked at the others. Many of Zion's Hill were also crying.

Maxine closed her eyes to regain composure, but that only brought back memories of those eyes – those sad, sad eyes.

Her sobs came anew.

***

Seth staggered along. His body no longer allowed him a full sprint.

He moved from shadow to shadow, staying in the dark as much as possible, refusing to stop. He couldn't stop.

Motion-activated lights eradicated the darkness. In that sodium-vapor glow, he felt exposed – caught. He stumbled away from it like a vampire at sunrise.

The prayerful of Zion's Hill must die. Or, you can take their place instead. Those words chased him like a dog after a rabbit.

He knew he could never hide from what he'd done – conspired to murder an entire church prayer group. There wasn't enough darkness in the world to hide from that.

He told himself he had no choice. He told himself that in the end, he didn't go through with it. But he knew the truth. He knew how close he'd come to killing the innocent. It was only his last-second gut reaction that turned the tide.

Plus, he knew what his heart wanted. He'd wanted the safety and prestige that the Kinship offered. And he wanted it so badly that he nearly sold his soul to get it.

He wiped the perspiration from his face with the ski-mask he now held. It smelled of body odor and guilt.

Seth wrapped the mask and his gloves around the gun. If anyone saw him, he didn't want that gun to be visible.

To his best knowledge, nobody had seen him. Maybe the Spirits were real. Maybe they were helping him out – keeping his visibility low.

Right. That couldn't be. If the Spirits were real, then they'd be against him now for sure.

He stumbled on a curb and fell to his knees. Then onto all fours. His body demanded rest. Fortunately, he'd fallen into a spot of deep shadow.

Every muscle twitched. Every nerve quivered. His breathes came loud – too loud. He struggled to hear, but all he heard was his own lungs chugging into overdrive.

He opened his eyes, not realizing he'd closed them. Bits of gravel stuck to his cheek as he pushed himself up.

I must have passed out.

His entire body hurt as he stood up, but at least his lungs were breathing normally. *You got away with it,* he dared think.

What's there to get away with? He countered his own thought. *You didn't do anything wrong.*

Yet, deep in his core, he knew how close he'd come – how in his heart, he'd wanted to do those horrid deeds.

You should be so lucky, he argued internally. *You've only bought some time. They'll find you. It's only a matter of time.*

No! he pleaded. *I had on the mask and gloves. The cops have nobody to identify.*

It's not the cops you need to worry about. That thought brought terror.

The Spirits are your problem. They know what you did or didn't do. And they know your intentions.

He ran, not knowing where he was going. Only knowing he had to run.

His own thoughts had become an enemy. He was right. Even if the authorities never find him, surely the Spirits would. *The prayerful of Zion's Hill must die. Or, you can take their place instead.*

He entered an unlit alley and slowed to a walk. It was utterly dark here.

He stopped, sensing something. "Who's there?"

Something WAS there. It didn't say anything. It didn't have to. Its presence was obvious by the hairs that stood up on the back of Seth's neck.

He turned to exit the alley, but the light at the end seemed so weak – so distant, nearly unattainable. Plus, the follower was here also.

"What do you want with me?" he hissed.

A light breeze touched his face, but nothing else happened.

"Who are you?"

No answer.

He extended his arms, feeling his way along. His fingers grazed something rough. *A brick wall?*

He followed the wall along the alley. *I just need to make it out of here.*

With every inch, his trepidation grew. Seth was sure that which lurked here was the same presence he'd felt back at the blood-letting ceremony – an evil presence.

Terror washed over him and he broke into a blind run which ended in a faceplant on the greasy-slick alley asphalt.

For a moment, his body remained still. The stench of alley waste permeated his nostrils and his face was warm with blood.

Regardless, he staggered to his feet. Something with claws grabbed him. He screamed and fought it.

The creature landed, hissed, and retreated. In the light at the end of the ally, a feline shadow appeared as the cat ran away.

It was only a cat. Seth didn't know whether to laugh or cry. He touched his face and confirmed he was bleeding, not profusely but enough.

Finally, he exited the alleyway. There was no sign of the cat. There was no sign of life at all. *Strange.*

His shirt was torn, smelled of garbage, and was damp with sweat and alley gook. Fortunately, his most cherished possession, his Jacobson jacket, was unbuttoned and still inside out.

He took it off, removed his shirt, and threw it back into the alley's darkness. Then, he put his jacket back on, right-side-out.

He kept the ski-mask and his gloves wrapped around the gun. Those items along with the cinch bag on his shoulder needed to be disposed with, but not like his shirt. These were tied to his crimes and needed to be "lost" in a way they'd never be found.

He trudged along the river walk, thankful and confused that even here, there were no bystanders. Even now though, he felt followed by the Spirits. They weren't going to let him go without a fight.

The prayerful of Zion's Hill must die. Or, you can take their place instead.

Seth staggered onto the vacant boardwalk which ran along the riverbank. Rivers had many purposes. For him, it would be a good place to lose a ski-mask, gloves, cinch bag full of clips, and a handgun.

His muscles quivered as he progressed along the boardwalk. He'd pushed himself to new limits tonight, and he wondered how much more he could endure.

Seth.

He spun around. Nobody.

Seth. It came again.

The voice came from within. Yet it was not his own. *Seth.*

He unwrapped the ski-mask and gloves from his gun and gripped it by the handle. What could bullets do in this situation? He had no idea, but it was all he could think to do.

Seth – Seth – Seth!

"Who are you?" Seth shouted.

His hand trembled along with the gun he held. He turned, trying to see all directions at once while simultaneously trying to remember his brother's instructions for firing such a weapon.

"Who are you!" he shouted again.

The lapping current of the river was the only sound.

"I know what you are," Seth dared say. "You're the presence from the alley. You're the Spirits I noticed at the blood-letting ceremony."

He stood still. All was quiet. All was still. The silence deafened him.

Seth! The voice screamed.

"What do you want?"

You failed us. It came quieter now, a sultry voice. *We were prepared to give you and your brother power. All you had to do was kill those at Zion's Hill. We, the Spirits of the Kinship would have given you all our power freely, if only you'd done that one thing.*

"Leave me alone!"

You could have had all your heart desired. If only you would have joined your brother in killing our enemies at Zion's Hill.

"Please, leave me alone," Seth whined.

It was a doable task was it not? It should have been easy to silence those prayers forever.

The clear night sky now filled with dark clouds. The moon disappeared and thunder rumbled.

Rain poured on Seth, stinging his injured face and soaking his clothes to the bone. "Leave me be!" he screamed above the ruckus.

Lighting struck, illuminating the riverfront in white-blue brilliance. That's when Seth saw them, the Kinship spirits – four of them, tall and dark. They appeared to be only made of shadow, unnaturally black, unnaturally tall.

They dove upon Seth, dragging him along the boardwalk as if he weighed nothing at all.

It felt odd, these shadow-creatures. They felt insubstantial, yet they gripped him like steel vices.

He fought hard, screaming until his throat burned. But his blows passed right through them. He tried to pry loose, but there was nothing to pry. Yet, they held him fast.

Then, he was falling from the boardwalk. He drew a breath just before hitting the rain-gorged river and sinking into its depths.

The Spirits remained with him. He pointed his gun at them only to realize he no longer held it, the gloves, or the ski mask.

Were they in the river? He thought. But these were the least of his worries now.

Now, we will punish, the Spirits hissed as he sunk deeper. *We will punish!*

The prayerful of Zion's Hill didn't die. So, you will take their place instead.

***

Jason ran until he no longer heard the sirens or saw the flashing of lights. The ensuing calm incubated his rage. *I save him from the streets, and this is how my brother repays me?*

He jogged along the edge of a vacant lot, keeping to the shadows, careful not to step on sleeping hobos or used needles. *How dare he! My own brother! My own flesh and blood!*

Jason took a deep breath and let it out slowly, but his muscles continued to twitch with rage. He stepped on broken glass, the crunch echoed loudly. In the unseen distance, a hobo moaned.

The mission was a bust. Nothing had gone right. *All due to Seth!*

He thought about the power which had been promised, the power denied him. *All because of Seth!*

He'd been with the Kinship long enough now to know somebody would pay for the mission's failure. *It wasn't my fault!*

Seth was to blame. But Seth wasn't here. He was. He didn't trust Cain to place blame correctly.

He didn't trust Cain period. Cain stood to lose a lot if the prophecy was fulfilled. If much power was given to Jason and Seth, where did that leave the high priest?

Regardless, Jason needed to return to the Kinship. He began walking in that direction.

No matter what, I'll reclaim what I lost. The prophecy will be met. I swear it by the Kinship spirits.

Also, I'll get my revenge on Seth.

***

Seth broke the water's surface, filling his lungs with precious oxygen. The Spirits had pulled him deep before letting him go. He had the feeling they were toying with him.

He coasted along with the swift current. Already, he was a considerable distance from the boardwalk. The glow of its streetlamps were mere specks.

He floated along in darkness, barely managing to keep his head above the surface, wondering where the current would carry him. He shed the cinch bag and let it sink into the depths, but letting it fall did little to decrease the weight pressing down on him.

He no longer heard the Spirits, but they were there. Just as before, he sensed their presence. "Leave me alone!" he shouted.

They didn't answer.

"Leave me!" he demanded.

They were out there. He imagined them circling like a school of hungry sharks.

Exhaustion took over. His limbs barely moved. He kept his nose and mouth above the current, but nothing more.

A wave smashed into him, causing a coughing spasm. He needed to get to shore, or die trying.

But how far away was the shore? He began swimming perpendicular to the current.

The water repulsed him. It was greasy, but not physically so. Seth realized this was what it felt like to swim with spirits. "Leave me alone!"

Another wave hit him, a large one. It crashed down, pulling him into the depths.

Seth sunk to the bottom. His feet drilled into the muck, up to his ankles.

Fatigued and starving for oxygen, he fought as best he could, kicking his feet free from the mire and swimming upward. He broke the surface and pulled in a lungful of air before another wave struck.

This time though, his feet didn't get stuck. Instead, they hit solid ground. Seth had found a sandbar. Fighting the current, he clawed into the sand and crawled against the undertow.

The sandbar was close to the surface and Seth was able to get air in-between waves. The rushing water pushed against him and he dug into the sand with all he had to keep from being swept away.

"You've got to do better than that!" he laughed his defiance.

But then a tree branch in the current hit him hard enough to dislodge Seth from the sandbar. He wheezed, trying to regain the breath the branch knocked from him, gripping onto it for dear life.

The rain spit. The thunder cracked. *Leave me alone!* he thought to himself.

The greasiness in the water confirmed the Spirits were still present. "Leave me alone," he said with little more than a whisper.

Pain radiated up his leg. Something snagged his foot.

He reached down to free himself. It was fishing line.

He screamed as the line became taunt, cutting into this waterlogged flesh. His heart pounded in fear, forcing blood through his veins.

The line pulled him against the current. He let go of the branch and got his fingers in the mess, protecting his injured leg as best he could.

"Let me go!" he cried.

Let me go! the Spirits mocked him.

The greasiness increased, grazing his skin. They were close now, touching him.

Seth shrieked, but there was nothing he could do to stop the Spirits. They yanked him below the surface and their touch covered his face.

His ankle throbbed where the line was digging in, but Seth didn't scream, not now that he was submerged.

He hit bottom, but they kept pulling. He was sinking into the mud – being buried alive.

Their greasy touch fondled every inch of his skin. Fingers reached in his mouth, tasting of death, forcing the river in.

His thoughts were slower now, less sensical. *Leave me alone! Leave me a scone! Sleave me a bone? Dream me a moan???*

The depths were dark, dark as the grave. He exhaled.

The darkness parted. A sickly green glow replaced it, an overly ripe avocado light – depressing beyond imagination.

The Kinship spirits took form. They surrounded him, ghastly creatures of elongated shadow, appearing black in the avocado light.

They grabbed him. Their touch here didn't compare to the greasiness of before. This was 10 times worse, a 100 times worse, infinitely worse.

Their eyes radiated neon green, like emeralds on a background of black velvet. And they laughed.

Their laughter mimicked their touch – unbearable. Yet, Seth bared it without option.

The emerald-eyes of the nearest one stared hard. The face was black as onyx. It's skin, wrinkled and shiny like a raisin.

Those eyes continued to torture him. The laughter continued to taunt. *You will be ours!* Seth heard it speak from within him.

He shook his head. *No!*

To that, their laughter doubled. They swarmed him, clamoring over each other, clawing and biting like a pack of hungry dogs. Seth shut his eyes tight, but they pulled his eyelids back open, shining their emerald peepers into his own.

Seth was dying. His oxygen was depleted. The Spirits would soon have him.

Inexplicably he thought of the sign outside of Zion's Hill. *Call on Jesus – He alone can save!*

Save me, Jesus!!! Seth's last thought. *You alone can s…*

***

"Somebody just called out to Jesus," Jasmine said.

Both Pastor Pete and the police officer he was speaking with turned toward her. "What?"

Jasmine smiled. "Somebody just called out to Jesus!"

Pastor nodded. The officer just continued the conversation he was having.

So what, Jasmine thought. *I don't care if I sound crazy. Somebody called to Jesus for the very first time, and that's worth celebrating.*

***

Save me, Jesus.

Seth no longer felt the Spirits presence. Where they went, he didn't know, but he was glad to be free of them.

He pushed upward, expecting to break the river's surface any moment, but that moment didn't come. *How deep am I?*

He swam harder now, struggling with all that remained in him - confused. Then, off to his right, he saw something

It was a light, distant – only a pinprick in the darkness. But it drew him and he swam toward it.

The light grew brighter. He stopped swimming. Yet, the light continued to grow larger. It pulled him like a moth to the flame.

Despite the situation, Seth felt calm – unnaturally calm. He glanced behind where everything was darker. He barely made out those emerald orbs. The Spirits were still there – watching but not following. They stayed just beyond the reach of the light.

Seth looked harder and noticed something there with the Spirits – something suspended in the water. Whatever it was, it preoccupied them.

Seth stared hard. The thing with them felt familiar somehow. It was large – *a dead catfish? Why would the Spirits be so enamored with a dead fish?*

As soon as that question popped into his head, the answer came to him. *They wouldn't.*

That's when Seth noticed the fish's tail. It wasn't a tail. It had two feet.

The current turned it toward Seth. *No! It can't be!* But it was. *It's me!*

He saw it all now. The bloated face was his. The lifeless body was his. The ankle, still tangled in fishing line floated listlessly in the depths.

But if that's me? He couldn't think he was dead.

Strangely, the sense of calm continued. He turned away from his body and the Spirits surrounding it.

The light pulled him faster now. He coasted toward it like iron to a magnet.

Seth realized he was no longer in water. He glided through air, only it wasn't really just air. He couldn't explain it.

At that moment, nothing mattered. There was him, the growing light, and nothing else.

Seth entered something akin to a tunnel. The light blazed from the far end. It continued pulling him.

The calmness within almost made him forget about the Spirits back in the darkness and his body floating among them. They were still there. He sensed it, but their presence didn't bother him.

He was nearly at tunnel's end. The light was mesmerizing. Seth reached for it, but as light often is, he couldn't touch it. He felt it's warmth though – like the heat of a summer morning before it got too hot.

The light, or something within the light called him. It didn't call with words, but it called and Seth felt the need to run toward it. His sense of calm radiated from it.

He heard a noise. It broke the silence like a hammer through glass.

It sounded something like a choir singing, and yet nothing like that at all. It was totally unique, something more than anything he ever heard before. Seth almost caught the lyrics, but somehow its meaning eluded him, just beyond his range of understanding.

Seth was drawn to the sound. He yearned to sing along, to join the throng. Yet he didn't. He didn't know how.

The tunnel ended abruptly, opening into a seemingly endless expanse. Here, the light was everywhere, brilliant but not blinding. Also, it was so perfectly lit that no shadows existed – only light.

There was something in the distance. He glided toward it.

He came before a great throne, and sitting upon it, was one beyond description. This was the source of all the light.

Seth's calmness teetered. The seed of fear germinated. He couldn't help it. The one before him demanded to be feared.

Unquestioningly, this was a king. Seth bowed with his face to the ground.

I should hide. There was nowhere to hide from the one on the throne. The light prevented it.

This was a place of justice and the throned one sat as judge. Seth couldn't explain how he knew this. He simply did.

Seth's calmness teetered further toward fear. *This one knows what I've done.*

That thought unhinged him. *He knows I was in on the plan to murder Christians.*

A hand rested on his shoulder. Instantly, his calmness returned.

Seth looked up at the one who'd touched him. He wore a white robe and held a shepherd's crook. Long white hair and matching beard covered his head and lower face.

The shepherd emitted light, as much as was coming from the one on the throne. Seth squinted to see him better – desiring to see him more clearly.

The shepherd kept his hand on Seth's shoulder, guiding him away from the throne. He wanted to ask him who he was, but couldn't find his voice.

Seth glanced back. The throne and the judge who sat upon it was still there, but distant.

All was still. All was peaceful.

Here, reality felt a thousand times more real than anything Seth had ever experienced before. The light was brighter. The whiteness of the expanse was whiter than white. The smell of the shepherd was like fresh linen. Everything was more without being too much.

The shepherd gestured with his crook and Seth's gaze followed. In the distance, was stormy darkness. It was very far off. Still, the sight of it disturbed him.

The shepherd guided Seth closer to the storm and Seth resisted. Here in the light, he felt safe, but that storm seemed dangerous.

Thunder rumbled from it. Bolts of lightning emanated from the black clouds. As he drew closer, the smell of rot and rain entered his nostrils.

They stopped on the edge of a deep and terrible chasm which separated them from the storm. The shepherd pointed once more with his crook and Seth stared hard across the chasm.

Within the darkness, emerald orbs became visible – the eyes of the Kindred spirits. Seth closed his eyes.

When he opened them, something new was afoot. Suspended over the middle of the great chasm, Seth saw his own body just as he'd seen it in the river previously.

It hung there, floating on the air itself. The body was bloated. The ankle still had the fishing line around it, slicing into the flesh.

The smell confirmed decay. With a sound of a loud kiss, the fishing-line foot came off, falling into the chasm's depths.

Seeing his own body disturbed Seth. But not as much as the brewing storm on the chasm's far side.

A figure emerged within the clouds – a silhouette darker than the storm itself. It sauntered right up to the very edge of the chasm.

Its green-emerald eyes glared at Seth. This spirit was larger and blacker than any he'd yet encountered. Despite the chasm separating him, his unease grew. It grinned a sadistic grin and licked its chops with a black, forked tongue.

"You have no place here Lucifer." The shepherd spoke for the first time.

Seth shivered at the sound of that voice. The shepherd spoke with confidence and authority.

"I have rights to this man. He is mine," Lucifer countered with a voice like thunder. He reached for Seth's suspended body, but it drifted just beyond his grasp. "He aligned with my spirits, and therefore with me."

Lucifer retracted his hand. "He's mine!"

The shepherd casually shook his head.

"Oh, good shepherd," Lucifer mocked. "Do you dispute it? Can you disprove where his loyalties fall? Did he not listen to my servant Cain? Did he not go with his brother to kill your people at Zion's Hill? Did he not…"

"Enough!"

The shepherd's voice was like the roar of a lion and Lucifer instantly shrank back into the darkness of the storm. He was still there though. Seth could see those green eyes piercing the darkness and seething with rage.

"None of that is remembered," the shepherd continued. "He called on MY name and has therefore been redeemed."

Lucifer cautiously reemerged from his hiding place. With him came others – his entourage. They stood at Lucifer's side, eyes glowing green and forked tongues tasting the air.

"Relinquish my slave!" Lucifer seemed braver now that his minions had joined the ranks.

"No! He is mine!"

Lucifer stumbled back along with all the others – as if the shepherd's voice had physically shoved him.

"Be gone," the shepherd commanded.

Lucifer's green-glowing eyes glared out from the clouds for a moment. Then they disappeared into the darkness along with all the rest.

A second later, the storm retreated. In the far distance, Seth could see it brewing, but he no longer feared it.

Suspended over the chasm and between the two lands, Seth's body remained. He watched it in wonder.

After a time, he looked at the shepherd. It was just the two of them here as far as Seth could tell.

For the first time, Seth noticed all the shepherd's scars – so many scars. They were on his wrists, his feet and his brow. They looked deep, but old – heeled.

"Consider my scars." The shepherd wasn't looking at Seth as he spoke, but at Seth's body dangling in the middle of the chasm. His voice no longer sounded like thunder. The rage was gone from it. He spoke gently – tenderly. "Do you wonder about my scars?"

"Yes," Seth answered.

"Behold child, your body hangs in the middle between two destinations."

Seth looked at his floating body.

"You must choose a side," the shepherd continued. "You cannot exist in the middle of the chasm indefinitely."

Seth nodded, but wasn't sure he understood.

"Go to those at Zion's Hill. They will instruct you in the meaning of my scars. They will help you choose the correct side of the chasm."

Seth trembled. "They won't accept me, not after what I did."

"But, I thought you were wondering about my scars?" he added with a kind chuckle.

Seth nodded.

"Those at Zion's Hill have the answers you need."

Seth wanted to say more, but the shepherd continued speaking.

"To learn about my scars is to learn about me. And to learn about me is to learn of the one who sent me – the one on the throne."

"I…"

"You must learn what I've done for you and what is expected of you."

"I don't want to go back," Seth uttered. "I want to stay here."

For just a brief moment, something akin to sadness, but not quite sadness, flittered across the shepherd's face. "The time isn't right for you to stay here. You must do the work assigned, and you must learn the meaning of my scars."

Seth looked away because his eyes felt hot and he didn't want the other to see him cry. "This is where I belong."

"Someday. Not now."

Those words broke the dam and Seth's tears trickled down his cheeks. The shepherd wiped them away with the hem of his robe before they fell.

Seth looked up and was surprised to see the shepherd weeping too. "Don't cry little one. I have prepared a place for you here. When the time is right, you will come to stay."

Seth nodded. The shepherd smiled.

"It's time you go. Learn from those at Zion's Hill and what it means to have my name written upon your heart."

"What is your name?"

The shepherd smiled. "You called me from out of the depths. How can you ask this question now?"

Save me Jesus. Seth recalled.

Seth began to drift away. He blinked and found himself back in the tunnel, only now he was going the opposite direction, away from the light.

Darkness surrounded him once more and a chill overwhelmed him. He closed his eyes to protect them from the cold.

Seth spasmed. His muscles burned. His limbs convulsed. He curled into himself to conserve heat.

His ankle throbbed. The fishing line dug in.

He opened his eyes. Water lapped against his cheek. The stink of the river was strong.

He sat up, shivering. Mud covered him except for the parts of him that remained in the shallows.

Daylight burned his eyes. Seth tried to shield them, but his hands were numb with cold. Every movement felt impossible.

The sun was rising. Morning was breaking.

Seth staggered to his feet. The pain in his leg – excruciating. He pulled up his pantleg. The fishing line was gone, but evidence of its existence remained.

He touched it gingerly. He would need to disinfect it. But not now. Now, he just needed to survive.

He rubbed his arms together to get the blood flowing. *Geez, I need a shower.* But that would have to wait as well.

He looked around. As far as he could tell, he was alone.

He hobbled forward, wincing from the pain in his ankle. The coldness in his body numbed him somewhat. He took a second step, then a third.

I escaped death. No. That's not quite accurate. *I've been allowed to live. I've been given a second chance.*

He remembered standing before a judgement throne. He remembered the grace and mercy Jesus had offered him.

You cannot exist in the middle of the chasm indefinitely.

The shepherd's words rang true. He would not stay in the middle. He'd choose a side – the right side – the side of truth.

Seth had washed ashore under a bridge – a busy bridge. He could hear the traffic rumbling above him. He must still be in the city.

He limped out from under it. Indeed, he was still in the city and in view of the downtown skyline.

Seth climbed the embankment. Every step shot pain up his injured leg. By the time he reached the top, he was crying.

He dropped to the ground. He needed food. He needed water. He needed to go to those at Zion's Hill.

CHAPTER 3

Pastor Pete Jones slumped in his chair with his chest, arms, and head sprawled out upon the desk's surface. A drool puddle expanded from his snoring mouth.

His nightmare jolted him awake. It was about his late wife.

He stood up and stretched his spine. "I'm getting too old to sleep this way," he moaned.

He slept here often. It was hard going home and sleeping alone in a bed that once held two.

"Lord, if I could have just one more day with her."

He grabbed a fist-wad of tissues from the box on his file cabinet and wiped up his drool puddle. Last night still haunted him.

He sat back down, running his fingers through his hair. *That bullet almost got me.*

By the time the police finally wrapped thing up, it was early morning and he was too wound up to sleep. So, he came here to the church office to pray.

At some point, he'd nodded off. Pete glanced at his wristwatch. *Two hours is better than nothing.*

Remnants of his nightmare made him frown. As always it was about Beth and finding out she had terminal cancer. He didn't know why he had to relive what actually happened in his dreams.

She'd died more than three years ago now. *Can that be right?* Pete wondered.

Time seemed to fly and stand still at the same time when it came to the event of Beth's death. Sometimes, it seemed like she should still be here and he'd come home to find her waiting and asking how his day was. Other times, it felt like a lifetime ago since he'd seen her, touched her, been with her.

They'd always wanted children, but wanted to start the church first. They were young. There was time. At least that's what they'd always said, until...

He missed her fiercely. Beth was his soul-mate. He loved everything about her. Plus, she was so full of the Holy Spirit.

He wiped tears away. *You left me too soon Beth.* He thought those words often.

Pete didn't blame her of course. She didn't ask to get cancer – nobody ever does.

Cancer is a strange curse. It gives you good and bad days. Overall, Beth remained vibrant, almost to the very end. Eventually though the cancer started giving her more bad days than good, and when that happened, it tore Pete apart.

Near the end, the doctors gave them little hope. Still, they clung to what little remained. They prayed for a miracle. They prayed for healing.

In the end, God did end Beth's suffering. But it left Pete struggling with his own pain. *Lord, if I could have just one more day with her.*

He stretched his muscles, trying to work out the kinks and stiffness. "I'm getting too old for this."

He thought about the masked men with guns and thanked God they'd gotten into some kind of disagreement that led to the bullet missing his head. Also, their little spat wasted time. They had to flee without killing anyone.

He started praying once more. He prayed for those men, that they might have their eyes opened – that they might follow Jesus.

From prayer to sleep he went. Two hours might be better than none, but it wasn't enough.

***

This is ridiculous.

Seth limped toward Zion's Hill. He'd stopped along the way at a free clinic and shelter. There, he'd gotten a shower. Also, he'd picked up a shirt at the free store. It said "Avoid the Noid" and had a weird cartoon character on it that was probably some kind of trend years ago. Plus, they disinfected his ankle with alcohol and wrapped it with clean gauze. Still, the wound hurt with every step.

This is just stupid.

A few hours after climbing up from the river bank, his dream was losing detail. *Why am I going back to the scene of the crime?*

The shepherd said these people could teach him something. Now though, it seemed to be the last place he should go.

Go to those at Zion's Hill. They will instruct you in the meaning of my scars. They will help you choose to which side of the chasm you should go. He remembered that part still.

He stood in front of the church. *Zion's Hill Church: Call on Jesus – He alone can save!* He read the sign. With a shrug, he opened the door and entered.

Seth leaned on the candy counter. His hands trembled. The perspiration dripped down his face. *This isn't a good idea.*

Go to those at Zion's Hill. The shepherd's voice rang in his head, spurring him onward.

He took a clumsy step and knocked over the easel with worship times listed on it. The whole thing toppled to the ground with a crash.

Seth stood mid-stride, still as stone as quiet took back over. This wasn't how he wanted to be discovered. *Had anyone heard?*

He waited.

***

Pastor Pete woke up with a start. Something had startled him. *A crash.*

It'd come from the lobby. Somebody was out there.

Normally, Pete wouldn't be too nervous. He left the doors unlocked whenever he was here. He never wanted anyone to feel unwelcome entering God's house. But having nearly had his head blown off just hours ago had put him on edge.

"Hello?" he called out.

No answer.

He stood from his desk. "Hello?" he said louder.

Nothing.

***

Seth heard the voice calling. He stood still as a statue, knowing the right thing to do is to respond, but fear took away his voice.

"Hello?" the voice came again.

This is a mistake, he thought to himself.

No, he countered. *The shepherd told me to come.*

Against his better judgement, he proceeded beyond the candy display and down a hallway where the voice had called from.

With every step, self-defeating thoughts entered his mind. *This is the stupidest decision you could make. Whoever's here will identify you. You'll go to prison for sure.*

They won't identify me, he argued with himself. *I was wearing gloves and a mask. And nobody will ever find them because they're in the sludge at the bottom of the river, weighed down by a gun.*

What about your jacket? He countered.

It was inside out. Plus, nobody saw me close up.

What if you're wrong?

Seth stopped, grabbed fistfuls of his hair and pulled, not so hard as to rip any out, but to gain perspective. *The shepherd told me to come.*

He took off his jacket and tied it around his waist. He couldn't bring himself to get rid of his most prized possession, but he could wear it in a new way at least. Seth looked down at himself. *What in the world is a Noid anyway?*

He passed by the theatre, the place where he'd almost committed murder with his brother. He looked in just long enough to verify the owner of the voice wasn't there. It wasn't. He kept going.

At the end of the hall was another door. It was ajar just enough to see light coming from the room beyond.

"Who's out there?" A man's voice said.

This is your last chance to run.

He paused and realized he'd been running his whole life. He ran from Amanda. He ran from the Kinship. He ran from the Spirits. He ran from the police. He ran from his own brother.

I'm tired of running.

And with that, he pushed the door open.

***

Pastor Pete almost convinced himself that the sounds were only his imagination. So, he flinched as the stranger entered.

The man looked like he lived in the gutter. For some reason, the olive-green jacket tied around his waist drew his attention. He didn't know why.

The man's pants were stained. His shirt was from a 1980s pizza-chain promotion. Strangely, his hair looked relatively clean. He took one tentative step and Pete noted the limp.

Pete found his voice. "Can I help you?"

The man opened his mouth, but no words came.

***

Seth swallowed hard. The morning sun poured in from a window on the far wall. Silhouetted against that light the man was little more than a shadow.

The shepherd told me to come. The shepherd told me to come. The shepherd told me to come. He wanted to say it out loud, but those words sounded weird now.

"What do you want?" The man asked tensely.

"The shepherd told me to come." *There. I said it.*

"I beg your pardon?"

Seth's words came now in a jumble. "The shepherd told me to come so that I can learn about the meaning of his scars."

The man didn't answer. Instead, he walked out of the sun's path.

The pastor. Seth heartrate doubled.

"Did you say the shepherd told you to come?" he asked.

"Yes?"

"Are you asking me or telling me?"

"Yes." Might as well be confident. There's no going back now.

The pastor came nearer and looked Seth directly in the eyes.

He recognizes me. I'm cooked.

"Nice jacket you have there."

Seth readied himself to fight his way out of here if it came to it. "It's just an old Army jacket."

"Were you in the Army?"

"No. It was a gift."

The pastor smiled. "It looks like a nice jacket."

Seth nodded. The man made no sudden moves, but Seth remained vigilant.

A small voice came from behind him. "If the shepherd told you to come, then it must be your time to be born again."

Seth spun around. Before him stood one of the oldest, most frail-looking women he'd ever seen.

She couldn't have been a hundred pounds dripping wet. Here snow-white hair was piled into a neat little bun on top her head.

She leaned against a cane, staring up at him through thick lenses, a smile on her face.

She extended her hand. "I'm Jasmine."

He scratched his head with one hand as he shook hers with the other. *You've got to get out of here,* his inner voice screamed. *She recognized you for sure.*

"Pastor," Jasmine said. "He's here to be born again. If the good shepherd sent him, then he's got to be coming to be born again. Praise Jesus!"

Keeping a grip on his hand, she squeezed by him. "Come on in," she pulled at him. "Make yourself comfortable."

Seth didn't move.

She turned and looked at him quizzically. "We're all just one big family here. Might as well get used to us."

The pastor chuckled. "I'd do as Jasmine says. I don't know if you realize you were coming here to be born again, but Jasmine's our prophetess. If she says that's why you came, then that's why you came. There's no use fighting it."

Seth remained in the doorway. "What does it mean to be born again?"

"Being born again" he answered, "is what happens when one gives their life to Christ. Their old self dies, but they are given a new life – a free life. They're born again."

Seth nodded, but scoffed inwardly. *If they only knew what I am. If only they knew who I am – their would-be murderer.*

"You are here to be born of water and the spirit," Jasmine added.

"A new creation," the pastor chimed in.

Seth took a step back. It was a mistake coming here. He couldn't be saved if he wanted to, not after what he'd almost done to these people.

He didn't run, but turned and began walking away. Jasmine's voice followed him down the hall. "Jesus is my good shepherd.

He can be yours as well. All you've got to do is trust in him, and in him alone."

The shepherd? Seth stopped in his tracks.

***

Jason sat in utter darkness, frowning. Now and again, a curse hissed through his tight lips.

He was in the inner room – a slightly modified walk-in closet. It had no windows. The rod for hanging clothes had been removed. The walls were bare masonry block. The floor was poured concrete.

Also, the original closet door had been replaced. It was of reinforced steel. On the outer side, there was a drop-bar lock, also made of steel.

The door had a knob. Jason found it in the darkness. It turned but didn't release the lock.

There was no light fixture in here, a modification by design. The Kinship used this space for those requiring introspection, and light was a hindrance.

Jason's rage flared. *Introspection,* he thought. In reality, it was for those who'd failed the Kinship. *Punishment, not introspection.*

I shouldn't be here. His rage was just below the surface now. *It wasn't me. It was Seth that failed.*

Cain's words reverberated in his mind. "You and your brother failed together. You will also be punished."

I blame you both. Jason's thoughts had venom. *I blame you Seth for your weakness. I blame you Cain for your poor judgement.*

"You'd allow the innocent to suffer, Cain?" He shouted. His voice reverberated through the small space, echoing off the steel door.

"And what about you, Kindred Spirits?" he dared add. *You were there. You should have spoken to Cain in my defense. But you remained quiet didn't you – kept your lips tight like a clam's.*

He waited for the Spirits to reply, but none came. *Figures. I'm only half a prophecy. Why would the Spirits care about me?*

Screaming, he kicked the door. He threw fists at the wall. He jumped up and down. But nobody heard. *Nobody cares.*

Breathing hard, he sat back down. "Seth, if you'd only done as told," he mumbled hoarsely. "Then, I wouldn't be here in this room. Instead, we would be ruling the Kinship." He thought about Cain. "And my first decision as leader would be to throw Cain in here for a little introspection time of his own."

But you hadn't done as told, did you? Jason inhaled deep, calming breaths. *And now things are going to get bad.*

Time passed in the inner room and slowly Jason's scowl became more sorrowful. "Even after all I've done to help you," he mumbled. "I saved you from Mother. I saved you from the streets. I took you into the Kinship." He was shouting now, "And this is the thanks I get!"

Silence reigned. For how long? Jason didn't know. The inner room had no clock. "This isn't over dear brother," he hissed after a time. "Not even close."

Jason wiped away his tears. "I'm the stronger brother," he said to the empty darkness. "I will overcome the weaker."

***

Cain leaned against the steel door. He sensed Jason's anguish only a few inches away on the other side and it made him smile.

Above him, a single string of bare bulbs ran the length of the building's main hallway. The hallway curved slightly until the bulbs were lost to view.

Cain hadn't led on, but he didn't care much for the spirit's prophecy about the brothers. *Where would it leave me?* He wanted to know and was therefore happy it hadn't been fulfilled.

It would mean an end to my reign, he answered his own question. He thought about the priest before him and what had happened. Kinship changes of power never come without bloodshed.

Cain's smile widened because the brothers had failed in their mission. All would remain, at least for the time being.

This was a test of loyalty. He saw that now. *The Spirits wanted to see if I'd bend to their desire even if it meant my own death.*

Pride enveloped him because he'd passed the test. He'd willingly risked death for the Spirits.

And now he hoped to be rewarded. *I wish my reign to never end,* he dared think. *It's not too much given the price I paid.*

The Spirits didn't answer. They would when the time was right – perhaps through the rolling of bones or through some other ritual. Cain wasn't worried. They always answered eventually.

He pressed his face against the steel door. The coldness of it permeated his skin. He wondered about the soul on the other side – one half of the duo.

The other was still – somewhere. Cain didn't know where, but the Kinship would find him. They always did.

And when we find him, Seth will wish otherwise.

***

Jason grew quiet. Earlier, he'd felt so alone.

Now, he sensed they'd come – the Spirits. They surrounded him, protected him.

They hadn't come to punish him even though that was the reason he'd been put here in the inner room. They'd come for something else. He wasn't sure what.

Give it time, Jason, their words came through his thoughts. *Be patient. Give it time.*

The Spirits had spoken to him before, not often, but enough. He knew their voices and they knew him by name.

Nobody knew of this line of communication, at least he'd never told anyone. *Give it time,* they said again.

"I don't understand," Jason mumbled.

Give your brother some time. And give Cain some time. Like the crouching tiger waits for the perfect moment to pounce, so you will wait.

And be rewarded?

Of course, they answered.

Jason frowned. Patience was a virtue, but he wasn't a virtuous person. He wanted to pounce now, but he trusted the Spirits.

Wait, and you will be rewarded.

"Okay. I'll wait."

***

Cain pressed his ear right up to the steel door. Above him, the bare bulbs swayed by barely-there air flow, suspended by a single wire running the length of the hallway.

He thought he might have heard something. The steel was thick, but the inner room wasn't airtight. Sound did travel from time to time.

Cain listened, barely breathing, trying to stay as silent as possible. The Spirits were near. He sensed that much. But they weren't talking to him, at least not yet.

If not me, then who? The answer popped into his mind almost the moment that question was asked. *No.*

It suddenly became urgent that he release the prisoner. Fuming, he hoisted the drop-bar lock away and grabbed the door's knob.

The knob turned under its own power. Somebody was opening it from the far side.

CHAPTER 4

One Year Later

Seth smiled as he stood in front of the congregation. He did this often. Smiles were great for hiding behind.

This was a momentous day. He looked at every face in the chairs. All of Zion's Hill had come. They were all looking at him, filled with joy.

Of course, he could never tell anyone about his relationship with the Kinship or the fact that he'd come close to killing them all. What would happen then? He couldn't risk being turned in, arrested, sent to prison – not now that life was going so well.

Also, he couldn't risk leaving the church. *The Spirits would sure like that wouldn't they?* Without the church, he was a sitting duck – as good as dead.

He had a new faith. He had a new life, a new girlfriend. Zion's Hill had become the family he'd never known, and as long as he kept his past hidden, it would likely continue.

Seth took no chances. He kept clear of the Kinship and also Jason.

The later was difficult. Zion's Hill taught him about a God that loved him so much he'd sent his only son Jesus Christ to die for his sins. He knew Jason was still living the sinful life, ignorant of the gift God offered. He wanted to rescue him.

But what if I expose myself in the process? he always concluded.

He often pondered the Kinship Spirits. He knew now that they weren't Spirits at all, but demons led by Lucifer himself.

He understood now why those demons wanted him to kill those at Zion's Hill. To them, Zion's Hill was an enemy stronghold within their turf. The prayers of the faithful were strong here and strong prayers are bitter poison to demons – torturous and power inhibiting.

That's why they'd tried to kill him in the river. This failure must have been infuriating to them.

Why had God showed him mercy? He couldn't understand it. He didn't deserve it, but was grateful nonetheless.

A year ago? Some days it didn't seem that long. Other days, it felt like a lifetime. One lesson learned: accepting Jesus was easy. Following him was difficult.

Pastor Pete told him all Christians have a target on their back the moment they accept Christ. *He didn't know half of it.*

Regardless, he drew strength from the Bible which he kept in one of his Jacobson jacket pockets whenever he wasn't reading it.

Now, as he looked out over the crowd assembled in Zion's Hill, his fears of the past were barely a memory. This was a big day, his baptism.

Maxine sat in the front row, smiling her captivating smile. Whenever she did that, his past nearly melted from memory.

Over the last year, they had become close. *And it all started with that first smile,* he thought now.

She held up her left hand and waved timidly, her smile growing. The ring on her hand glimmered in the light. The diamond wasn't big. It certainly wasn't flawless, but it was what he could afford.

He'd worried she wouldn't accept it because it was a cheap ring. But Maxine wasn't his mother, Amanda. She didn't live life to take away from others. She was different.

He felt weak in the knees as he stared at her from his place in the front of church. Soon, they'd be up here together, tying the bonds of holy matrimony.

She's certainly better than I deserve, he thought. And for a brief moment, his past haunted him, but he pushed it away. *This is my life now,* he thought as he pushed those memories deep down in the darkness of his being.

Staring at Maxine, he barely noticed that Pastor Pete had started the baptism ceremony. Once he did notice though, he forced himself to pay attention. The sacrament of baptism would not be disrespected by his short attention span.

Seth was guided to the horse tank which Zion's Hill used for 'the dunking' as Jasmine so fondly referred to it.

He stepped into the tank, his pantlegs drenching. The water was a perfect room temperature. With the help of Pastor and an elder, he lowered himself into the water.

Pete placed his hands on Seth's head, and leaned him back into the tank. Seth went under the surface, and a bad memory from a dark place in his brain emerged.

No! he thought, forcing away the memory of demons dragging him into the depths. *The good shepherd saved me then. He'll save me now. He'll save me always.*

He purged that memory from him, refusing to soil his baptism with it. Even under the surface of the horse tank water, he could hear Pete. "Brother Seth, I baptize you in the name of the Father, and of the Son, and of the Holy Spirit."

Seth was happy as he rose up from the water. He knew Jesus, his shepherd. He'd been forgiven of every sin.

Just then, a voice within asked, *Are you though? Every sin? Even attempted murder?*

Seth ignored it and smiled broadly. Smiles were great for hiding behind. Plus, he really was happy.

***

Jason woke up, although he hadn't been asleep – not really. He looked at the digital clock near his bed which confirmed he's been lying here for hours, mostly in that twilight realm.

His insomnia was chronic, developed back when he shared the house with his mother and her parade of strange men. He never trusted any of them, which made him a light sleeper.

Tonight though, it wasn't strange men or neglecting mothers that kept him awake, it was his brother. In fact, he'd lost a lot of sleep over the last year because of Seth.

During the day, he could nurse his grudge, but at night, when all was quiet and dark, his rage affected him like an energy drink.

Tonight, like many other nights, he'd spiraled down the tornado of anger. Because of Seth, he'd become the Kinship's joke – he, the one the prophecy spoke of – a joke!

Cain especially taunted him, treating Seth like some leper. He was only a smidge above being untouchable.

It shouldn't be like this, he thought. *If Seth had only done as told – if he'd only done his share in the killing, then the prophecy would have been fulfilled.*

Jason's sweat dampened his sheets. The acrid stench permeated his nostrils.

Then Cain would be the outcast, not me!

Soon after Seth's departure, when everything first started going bad for Jason, he'd considered abandoning the Kinship as well. But where could he go?

The streets were unsafe for an AWOL Kinship member. *Correction, downright dangerous.*

Word travels fast on the streets. Especially when the messengers are spirits.

Besides, he knew so few people. Amanda was in no position to protect him. The police would be no use. Seth? He was probably dead already.

Jason tried kicking his sheets away, but they were sticky with perspiration. He kicked harder – cursing.

Calm yourself.

Jason immediately grew still. The Spirits often came to him when he was at his worst.

You're not the outcast Cain claims.

I know that. Why won't you tell everyone that?

The Spirits sighed. *Cain is our priest. He is our voice. We've told him, but he chooses not to listen. He fears you, Jason.*

Give it time. Your moment will come. Just be patient.

And with that, Jason finally fell asleep. Dreams danced in his head – dreams of vengeance.

CHAPTER 5

Two Years Later

Seth lay in bed, staring toward the ceiling. It was dark, but not completely. The streetlamps outside permeated the sheer curtains, casting the room in ethereal hues.

He often struggled with sleep, a product of his past. This was when his secrets confronted him the strongest – when he felt most ashamed for keeping the truth about who he used to be away from those who mattered most now.

I can't tell them. He couldn't risk it. These people of Zion's Hill loved him like a brother. Maxine loved him too. He couldn't risk throwing that all away.

Please God, take this from me, somehow.
He'd prayed such things so many times over the past two years. Sometimes though, prayers aren't answered right away in the way one wants them answered.

He stared up at the white-plaster ceiling, virtually shaking with anxiety. So many things haunted his nights: his brother, his childhood, his mother, and of course the fact that he once contemplated murder to save his own hide.

This isn't healthy.
He knew this, but he'd hidden for so long now. If felt impossible to escape it now.

Guilt crept in like a burrowing worm. Here he was, married to a beautiful woman, accepted by God and his church family – so unworthy of his blessings. And all the while his brother remained in spiritual darkness.

He'd often thought about rescuing Jason. But did his brother even want to be rescued? Plus, finding Jason would be akin to digging up the past, and he couldn't do that.

Maxine started snoring lightly. He turned and looked at her. She was so beautiful, bathed in the fragile light of the outside lights.

Who am I to be so blessed?

They were coming up on six months of marriage. Still in the honeymoon phase, some would say.

Six months, or sixty years, he knew his love for her would never fade. Her dark skin glowed in that light. Her light snoring was like music in his ears. Her black hair haloed her face like that of an angel's.

"I can't risk losing you," he whispered. *I won't.*

He couldn't understand what she saw in him, a man with a past he never shared.

He did share some, as much as he dared, but his deepest secrets remained under lock and key. *Indefinitely.*

Fortunately, she'd never been overly inquisitive about him. He never thought he'd find somebody that would love him for who he appeared to be without asking who he used to be. But that was who he'd found in Maxine.

He watched her sleep until his own eyes grew heavy. Until sleep came for him too.

***

The Spirits spoke often. *Give it time. Your moment will come. Just be patient,* they said.

So, Jason waited. The Kinship continued under Cain's leadership and they all treated him like an outcast.

Give it time. Your moment will come. Just be patient.

Two years of biding one's time isn't easy. He endured ridicule from Cain. He put up with pointing and laughing from the Kinship. He'd endured hours upon hours in the inner room. But he took it stoically because the Spirits had made him a promise – one he believed with all his heart.

He grinned. *When that time comes, woe to those who poked fun.*

Give it time. Your moment will come. Just be patient.

Nobody knew the Spirits spoke to Jason. Because why would they speak to such a plebe in the Kinship ranks. He kept those cards close, ready to reveal them when the time was right, but not a moment before.

During this time, he realized the Kinship wasn't his family. It was all just a front, a sham – a shell company hiding the truth. No, the Kinship was just a people to be exploited. Cain figured that out, and so had Jason, but everyone else seemed oblivious.

Give it time. Your moment will come. Just be patient.

The Spirits were his family. He knew it was true. They told him so.

This was the benefit of spending so much time locked in the inner room. By no means was it the torture Cain meant it to be. No, this was time for Jason to meet with his true family.

You deserve another chance, they said. *Another chance to prove yourself.*

Jason answered without hesitation, "I'll do whatever you ask of me."

The prophecy can still be fulfilled. It must be fulfilled.

"What do I have to do?"

Find your brother. Convince him to join us. Then the prophecy will come to fruition. All power will be yours.

Jason's eyes widened. "My brother is still alive?"

He is both alive and dead.

"I don't understand."

We allowed him to live after running from us. But, until he renews his allegiance, he's dead to us.

Jason nodded.

"And what about Cain." That name rolled off his tongue like a bitter pill.

Cain is nothing if you gain power with your brother. You will reign as priest.

Jason smiled. They said he could reign as priest, not he and his brother together. Their choice of words was not lost on him.

Jason thought of the moment Cain would discover everything and his smile stretched wider. Of course, he'd only allow Cain to learn of his demise once it was too late to thwart his coup. And then, the tortures he'd make that man endure. The thought made him sigh.

Do you hate Cain? The Spirits inquired.

Yes, Jason answered in thought.

Good. Do you hate your brother?

Jason paused. He was unsure how to answer. After all, Seth was a vital part of the prophecy.

Do you hate your brother? They pressed.

Yes. It felt good to say.

Hate is good because it keeps you sharp. However, you must control your hatred of Seth. He is your brother and you will need him to fulfill the prophecy.

What if he refuses to join me? What if he runs like last time?

For a moment, there was silence. Then, *Prophecy is prophecy. It cannot be altered. The power can only be obtained if your brother joins you.*

And if he won't?

There are ways to persuade.

Seth cannot be trusted.

Prophecy is prophecy, they repeated.

Jason didn't respond. He held Seth responsible for all the things done against him because if Seth had just done as instructed, then Jason would be ruling the Kinship today instead of being Cain's whipping boy.

Do not fret. Between you and your brother, you are the stronger. Once the prophecy is fulfilled, you'll rule and he'll be your servant.

He'll be my slave.

As you wish. But you're putting the horse before the cart. First, Seth must be brought back into the Kinship.

Jason nodded.

So, where has my brother been these last two years?

You won't believe it, the Spirits answered with a chuckle.

Try me.

He's defected to the enemy.

Zion's Hill?

Precisely.

Tell me more.

And, so they did.

***

Seth kept his head down as he walked. The sky was dark with clouds. The day was gloomy – the kind of weather that made one drowsy.

Seth didn't need any help in that department. Last night had been a bad one. He picked up his pace to keep from nodding off.

Glancing back, he could still see the edge of the front porch of the little bungalow that he and Maxine shared. It wasn't much, a one-bedroom, one and ½ story, built in the 1920s along with the rest of the neighborhood.

He and Maxine fell in love with it for a number of reasons. It had large windows. It had an open floor plan with maximum charm. And most importantly, it was in their price range.

On their budget, housing options were limited, but Maxine really wanted a house in lieu of an apartment. It was the American dream after all.

Theirs was a blue-collar neighborhood filled with more or less honest folk – hard-working folk. Plus, it was only a couple blocks from Zion's Hill.

Carrying a bagged lunch, He headed toward the bus stop which would drop him off near work. Inside the bag was an apple, a bologna sandwich on white bread with mustard and a slice of Swiss, and a fruit punch flavored Little Hug brand fruit drink.

He didn't have a lot of good memories related to his childhood, but getting Little Hugs at the food pantry was one of them. They reminded him his childhood wasn't complete garbage. Plus, they were cheap, so he could afford the nostalgia.

He wore his Jacobson jacket, turning up the collar against an unseasonable chilly breeze. The sky looked angry. He hoped the rain wouldn't start until he was on the bus.

He did have an umbrella with him, but if the wind really got going, it wouldn't do him much good. Already the gusts were strong enough to momentarily slow his pace.

At least Maxine won't be caught in this. She left for work two hours ago, driving their one car – a twenty-year-old Ford Fiesta.

The car had seen better days. It had more than 140,000 miles. The factory color was red, but had since sun-bleached to a pinkish form of red. But it ran and that's what they needed.

Maxine's commute was 45 minutes each way and her job didn't pay a lot, but she didn't mind because it was in her sales and marketing degree field.

She liked the work and her supervisor was very encouraging. If she stuck with it, her clientele would grow and the pay would increase. That was her hope anyway.

Thunder rumbled, low and ominous. Seth increased his pace to a slow jog. He could physically feel the temperature dropping by the second. *This is going to be a doozy of a storm.*

With his lunch in one hand and his umbrella in the other, he hugged his Jacobson jacket as tightly to him as possible. Still, the wind whipped it around, as if trying to steal his prized jacket.

The only part of that jacket that felt anchored was the right side, because that's where the pocket was that had his Bible.

These days, he rarely went anywhere without his Bible. Reading it was something of an obsession – he couldn't get enough of it.

It was a gift presented by Pastor Pete on behalf of Zion's Hill and had been given to him the day of his baptism. It was also his primary weapon against the Devil's schemes.

Dust stung his face as the wind picked up. He lifted the collar to block it. That's when he heard something.

It was barely audible above the howling wind. *Somebody's crying.*

The cries rode on the wind and Seth followed them. They were long, sorrowful sobs.

The landscape had changed a few blocks back. He was no longer on a street of single-family dwellings.

This block had seen better days. The old 19th century brownstones still had their ornate windows and regal front stoops, but they looked worn. Plus, some of the windows revealed vacancy. This was clearly a block in decline.

Garbage blew along the sidewalk, swirling in the growing wind. The crying was louder here. Seth followed it to a place where a front stoop provided relief from the wind.

Here was a sobbing man.

Seth knew the type. His clothes, unkept hair, and beard gave him away. He had a grimy backpack sitting beside him, bulging with belongings. Also, here in the shelter of the stoop, Seth could smell him – body odor and cheap bourbon.

The man hadn't noticed Seth's presence. He remained hunched to stay warm – to protect himself from the coming storm.

He wasn't dressed for the weather. His jeans were torn. His flannel shirt was thin and missing buttons. His shoes were held together by wrappings of duct tape.

The man trembled as the wind picked up and he began to cry harder. Seth suspected he was detoxing. He'd seen it before in some of the men Amanda brought home.

He who has two coats, let him give to him who has none. He'd read that in his Bible just that morning. It never stopped amazing him, how God's word spoke to those who believed. It was something very different from that of the Kinship, but not less powerful.

But I don't have two coats, he said to himself. *I only have my Jacobson jacket.*

You can get another jacket, he argued with himself. *This man needs one now.*

But, it's my jacket. Mother gave it to me…

Even as he argued, he knew what he'd do. He'd do the right thing.

Seth approached the man slowly. He removed his jacket and draped it over the man's shoulders.

The man jolted. His eyes gave away the fact that he'd not noticed Seth's presence until then.

"You look cold," Seth ventured. "Take my jacket."

He almost took it back. This was his jacket. It'd been with him through thick and thin.

You shall love your neighbor as yourself, another scripture popped into his head. He'd noticed this happening more and more as he read his Bible more often.

"Your jacket?" the man mumbled.

"It's yours. You need it more."

"God bless you."

"May God bless you too," Seth replied.

"I have nothing to give you," the man mumbled.

Seth looked into the man's eyes. They weren't clear. He was obviously still a little drunk or high or both. "It's ok. I'm giving you this because Jesus has blessed me. I want you to have it."

Seth began to walk away, then he turned back. *I forgot my Bible in the pocket.* He almost asked for it back – almost.

You can always get another. He told himself. *And this man needs it more than you.*

"Have you eaten today?" Seth inquired.

The man's face told the answer.

"Here." He handed the man his lunch. He'd get something a McDonalds if he got hungry.

The man wiped tears away. "Thanks."

Seth turned and walked away. He got to the bus stop just in time. He was cold, but it didn't matter.

He took a seat near the rear of the bus and was already starting to warm up. *This is going to be a good day.*

He could feel it.

***

Jason told Cain why they needed to recruit the Kinship defector. Cain listened with the air of derision usually reserved for the Kinship outcast.

Jason hadn't wanted to tell Cain at all, but the Spirits were insistent. *If he's included, then he'll be less likely to realize his days are numbered,* they said.

"How do you know your brother is still alive let alone residing at Zion's Hill," Cain scoffed.

Seth paused. He didn't want to give away the fact that the Spirits told him. Cain thought he was the only one the Spirits spoke with. Proving him wrong could end badly. "I saw him on the streets and followed him to the church."

"And why do you think he'll come back?"

Jason chose his words carefully. "We'll do what we can to persuade him. If he refuses, we'll take him by force. Regardless, the prophecy must be fulfilled."

Cain didn't argue which destressed Jason just a smidge. He smiled at the priest, but inside, his rage was rising. *Your days are numbered Cain,* he thought but dared not say.

Cain stroked his beard, thinking. His eyes stared hard at Jason. His poker-face was unreadable.

Is he on to me? Jason could actually feel his pulse speed up.

"Do it," Cain finally said.

Jason exhaled the breath which he'd been holding in without even realizing it. Then, he left Cain's presence.

***

Cain regarded Jason as he left. The man seemed nervous.

Jason hadn't been able to maintain eye contact – a clear giveaway. Also, his breathing was short and his eyebrows were twitchy.

That could just be the result of Jason, a Kinship outcast, daring to speak with the high priest. *Or, was it something more?*

He's not telling me everything. Cain puzzled. *Why?*

Because he's looking out for himself. Cain answered his own question.

The fulfillment of the prophecy was worth its weight in gold to Jason, but was worthless to Cain. In fact, Cain stood to lose everything if it was fulfilled.

He'd destroyed many lives to get to where he was. He'd destroyed countless more to keep his position. He wasn't about to go on the chopping block himself.

Why do you want me to go? He inquired of the Spirits. *What have I done to displease you?*

He waited, but no response came. In the old days, the Spirits spoke with him daily. Such conversations – epic conversations. Back then, they idolized him – always whispering flattering things in his ears.

Times change. These days, the Spirits only spoke to him occasionally, and never directly. They spoke only through black arts like the rolling of bones and the reading of tealeaves. Never like they used to – never face to face.

Are they speaking to you, dear Jason? His eyes narrowed at that thought. *And if so, what are they telling you?*

"I won't go easily," he mumbled with clenched fists.

He schemed. *I'll go along with Jason for now. And when the time is ripe, I'll destroy him and his brother.*

A smile grew on his face. *They'll go down like all the rest. I'll dedicate their sacrifice to the Kinship spirits. Then surely, it'll be like old times again.*

Cain smiled. He liked his plan better than Jason's – far better.

***

Seth left work. The wind blew. The temperature fell. Soon it would be winter.

At times like this, he thought of his Jacobson jacket. It's been weeks since he'd given it away. It had been his security blanket for so long and honestly, he missed it.

He walked toward his bus stop, buttoning up his new padded flannel jacket which he'd gotten soon after losing Jacobson. Like much of his wardrobe, it was a thrift store find.

Whenever he thought about his jacket, he also thought of the one who wore it. He often prayed for the man. It was all he could do now.

The bus dropped him off in his neighborhood and he began walking toward his home. The wind was against him.

I should have stayed with him longer, Seth thought. *I should have witnessed to him – shared the gospel.*

He furrowed his brow. *I shouldn't have been so much in a hurry – so intent on not missing my bus.*

The wind changed direction and he staggered. *I'll try harder next time,* he prayed although he knew it wasn't him that did anything. If the man was to be saved, he would be saved. Still, he wanted to do better. *I will do better.*

Maxine worked long hours. She had to if she was going to build up her clientele and find success. Seth's routine was fairly standard here. He'd come home, clean up a bit, and then start cooking supper so it was ready when his wife got there.

He stood in front of their bungalow, struggling open the mailbox at the curb. The wind made this difficult. It was a full-blown gale, pulling at him, making him stumble.

Only a few envelopes were inside the mailbox. Two were sales pieces addressed to "current resident".

He moved these to the bottom of the stack and froze. The last envelope caused his world to spin. He grabbed the mailbox for balance as his body began to shiver, not from the wind but from his nerves.

The "current resident" pieces fell from his grip and blew away in the wind. He didn't retrieve them, but continued staring at that third envelope – his eyes wide like saucers.

This envelope had no stamp and didn't come via postal service. Two words were written on it.

From Amanda.

He tore it open with trembling hands.

***

"Amanda old gal, you never were much of a housekeeper," Jason mumbled as he glanced around in disgust.

He hesitated, finally choosing the least-stained spot on the threadbare couch. *Hope I don't get a disease,* he said to himself as he sat.

This couch had followed Amanda since he could remember, one of the few constants in an otherwise everchanging life.

It's been a while, Mom. Yet, even after so much time, some things never change.

Unlike his brother, who he'd assumed was dead, he'd kept track of Amanda, albeit covertly. Why? Because perhaps one day, she would prove useful to him.

That day arrived.

It hadn't been hard to track her. Many of her current and past men were Kinship members. And the sort of men she kept liked to brag, even if it was only to the group's main outcast.

Jason swallowed hard. The smell alone was rough. The sight was rougher.

His disgust went deeper than his senses. *Memories.*

He shook his head. He'd not allow his past to haunt him. *What about you, brother? Will you come, or are the memories too distasteful?*

Jason hoped he'd show. He needed him to show. He tried to convince himself. *A mamma's boy like Seth wouldn't be able to stay away if he tried.*

He used to ask the question often: Why did Seth cling so long to his mother's apron strings?

He couldn't understand it. They'd both endured her abysmal mothering, her cold neglect.

He counted on his brother's soft heart for Amanda now – his weakness for her. *Amanda is the bait. Let's hope the fishing's good. Let's hook a live one.*

The prophecy needed fulfillment. Cain must be deposed. *And it'll all start with a meeting between brothers.*

He shifted his weight. The couch protested with the twang of bent springs.

Where are you? he wondered.

It was strange to think that not long ago, Jason assumed his brother was dead. Now, just a short time later, he knew quite a bit about Seth's life.

It was easy finding out Seth's address once the Zion's Hill connection was discovered. It was just a matter of obtaining a copy of the church's directory. This was no hard task. Even in the digital age, Zion's Hill still printed physical copies. It'd been easy to sneak in under disguise and steel one.

Inside the directory, Jason discovered where his brother resided. There was also a photo. *But who's the woman pictured with him?* He wondered. *Maxine? Well brother, I wonder why I wasn't invited to the wedding?*

He shifted weight again and a couch spring stuck him in the butt. That brought him back to the present.

Knock, knock, knock. Somebody was at the door.

Jason smiled. *Hello brother, I see you received your letter.*

He didn't get up to answer the unlocked door. Neither did he bid the knocker to enter. No, Seth would come to him as a first act of submission to the superior sibling.

He heard the door unlatch and open. "Mom?" the voice of his weaker half drifted in. "Are you home?"

Jason smiled but said nothing. *You came crawling back to Mom just like always. Just like I knew you would.*

He heard the door groan as it opened more fully. Then, footsteps on creaking floorboards. *Come on in, brother. Let's have a little family reunion.*

Jason could hardly wait.

***

Seth's knocks went unanswered. He steadied his hand and turned the knob. Finding it unlocked, he opened the door just a little, then all the way, and took a step into the house. "Mom, are you home?"

The first thing he noticed was the stench. He stifled a gag.

He held his mother's letter. His fingers trembled as they gripped it, as if it weighed more than what paper and ink should.

He entered further into the home. With every step, the smell grew worse. He found the combination of incense, body odor, and weed, to be both familiar and repulsive.

He grimaced. Countless memories bombarded him. They were mostly bad ones which he'd tried for years to repress. The tears came now as they resurfaced.

Here, two brothers were forced to grow up too quickly – required to be self-sufficient too soon. Hard lessons were learned – some were extra hard to learn because they should have been taught by a father figure.

But father was absent. So was Mother, more or less.

Seth prayed, *Jesus, help me.* His tears clouded his vision, not that it mattered. He could have navigated the entry way blindfolded. This had once been home, like it or not.

He looked at the envelope in his hand. Perspiration darkened it where his sweaty fingers gripped. *Please Jesus, give me strength.*

He still cared for Amanda. He couldn't explain why. She was self-centered, egotistical, and ignorant of her children's needs. *But she's my mother, the only one I'll ever have.*

Because he was now saved and because she WAS his mother, he'd prayed for her a lot – hoping she'd come out of the lifestyle she led and turn a new leaf. He'd prayed for strength to visit with her, to offer his help – but hadn't been able to bring himself to that point. Too many bad memories held him back.

But now, she's sent the letter.

When he'd read her letter, his legs suddenly felt rubbery and he'd held onto his mailbox for balance. Amanda's words generated both fear and courage simultaneously.

This is no time for cowardice, he'd said then and forced himself to go to her.

Now, he was wondering if he'd made the right choice. This place held so many bad memories.

He looked at the walls of the entryway. They were stained dark with age and cigarette smoke. There was a crack in the plaster near the doorway where somebody's head and once hit the wall, the result of two men fighting over his mother.

To this day, he didn't understand why men fought over her. She only ever used them.

He thought about it. The using went both ways. Everything between Amanda and her men was a quid pro quo, an exchange of drugs, sex, and money.

He wiped away the tears. They'd stopped flowing now. His face felt hot.

A crinkling sound entered his ears. He was crumpling Amanda's letter. His grip was so tight that his fist quivered under the pressure.

He inhaled deeply, calmed himself, and relaxed his hold on that envelope. *Dear God, help me overcome this.*

"Mom?" he called out once more. "Amanda?"

Silence.

Maybe I'm too late. What if writing the letter was the last thing she did before dying?

Ahead, the entryway turned left. Then, if he remembered right, he'd be in the living room.

He remembered the living room particularly well. Amanda always kept the drapes closed here. They were heavy drapes. No light got through. She liked it that way because her hungover brain didn't like the light.

I'll whoop you good, he remembered her screaming at him once when he tried to open the drapes.

The tears came once more. *I just wanted to see outside. That's all.*

With resolve, he forced himself to walk toward that corner in the entryway – to turn and enter the living room. *I've come this far. I can't turn back now. I owe it to Amanda? No. I owe it to myself.*

He rounded the corner. "Mother, I've come…" his voice dropped dead. The one sitting on the couch was not Amanda.

"Where's Mother?" he asked, trying hard to stifle the fear in his voice.

***

"How would I know where Mother is?" Jason responded.

He intentionally smiled as toothily as possible. *Nothing's changed in you over the last two years. Nothing at all. You're still just a mamma's boy.*

Seth's eyes narrowed and Jason could feel the lack of love. "Don't look so angry brother," he said sweet as syrup. "We have a history, you and me. We've been apart for a long time. How long's it been anyway?"

"Where is Amanda?"

"I already told you I have no idea." He paused. "Two years, can that be right? Has it really been that long since we last saw each other? Where has the time gone?"

"What have you done with her?"

Jason inhaled deeply. "You're not going to let this go, are you? Obviously, she's not here."

If Seth's eyes were cobras, they'd be spitting venom. His breathing was audible, as if he was about to explode.

Jason added, "I'm not her keeper you know."

Seth's stomped his feet hard enough to cause a cloud of dust to rise from the shag carpet. "Don't mess with me," he spat.

Maybe my brother has changed a bit. Maybe he has some bite after all. "You know her reputation. She's a bit flaky – could be anywhere really." He saw what Seth held. "I see you received the letter."

Seth's voice dropped an octave, "How would you know what this is?"

"Oh, brother," Jason chuckled. "Don't you recognize my handwriting when you see it?"

"You? You! You wrote this?"

Jason closed his eyes. "I want to start over – be the mother I always should have been," he said with a high voice. "I'm trying to stay clean, but I need help. Right now, I don't know if I can do it. Maybe I'd be better off dead. Come fast. Please help me."

Jason knew he was reciting the letter pretty accurately. After all, he was the author.

He opened his eyes. By the seething expression on his brother's face, he knew he'd struck a nerve. This knowledge gave him great satisfaction.

"You wrote the letter!" Seth's voice rose.

"I believe that's been established. Now, can we please move on to more important things."

"Why? Why would you do something like this?"

"Okay, I guess we can't move on yet," Jason chuckled. "I wrote it because I need to speak with you."

Seth glared.

"And I don't think you would come if I told you the truth."

"What are you talking about," Seth spat.

"I mean, it's me, the brother you abandoned at Zion's Hill. I'm the one you deserted remember? Would you respond now if I wrote you a letter asking to meet? I doubt it.

"However, you've always been a mamma's boy. I bet myself you'd come for her. And guess what? I was right. Here you are."

Seth didn't say a word. His body language said it all.

"But now that you're here, maybe we can talk."

"What did you do with Amanda?" Seth asked, his voice trembling. "This is her place. She's not here. What did you do with her?"

"Only what needed to be done."

Seth screamed, "What did you do with her!"

Jason wanted to beat some respect into Seth. *Give it time. Your moment will come. Just be patient,* he remembered what the Spirits had told him. "Your fascination with Mother is a little off-putting, I have to say. It's something to consider working on, in the interest of self-betterment if for no other reason."

Seth's voice came low, almost a whisper, "What did you do with her?"

"You really aren't going to listen to a thing I have to say until we address this are you?" He forced his voice to remain calm, jovial even. "I've missed you, brother. Despite your mamma-issues, and other quirks, I've missed you." He paused, "You want to know what happened to Amanda? Fine, but first, we have business to discuss."

Jason patted the vacant spot on the sofa. "Have a seat, let's talk."

Seth didn't move.

***

Maxine pulled into the driveway, turned off the ignition, and listened to the engine tick as it cooled. *Is it time for an oil change?* She wondered about the old Fiesta.

It was time, but she dreaded scheduling it. The mechanic she took it to was good, but it was always disheartened for her to get the list of items that needing fixing or replacing.

She needed a car. This was the car they could afford. And yet, they never had the money to keep it running in good condition.

She exited the vehicle and walked up the porch stairs to the front door of the bungalow she shared with Seth. She unlocked the door and stepped inside, glad to be out of the weather. It wasn't too bad of a day, but cold, a hint of winter to come.

For a second, she just stood there, warming her arms by rubbing them. Besides the sound made by that friction, the house was quiet.

"Seth?"

No answer.

"I'm home."

She paused – nothing. Maxine breathed deep. It was unusual to not be smelling something delicious wafting from the kitchen when she came home.

She walked from the living room to the kitchen in back. That space was clean and vacant.

The hairs on the back of her neck bristled as she reentered the living room and climbed the steps to the bedroom and bath.

"Seth?"

No Seth. She rubbed the back of her neck to calm those bristling hairs. *Maybe he had to work late,* she told herself.

He'd never worked late before. His job was a punch-in, punch-out kind of arrangement with set hours and no overtime.

Maybe he got home and had to leave again for some reason.

She reentered the kitchen and checked the table for a note. They only had one cell phone which she had for work, so this was how they communicated.

There was nothing on the table. She checked the floor, hoping one had fallen. Nothing.

He probably didn't feel like cooking and is getting takeout from the Hung's, the Chinese restaurant a few blocks away. Sure, that makes sense.

They rarely did this without discussing it first. They didn't have much money to spend on such things. Still, it was possible.

Wherever he was, Maxine hoped he'd return soon. Not knowing was the worst. Plus, she was hungry.

She stepped onto the porch and looked as far as she could see down the street in the direction of Hung's. *Where are you?*

A white utility van drove by and parked two houses away on the opposite side of the street. Other than that, the road was empty.

She furrowed her brow, turned and went back into the house and closed the door. *Where are you, Seth?*

***

"That's the deal on the table, brother."

Seth's head swam.

"Take it or leave it." Jason's statement felt final.

Two years ago, maybe he would have considered Jason's offer. But Seth was saved now. He knew what the Spirits were. He knew the truth and so could never go back to the Kinship. But how could he tell Jason this without angering him further?

"I hate to put pressure on you, bro," Jason chuffed. "But this is a limited-time offer, and it's about to expire."

He stared at Jason. The man appeared so confident as he sat there on the old couch. "Are you with me or against me?" he said with a smile

"Neither," Seth answered.

"I'm afraid that's not an option."

"But it's the truth, Jason. Let me expla…"

Jason interrupted. "That's just the sort of luke-warm answer I'd expect from somebody in the Zion's Hill sect."

He knows about my relationship with Zion's Hill?

Jason grinned as he put his arms up on the back of the couch, exuding the confidence of a master salesman moving in for the close. "Oh yes, I know all about your religion and friends and lies they've told you."

Seth shook his head. "They aren't lies. If you give them the chance, you'll see."

Jason's smile vanished. "You've been brainwashed," he spat. "Think about it. I'm sure they've told you how powerful your Jesus is. I'm sure they've told you all the stories out of their Bible about how great is their god's power. Here's the thing though? What evidence have they shown you?"

Seth stood there trying to organize his response.

"Surely the Christian God has shown you His power. What evidence do you have?"

"I…"

"And before you answer," Jason interjected. "Think of the evidence you've been shown by the Spirits. Think of the bloodletting ceremony. Did you not feel their presence there – their power?"

Memories of his haunting in the river bombarded Seth. The Spirits did show their power that night. But so did Jesus. *But how do I convince Jason of this?* The man had clearly taken his side – the wrong side of the chasm.

"I've seen true power," Seth finally uttered. "I've seen it first-hand. It's far more than anything the demons of the Kinship possess. It's real power. It's real salvation."

"It's real snake oil – nothing but smoke and mirrors."

"Just give it a chance. I'll show…"

"You talk about power," Jason hissed. "You don't know what true power even is. In fact, neither of us has seen true power. But, if the prophecy is fulfilled, then we will see it. Just think, all you have to do is join me and it becomes ours for the taking."

This wasn't going well. If he'd been more prepared for a head-on collision with Jason, maybe things would be going better, but he thought he was meeting his mom who, according the forged letter, was potentially in a mood to listen. "The power of Jesus is greater than anything your prophecy can deliver," was all he could say.

"Oh really? Show me."

"What?"

"Show me this power. Show me it's greatness, and I'll believe."

Seth shook his head. "I used to be just like you. I used to need proof of power. Now I live by faith, knowing that someday my faith will become sight."

Jason scoffed. "Just another Christian delusion."

Seth looked down at the letter he held. "You still haven't answered my question."

"What question?"

"Where's Amanda?"

"She's dead."

Those two words hit Seth like a sledgehammer. Jason's ear-to-ear grin sickened him and he felt the urge to beat it off his face.

"I killed her."

"You---," Seth had no words. His hands began to shake and he clenched them into fists, tight and formidable.

"And the same will happen to your precious wife unless you reconsider your loyalties."

A lump caught in Seth's throat. *He knows I'm married?* He thought about the letter he'd found in his mailbox without postage. *He knows where we live.*

"You don't want to put Maxine in harm's way, do you?"

He knows her name? Seth's legs became rubbery and he grabbed the wall for support.

"Think long and hard before you make a final decision brother," Jason's voice came to him as if through a long tunnel. "If you still think your Jesus will save you from the Kinship, then by all means, put your trust in him. But, if your wrong, I'd hate for Maxine to pay the price."

The room began to spin. He needed to get out of there. He needed to save Maxine!

"Just make the right choice and nobody gets hurt."

Seth staggered away from Jason, toward the door. He needed to leave now – before it's too late!

As he stumbled out of the living room and toward the entry way, he heard Jason's voice. "It's in your court, brother. Everything's in your court."

He ran out the door, leaving it open.

"The offer stands for now! But it won't last long! Make your choice!"

He ran toward home. He needed to get there first – before it was too late.

He had no phone. He had no car. He was no Olympian and it was a long way to sprint, but he'd do what he had to do, even if he died of exhaustion.

Make your choice! Jason's voice rang inside his head. *Make our choice!*

He ran toward home as fast as his legs could propel him. *Make your choice!*

***

"Well, that went downhill in a hurry," Jason said to the empty room.

He sat there for a moment, savoring his little victory, relaxed and unrushed.

He'd been surveilling Seth since the moment he learned the man was still alive and was almost certain his brother didn't have a mobile phone. And if he had no mobile phone, he couldn't easily relay a warning to Maxine.

He was confident Seth wouldn't go to the cops. The fear in his brother's face showed he understood calling the police meant Maxine would be dead before they ever arrived on the scene.

Jason withdrew his smartphone from his pocket and dialed. It only rang once before being answered.

"It's me," he said into the receiver. "No, just like we figured, he didn't bite. Yes, he's on his way there now. Yes, initiate the plan immediately. You have 15 minutes."

He'd ran from his brother's house to Amanda's place three times over the last couple days. The test results were in. It took 15 minutes.

He stood up and the old couch groaned. He reached for the ceiling, stretching his muscles.

"Why do you always make the wrong choice, brother," he uttered. "You should have just agreed to join me." He paused and crossed his arms. "Now your wife will pay a hefty price."

CHAPTER 6

Pamela hung up the phone and handed it to Big Steve. "Looks like the mission is on. We have 15 minutes."

Steve nodded. He and Pamela were the two newest members of the Kinship. Therefore, they'd been assigned this mission to prove their worth – their loyalty.

Pamela could tell Steve had the same excitement about the fact they were going in. This was their moment to shine – to start climbing the Kinship ranks.

15 minutes. Tick, tick, tick...

Pamela knew it could be done in that amount of time. She and Big Steve rehearsed it a hundred times over the last 24 hours. It could be done in 15 minutes, but no dilly dallying.

"Time's ticking," she said, handing Steve two magnetic signs that were sitting between them in the van. Both signs read *42nd Street Laundry Service.*

Big Steve also grabbed the large, dark gray linen sheet from behind his seat. He wadded it up as tightly as possible. Together, they exited the white, windowless utility van which they'd parked across the street and a couple houses down from their target.

She nonchalantly glanced up and down the street. It was vacant. That was good. They didn't need witnesses.

Steve joined her. "The signs are on the van."

Pamela nodded and glanced around once more. *I hope nobody's watching.*

Big Steve, with his freakishly large size, would certainly stand out in someone's mind if the police question neighbors later. The man was a natural for intimidation tactics, but not so much for espionage. But all new Kinship members did grunt work regardless of size.

15 minutes. Tick, tick, tick...

They crossed the street and angled toward the little bungalow with the Ford Fiesta parked in the driveway. The key was to not draw attention.

She frowned as she walked because Big Steve was with her and looked more like an escaped gorilla from the Zoo, than your average Joe. *Why did it have to be Big Steve? What deplorable thing had she done in a past life to warrant this punishment now.*

She glanced at him, but he didn't look back. The sheet he carried distracted him. It kept unfurling from his spade-shovel-sized hands and billowing in the breeze.

She rubbed her temples. *He's as uncoordinated as he is large.* "Keep that under control, will you?" she snapped.

Big Steve didn't respond. But he did wrestle the sheet back into his grip.

She led Steve up the driveway. The Fiesta was an old model that had seen better days. The vehicle was empty.

She climbed the porch stairs. She heard Steve follow, sounding like Frankenstein's monster. "Can't you do anything quietly?"

She wanted to say more, but refrained. He furrowed his brow in annoyance. She didn't need anyone that size being annoyed at her. It would be hard, but she needed to hold her tongue. *The mission came first.*

Fifteen minutes, and counting.

***

Maxine made herself a grilled cheese while she waited for her husband to return from wherever he'd gone. It wasn't really a meal, but it would tide her over until Seth got home.

She sat at their kitchen table, nibbling nervously at the sandwich. *Where are you, Seth?*

She checked her mobile every few minutes – no messages. She did the same with her land line with the same results – nothing.

He's an adult, she told herself. *He probably had to leave for some legit reason. He'll be walking in the door any second and we'll all have a good laugh about how worried I'd gotten over nothing.*

A noise made her jump. Somebody was at her front door – knocking.

She got up and started toward the door. *What if it's the police? What if they're here to tell me something bad has happened to Seth?*

Shut up! She chastised herself. *Don't go putting the cart before the horse.*

She peered through the front door's peephole. It wasn't the police.

It was a man. *Was it a man?* The guy looked like Goliath.

She observed him and felt those hairs rise up once more on the back of her neck. Something about this guy was off. For one thing, he shifted weight from one leg to the other too often, as if he had no business standing there on her front porch.

He held something that kept escaping his grasp. *A sheet?*

Whatever it was, the guy was struggling to keep it wadded up in his catcher's mitt hands.

She held her cell phone, keeping it at the ready. Calling the police seemed a bit pre-mature. The man's size was intimidating, but there's no law against being large.

Whatever you're selling, I'm not buying. Just go away.

But he didn't go away. Instead, he knocked again, louder than before.

***

Everything was going to plan. Pamela could hear Big Steve knocking. His bowling-ball-sized fists were quite handy in certain situations. Meanwhile, she moved into position at the rear of the house.

She moved quickly. Time was of the essence and she couldn't afford even one delay if she wanted to be gone before the 15-minute timer ran to zero.

Pamela approached the back of the house, keeping below the windows, staying silent – hoping no neighbors saw. She heard Big Steve knock again and smiled. Finally, his sticking-out-like-a-sore-thumb syndrome was paying off.

She reached up and tried the back door's knob. It was locked.

She retrieved the locksmith kit she carried in her hip pocket and was opening the door in less than 10 seconds. *Click,* went the latch as it disengaged.

She pushed the door open slowly to avoid creaking, and only far enough to slip into the kitchen. Pamela listened. Steve's knocking continued.

She tiptoed past the stove, refrigerator and sink. Using the table for balance, she slid toward the entrance to the living room.

Not only could she hear Steve's knocks, but she could actually feel them vibrating through the floorboards. *That man doesn't know his own strength.*

Her mouth watered. The grilled cheese on the table smelled delicious but there was no time to take a bite. Time was running low. She pulled a sealed envelope from her back pocket and put it on top of the sandwich.

She peered into the living room and saw the wife just where she suspected she'd be, staring out the peephole at Big Steve.

Moving like a prowling feline, she approached the woman. Pamela noticed the cell phone in her hand. *This is going to be tricky.*

Slowly, she drew nearer, past a staircase leading to the upper floor, past the television mounted on the interior wall – every step was one step closer to her prey.

The woman shifted slightly.

Pamela froze.

For a moment that felt like eternity, everything seemed stuck in time.

How much time is left? Five minutes? Four?

Pamela forced her body forward. She couldn't afford to waste any more time. The husband could arrive any moment and they needed to be gone by then. Fortunately, the carpet muffled her footsteps.

Pamela withdrew the bottle of chloroform from her fanny pack along with a handkerchief. While continuing her predatory prowl, she opened the bottle and wetted the handkerchief.

The slightly sweet smell of the chemical permeated the air. She closed the bottle and replaced it in her pack. *Almost there.*

She'd only get one shot. She needed the element of surprise. Closer, closer she crept.

Steve kept knocking.

The woman kept staring out the peephole.

Pamela prepared to strike.

***

Can't you take a hint? Nobody's home. Leave!

The salesman, or whoever he was, seemed determined not to move on. Maxine considered calling the police. *But was there probable cause? Was he loitering only if she let him know she wasn't interested in what he was selling?*

And why was he holding that sheet? It didn't make sense.

She checked the deadbolt and was relieved to find it held. He knocked loud enough now to rattle the plaster.

"That's it big boy," she hissed. "I'm calling the cops."

But she never got the chance.

***

Pamela grabbed the woman from behind, wrenching her wrist, twisting her arm until she dropped the phone. Her other hand simultaneously wrapped around her, cupping the handkerchief over the woman's mouth and nose.

She slammed the woman against the door and heard her breath escape. The woman pushed back, but Pamela had the element of surprise and leverage on her side.

The wife screamed, but those screams were muffled due to the handkerchief. Pamela dodged clawing hands and stomping feet. Pain radiated up her hand as the woman sunk her teeth into Pamela's finger. Undaunted, she slammed the woman into the door again.

Her victim grew weak as the chloroform did its job. In another second, she became limp, sliding down the door, landing in a crumpled heap on the floor.

Her arm stung where the woman's fingernails had caught her. The adrenaline masked the pain before. Now it felt like a hot poker had seared her.

During the melee, the woman's screams overpowered everything else. Now though, she heard Steve. "Pamela!" he shouted as he pounded on that door.

She fumed as she pulled the limp body to one side of the door. *That moron's going to get us caught.*

Before Pamela could open the door, it blew from its hinges with Steve bringing up the rear like an angry bull moose.

Pamela fell to the floor, reacting just fast enough to avoid being plowed over. Projectile splinters flew from the doorframe bouncing off her like angry wasps.

The doorframe clamored to the living room floor. Big Steve stumbled and fell on top of it, grunting as he landed.

She looked over the unconscious woman. She was unharmed. She wiped the perspiration from her brow and turned on Steve.

"What do you think you're doing!" she hissed.

Steve stumbled to his feet, confusion showing.

"If you'd hurt her," she jabbed a finger at the crumpled body beside the door. "It would be our hides."

Steve shrugged. "I heard a ruckus. I thought you needed help."

"Your 'help' almost landed us time in the inner room."

"It sounded like you were in trouble."

"Everything's under control!" she hissed through gritted teeth.

Pamela had more to say, but refrained. There couldn't be more than a couple of minutes to spare. They had to get scarce. "Lay out the sheet."

Steve spread it out over the fallen door. Together, they lifted the woman onto it and folded her up like a burrito.

Steve hoisted the burrito on one shoulder. He made it look easy even though Pamela knew the woman was probably a hundred pounds.

She struggled with the door, leaning it back into the doorframe as best she could. No sense in the damage being too obvious.

They stood there on the porch, listening. *No sirens.*

She glanced around. No witnesses were visible and no sign of the husband yet.

"Let's go."

Pamela led. Steve followed with the sheet that now looked suspiciously like a body bag.

Her heart pounded as she opened the back of the van and Steve slid the burrito in. She felt exposed here, but nothing could be done about it.

They got in. She started up the engine. They left.

"How's she doing back there?" she asked after a block or so.

Steve turned and looked back from the passenger seat. "I think she's breathing."

"She'd better be," Pamela replied. "It's our necks on the chopping block if we show up with a corpse."

"Do you think anyone saw us?" Steve wanted to know.

Pamela didn't answer. She'd taken about as much of Steve as she could handle.

He didn't ask again, and that was a good thing.

***

Seth ran home. His lungs felt like they were on fire. He stopped only once to throw up and wait for his vision to clear.

His thoughts chastised himself. *If only you'd been truthful from the beginning. Now, everyone you care about is in trouble because of your obsession with hiding the truth about your past.*

He staggered to his house and tripped on the porch steps, going down hard, skinning his shins.

The pain and exhaustion blurred his vision, but he pushed on. *I have no choice.*

His shins, sticky with blood adhered to his jeans. He took a step and they peeled away. He moaned, but didn't stop. *I can't.*

He grabbed the railing and pulled himself up the remaining stairs. He saw the door. His stomach wretched.

The door was free of its hinges, leaning against a splintered frame. "Maxine," he tried to say. But he had no wind in his pipes and it only came as a raspy whisper.

He wheezed as the tears came. *This can't be happening. Wake up!*

He wasn't dreaming no matter how much he wished otherwise. "Ma..." he tried calling for her. He couldn't.

Coughing hard enough to hurt, he approached the door. Leaning into it, he shoved it down, falling with it. "Maxi..."

I can't go on. For a second, he just laid there, face down on the door, letting the tears drip from the end of his nose.

I must go on. His arms trembled as he pushed away from the door. He stood, stumbling on the instability of the door, but refusing to fall.

"Maxine," he finally managed with enough force to be heard. "Maxine!"

Please, Jesus, let her be okay.

He leaned on the banister. "Maxine!" he called up the stairs.

He stumbled into the kitchen. "Max…"

The envelope on top of a grilled cheese sandwich stole his voice. *No. No, no, no…*

He picked it up as dread filled him from head to toe. *I can't bear it.*

But he had to. Maxine's life depended on it.

He broke the envelope's seal and removed the paper within.

Seth unfolded it, read it, read it again. Then, he set it down on the table.

His legs wavered. He sat down on a kitchen chair, rested his elbows on the table, put his head in his hands, and began to wail as the gravity of his situation sunk in.

And one thought overrode all the rest. *This is all your fault.*

***

Maxine moaned. Her head throbbed painfully with every beat of her heart.

She was afraid to open her eyes because she knew light would make the throbbing even worse.

She thought, *I was eating a grilled cheese sandwich. Why would that make my head hurt?*

Why was I eating a grilled cheese sandwich? She wondered. *Because Seth wasn't home to make dinner.*

It all came back to her then – everything. She opened her eyes, no longer caring what the light did to her.

But there was no light, none at all.

The darkness was absolute. *Are my eyes actually open?* They were. *Is this a dream?* she hoped.

She sat up and the throbbing did come. Dizziness and nausea forced her back down.

Despite her pain and excitement, she felt sleepy.

Of course you're sleepy, she thought as she remembered the antiseptic-smelling handkerchief someone had pressed to her face.

She fought to keep her eyes open, trying to recall details of her ordeal to keep awake.

The man on my porch was big. She remembered his hands. *They were the size of pie plates, and he held a sheet. Why would he be holding a sheet?*

Could you identify him in a lineup? She decided she probably could.

She knew far less about the other one, the one who'd snuck up behind her. She didn't even know if this one was a man or a woman.

She checked her pockets. They were empty. She had no keys. She had no phone. She had nothing.

She jolted awake, not realizing she'd nodded off. Part of her just wanted to go back to sleep. Her head hurt less when she slept. Also, she found the utter darkness disturbing.

The darkness was almost physical. Being in it was suffocating, as if a wet wool blanket was on her face.

It was a familiar feeling, identical to the one she'd experienced the night those gunmen infiltrated Zion's Hill. Memories of that night resurrected within her – frightened her beyond what she'd already attained.

She began feeling around in the darkness. Maybe something was there that would be of help. *Or something harmful.*

She had to feel around. It was all she could do, and doing nothing was akin to giving up hope. She would not give up!

She saw the glow of her phone's screen and reached for it. But when her hands got there, there was nothing. *The darkness is playing with me.*

She'd heard stories of people who, for whatever reason, had to endure long periods of total darkness. One of the effects was delusion and madness.

She thought she saw her cellphone screen light up again, this time a few paces further than before, but she didn't react. Instead, she closed her eyes. *I won't go mad. I know that's not real. It's what I want to see – what my mind wishes was real. But it's not.*

When she opened her eyes, the screen's glow was gone. *Nothing's there.*

She continued exploring her surroundings. The floor felt cold and hard, like concrete. She came to a wall, also cold and hard.

Maxine turned away from the wall and continued exploring in a different direction. She crawled along the floor, patting with her hands, feeling her way in the darkness.

Her fingers grazed something. It was warm and soft. She pulled back with a gasp.

Fear rose. Whatever she'd touched felt like something that lived.

She waited, but nothing lunged at her, nothing clawed or bit or spit. No noise came, not a growl, or a shriek – nothing.

Gathering her courage, she reached out once more. It was still there.

She ran her fingers along it. It was warm and covered in fabric. *Clothing?*

She came across something hard and smooth. It was small and round. *A button?* Came to mind.

She explored further. Past the button was the unmistakable shape of fingers. The flesh was warm. The thumb twitched.

Maxine whimpered as she withdrew, scooting away from the other until her back hit the wall. She cupped her hands over her mouth to muffle her breath, which came in loud rattling gasps.

"Who's there?" she managed finally.

Nothing answered.

"Who are you?"

She held her breath and listened. She could hear the other's breathing. It was steady, rhythmic.

It suddenly hit her. *Maybe the other one is like her. Maybe somebody drugged this other one too.*

"Um, if you can hear me, I'm coming back over. Please don't do anything bad to me. I don't mean any harm."

She scooted back to where she thought the other had been. She reached out and found the cuff with the button and the hand she'd found before. On the wrist she found a pulse, steady and strong.

Exploring further, she found a face. She touched lips – warm and moist. She found the nose and felt breath.

Once more, panic scratched at her, nearly tearing through the surface. "What's in store for us?" she asked the sleeper.

"Jesus, help us," she prayed.

She crawled away and found cold steel. *A door?* It wouldn't budge.

Somewhere in the darkness, the other began to stir.

***

Seth managed to stagger out the back door. He stumbled and fell, landing on his knees.

This is all your fault.

His heart beat ferociously, as if trying to escape his chest. He breathed in short, sharp gasps. His hand, still holding the note found on the sandwich, quivered with adrenaline.

Somewhere unseen, a bird chirped happily. Seth looked up into this tree, searching for the chirper. The happiness of its song was out of place here.

In the end, he gave up searching for the bird. He didn't have the energy to do anything about it anyway.

All your fault – all of it.

Upon reading the letter, the kitchen walls seemed to close in on him. The air felt thin, unbreathable.

Now, as he knelt in his back yard, he prayed that he'd wake up from this nightmare. In his gut though, he knew there was nothing to wake up from. This was real.

It's all my fault. That thought continued to pummel him like a ton of bricks to the head. *You can't escape your past. I was a fool to think otherwise. It found me and now Maxine's paying the price.*

The guilt of that statement pulled him to the ground. He fell forward, face down in the dirt, praying. *Please God, help me!*

He'd never again eat a grilled cheese sandwich, being forever associated with tragedy in his mind. The words of that note resonated in his head, permanently seared into his memories as if from a glowing red branding iron.

Dear brother,

If you're reading this, then you must have decided not to rejoin me and the Kinship. This of course is your choice to make but do understand that you also must live with the consequences of that choice. This is serious business. Without you and me together, the prophecy cannot be fulfilled, and the prophecy must be fulfilled!

Now, I hate to take such drastic measures, but you've limited my options. Your wife is with us. I hope that her abduction wakes you up to the seriousness of the situation.

Don't even think about alerting the police, or anyone else for that matter. If you do, then I can't guarantee your dear wife's safety. And even if you do alert the cops, I'm not sure anything would come of it – most of them are on our payroll anyway.

It's time to rethink your loyalties brother. You know where to find me – where the Kinship lives strong. Think it over, but don't doddle. Time's ticking and I don't know how long your wife will remain unharmed. I'll see you today.

I'll be waiting in the main room.

Best regards – ☺,

Your dear brother

The grass was wet from Seth's tears by the time he finally found the strength to pry himself off the ground. He knew what he had to do.

He went back inside and ate two granola bars he kept in the kitchen. Recent events burned calories and those yet to come would burn more. He needed sustenance.

He also downed an apple and large spoonful of peanut butter. He washed it all down with copious amounts of water.

The main room. It had been a long time since he'd been there. The last time, blood had been spilled. He prayed this time would be different.

Seth exited his house via the front door. He carefully fit the door into the frame to avoid anyone passing by from noticing.

Then, he started down the sidewalk. He didn't run this time. *I must conserve energy.*

He'd need it.

***

Jason stood in the main room of the Kinship headquarters building – a space that held fond memories. There was no light here except for that which drifted in from the entrance.

This was the very same room where he and Seth's blood mixed two years ago. *That was a great day – until it wasn't,* he thought.

The ceremony had been great. The Spirits' presence had been strong as blood was spilled and mixed. *But Seth destroyed all that with a single decision to run away.*

Now, he felt that feeling again. *The Spirits are near.*

There'll be no running away this time because he had Maxine, the proverbial insurance policy. *No. Seth wont' run, not without her.*

The only negative was that Jason needed his good-for-nothing brother at all. It was a bitter pill to swallow, but he'd forced it down. *This is the only way to fulfill the prophecy.*

For two years, he'd asked the Spirits if there was any other way. There answer was unchanging: *Bound by blood, you are greater together than the sum of your parts. You must be joined. The prophecy must be fulfilled. Prophecy is prophecy. It cannot be altered.*

Jason stared down at the concrete floor. In the dimness, he could just make out the blood stains left by their bloodletting. *There's power in the blood,* he remembered Cain saying.

And so there is. "Blood will flow again," he mumbled. "And this time, the sacrifice will be greater."

He looked up toward the entrance to the room. He could just see the first few bare bulbs which strung the length of the hallway. Along that hallway was the inner room.

Blood will spill again! he thought, staring once more at those two-year-old floor stains. Looking back up, he realized he wasn't alone.

A figure stood in the entrance. Backlit by the bare bulbs, he was but a shadow.

The figure neither moved nor spoke.

Seth? was Jason's first thought. *Could he have arrived already?*

A familiar voice came from the figure. "Jason," it said.

"Greetings, Cain."

Cain's shadow lengthened as he entered the room. "Your voice betrays you." He paused and smiled. "What's troubling you?"

You trouble me. "Just keeping my edge."

"Any news regarding your brother?"

Jason shook his head. He hated Cain and he hated acting the subordinate. *Be patient. Your time will come,* he told himself.

"What if he doesn't show?"

Jason took a breath to hide the hatred brewing just below the surface. "He'll show."

"How do you know? He doesn't have best track record."

Jason looked Cain straight in the eyes. "He will show."

Cain frowned. "For your sake, I hope he does."

Jason overlooked that thinly veiled threat. Prophesy was prophesy. It could not be changed. *Seth will show.*

Cain smiled once more. "If he does show, then it will be soon."

Jason nodded.

"We must have the sacrifice prepared prior to his arrival."

Listening to Cain give him orders stirred up his anger. *Bide your time,* he thought. *Do as he says for now.*

"Jason, did you hear?"

"Yes."

"You will address me properly."

"Yes, High Priest Cain."

Cain took a step nearer and even in that dimness, Jason could see a glimmer of anger in the high priest's eyes.

Bide your time. "My apologies," he said deliberately subverting his eyes. "It won't happen again."

Cain stared at him for what seemed an eternity. "Go, retrieve the sacrifice," he finally said.

Do as he says, for now, Jason advised himself. *And look forward to punishing him later.*

He gave a curt nod and left the main room. Jason didn't allow his curses to pass his lips until far down the bare-bulb hallway – well beyond the hearing of Cain.

Then he let them fly in a flood of rage.

***

Maxine flexed and unflexed her trembling fingers as the stranger in the darkness began to stir. A female voice filled the space, not words, just moans and incomprehensible mumblings.

She felt the cold steel of the door at her back, soaking the chill through her shirt and freezing the layer of perspiration on her skin. She reached up and tried the door again. It was still locked.

She stared into the darkness, searching for any movement. But the darkness was complete. The other could be standing right in front of her, inches away, and she'd not know it.

The woman, if it was indeed a woman, had gone silent once more. She listened hard, searching for any latent sound.

None could be heard. *Dear God, give me strength.*

She slid from the door to what she perceived to be the farthest corner. Even then, she couldn't be more than a few feet from the other. She had no way to know how big the space was, but it couldn't be much bigger than your average walk-in closet.

Time was meaningless here. There was no way to measure its passing. To Maxine, it felt like an eternity.

Hunger gnawed. She hadn't eaten her grilled cheese. Her last full meal had been breakfast. Her head felt light from hunger and the fear cocktail that surged within her.

Who put me here? she wondered. A more disturbing thought entered her mind. *And what do they plan to do with me?*

Fresh tears wetted her cheeks. *Jesus, give me strength.*

The other pulled Maxine from her thoughts. She was stirring once more.

"Hello?" Maxine uttered with barely a whisper.

The other grew quiet.

"Who are you?" Maxine inquired.

She could hear breathing – they came short and sharp, fearful.

"Please say something."

No response.

"Hello? Can you hear me?"

Feeling alone, the darkness pressed harder against her. New tears formed as she thought of Seth. *Was he okay? Had the people who'd taken her, taken him as well? Was it a coincidence he wasn't home?*

A loud scraping noise broke the quiet. Maxine covered her ears. It was like fingernails on a chalkboard.

The other let out a whimper as the steel door began to slide open. Maxine pressed herself into the corner, wishing she could just disappear.

Light flooded the room. Maxine shielded her eyes.

A silhouette filled the open doorway, backlit by a string of bare bulbs.

"What do you want with me?" Maxine asked.

"Get up," came the two-word reply. It sounded male.

"Who are you?"

The voice grew harsh. "Get up!"

Maxine obeyed. There was something familiar here.

The silhouette entered further until he was very close, inches away. But her eyes were still adjusting to the brightness. His features remained in shadow.

"Are you hungry?" he asked, less harsh than before.

Maxine didn't answer.

"You didn't get to eat your grilled cheese. So, you must be hungry."

Maxine said nothing.

"I brought you something."

He handed her a sandwich.

"It's tuna. I made it myself. Hope you like it."

Maxine didn't trust this man. What if he poisoned the tuna?

He added, "It's got pickles and extra mayo," as if that's why she was hesitating.

She still didn't take it from him.

After a moment, he let out a huff and took a big bite himself. "See, it's fine," he said through his full mouth."

She could smell the tuna as he spoke. She could feel bits hit her face.

He swallowed. "See, nothing's wrong with it."

He held out the remaining sandwich to her. "Now, eat."

Fear held her.

"Take it!" The harshness returned.

Maxine took it.

"Eat it."

She took a bite. She swallowed.

His voice calmed. "See, I'm not all that bad."

Her hunger took over. She ate the rest in less than a minute.

She knew this voice. *But from where?*

He gripped her upper arm. "Come with me."

Maxine glanced at the other. The light revealed she was indeed a woman. She was older than Maxine, maybe in her early forties. She appeared to be unconscious once more.

"She's not your concern," the man said. "Come with me now."

He guided her out of the room and into a long hallway lit with a single string of bare lightbulbs.

Here, she saw his face for the first time and everything fell into place – sort of.

"Seth?"

***

At that moment, Seth wished more than anything he could operate a manual transmission. Unfortunately, he'd never learned, eliminating Maxine's old Fiesta as a means of transportation. So now, he continued walking toward a place he hadn't been in more than two years – a place he always hoped he'd never have to return to.

It wasn't far from his house to the Kinship's compound, but he'd already exerted himself to his limits. His legs trembled with every step from both exhaustion and fear.

The Kinship's compound was actually an old warehouse. As it came into view, latent memories pushed to the forefront of his mind.

He wrung his hands together as images coalesced in his brain. He remembered the pain of the knife. He remembered the mixing of blood. He remembered the presence of the Spirits.

These thoughts brought shivers and gooseflesh. *I have no choice,* he said to himself. *You've got to do this. You owe it to Maxine.*

Shame and guilt overwhelmed him. *If anything happens to my wife…* he couldn't bear to finish that thought. It was his past that caused this. It was all his fault.

If only I'd been honest from the start. Maybe Maxine wouldn't have married him. Maybe he'd be doing time for attempted murder. But at least Maxine would be safe.

He drew nearer and the warehouse loomed larger until it took up his entire line of vision. Standing before that Goliath, he prayed silently. *God, help me now.*

He couldn't help but fear that building. He witnessed bad things there – things he wished he could unsee.

Please God, give me strength.

He feared more bad things were to happen in the future. And not just to him, but to the woman he loved.

"No!" he blurted. He wouldn't let these memories overcome him. He wouldn't allow what might be to destroy him.

He wanted to rescue Jason from all this too. *But if he hurts Maxine, then all bets are off.*

The guilt, shame, anger and regret piled on him, making it almost impossible to progress toward his goal. But he had to. Too much was on the line to run away.

He reached the main entrance. The last time he was here, he carried a bag containing a gun, ammo, a mask, and gloves. This time, he had nothing. *I can't believe I'm going back.*

He touched the handle of the steel-reinforced door. It felt cold in his grip, so cold it almost felt hot.

The door was unlocked. *Of course it's unlocked*, he thought to himself. *They're expecting me.* He pulled it open and stared into the entrance of the bare-bulb hallway.

To Seth, the hallway looked like the gaping maw of a giant serpent. He hesitated only a moment before entering. He could do nothing less.

With a hiss, the hydraulic hinge of the door pulled it shut. He heard the latch catch with a click. *No turning back.*

Memories flooded his mind. After two years, walking this hallway was like riding a bike – something you never forget.

He navigated deeper along the corridor. It was narrow. He could just touch both walls if he stretched his arms to their fullest.

Above him the string of bare bulbs lit the way. These weren't LEDs, but old-school incandescent bulbs. The Kinship had a storeroom full of them, or so Seth had heard. The string allowed for a bulb every ten feet and the heat generated by them was enough to draw beads of sweat on Seth's skin.

The unshaded light of the hallway created sharp contrast between light and shadow. Seth's crisp shadow went with him, passing from in front to behind as he traveled beneath each lightbulb. Also, the bulbs swayed slightly on the wire from which they hung, causing additional illusion of motion.

This environment disturbed Seth. But that was the point, he supposed.

Jason's letter had instructed him to go to the main meeting room. He knew the hallway led to it. In fact, all rooms were connected to this hallway. The main room was at its end.

What'll happen then? He didn't want to think of that. But the thought slipped in nonetheless.

Maybe I can reason with him. He didn't have much hope in that idea. Jason hadn't shown a lot of reason so far.

Maybe I can convince him to leave this cult. If that happened. It would be an answer to two years' worth of prayer. Still, it felt like a long shot.

Maybe I can trade my life for Maxine's at least. That seemed the most plausible, and something he'd do willingly enough if there was no other way. He owed his wife that much.

What worried Seth most was his brother's obsession with fulfilling the Kinship prophecy. For that to work, he'd have to join with Jason. *And that's something I can't do.*

Dear Jesus, help me through this. Amen.

***

Cain waited. Jason should be here any moment with Seth's precious wife in tow.

He sat cross-legged, centered in the middle of the main warehouse room. Directly beneath him, the floor was stained with two-year-old blood.

My how things have changed, he thought to himself. *I used to have such optimism.* But that was all before the twins arrived – before the Spirits started obsessing about prophecy.

Cain fumed. *Did you know Seth was a flight risk?* he wondered about the Spirits. He didn't think they did. The Spirits were powerful, but not all-knowing.

Also, he'd learned that they couldn't read his thoughts unless he wanted them to. This was a good thing because his recent thoughts were not in their favor.

He'd kept the remaining brother down, opposing the Spirits' obsession – keeping the prophecy at arm's length. It worked for a while. *Until Seth reentered the picture.* He didn't like this threat to his leadership, not one bit.

Now I have no choice but to go along with it, Cain thought. *For now.*

When the time was right, he'd crush this little rebellion. Even the Spirits would be caught off guard. Then, they'd have to acknowledge his worthiness of continuing as their priest.

About the brothers, *I'll need to kill them both at once – together.*

I only need patience. I only need to keep vigilant – watchful. Then, when the time comes, I'll strike them down. For that I'll need them together.

That was why he'd gone along with Jason's plan to get Seth to come. It was all playing into his scheme. *Soon, this will all be behind me.*

The Kinship revered prophecy. *I'll need the killing to look like an accident, or do it when nobody it looking.*

Cain stroked the floor with his hands, tracing the bloodstains that started everything in motion. A smile emerged on his face.

Just be patient. Bide your time. Then, when the time is right, slaughter them both.

***

"Seth?" Maxine gasped again.

Seth looked strange. She couldn't put her finger on it, but something was off. *Was it how he tilted his head when he looked at her? Was it the unusual, almost amused look in his eyes? What was it?*

He guided her down a seemingly infinite hallway. It was narrow with a string of bare bulbs overhead which ran down its center, eventually disappearing as the hallway curved.

"Wait," she said.

He stopped and turned toward her. She felt unease rise within her, a feeling she'd never before felt with him. "What is it?" he asked, annoyed.

"What about her?"

Seth replied, "What about who?"

"The woman in that room. She needs help. We need to help her."

Her husband's eyes chilled Maxine. "No, we don't."

"I don't understand." This wasn't like Seth.

A non-pleasant smile crept on his face, one she'd never seen before and hoped to never see again.

"What's going on," her voice came with a quiver. "What's wrong?"

"Nothing's wrong. In fact, everything is on the verge of being very right."

The strangeness in those words chilled her. She tried to pull from his grip.

He tightened his hold around her arm to the point of pain.

"Seth," she pleaded. "You're hurting me."

"Then stop resisting!" he shouted.

In shock, she did as he asked.

"And stop calling me Seth."

"Why?" Maxine managed to whisper.

"Because my name is Jason."

***

Pastor Pete was in Zion's Hill's sanctuary. He sat in the front row of seats where he'd been reading the scriptures until a strange feeling stopped him. *Somebody's watching me.*

Such feelings happened on occasion ever since that fateful night where he almost got his head blown off by masked gunmen. He turned and looked. In the back of the sanctuary stood Jasmine.

Pete smiled as he looked at her. She was so old, frail looking. The woman couldn't have been more than 90 pounds soaking wet. Yet, she conveyed an inner strength that Pete found encouraging.

He stood up and waved. She nodded but said nothing. Her face was stoic, and Pete found himself wondering what kind of message the church's prophet was about to deliver.

He walked into the center aisle. Her eyes followed his movements.

Jasmine appeared out of sorts. Her hair, which was normally kept in a tight bun, was disheveled. She still had the bun, but strands of hair wisped out from it in all directions. Her lips were pinched tight, her face looked tense.

She started toward him, using her cane as more of a crutch than normal. Plus, her gait was slower and her movements – labored.

"Jasmine," he called to her.

She nodded again as she drew nearer.

"Is everything okay?"

"I'm just glad I found you."

"What's wrong?" he wanted to know.

She was beside him now. "Much."

"Would you like to sit and tell me about it?"

She looked at the nearest row of seats, nodded and sat. Pete noticed her body vibrating minutely – trembling. It was so minute that he might not have noticed it at all except for those wispy hairs waving in the air, free from her bun. Those hairs twitched like Geiger counter needles detecting trace amounts of radiation.

He took a seat in the row ahead of hers. Then, he turned to face her.

She put her hands on the back of his seat and leaned forward so they were close. Whatever she had to say, was meant to be between them.

This close, Pete could see the extent of her stress. Her eyes were wild and twitchy. Her breathing was elevated. Her trembling body vibrated the chair he sat in which she was touching.

"Something dark is coming against this church," she finally managed.

Pete nodded. *Well, at least it's something we've delt with before,* he thought as memories from more than two years ago flooded his mind.

She continued, barely above a whisper. "This darkness – oh Jesus help me, it's dark and it has targeted three of us."

"Who's us?" Pete wanted to know.

"Three members of this church."

"Who?" Pete needed to know.

She didn't answer his question. "We must assemble the congregation. We must pray for their protection as soon as possible."

"We will. But who is it? Don't you know?"

She shook her head. "It hasn't been revealed."

Pastor Pete opened his mouth, but wasn't sure what to ask.

"Call the congregation. We must meet. God himself has decreed it. Perhaps, those in Satan's crosshairs will be revealed then."

Pete nodded, stood up and jogged to his office. He needed two things: his cell phone and a copy of the current church directory.

When he returned, Jasmine was still where he'd left her. Her head now rested on the back of the chair in front of her. She looked up as he approached. Tears were streaming down her face. "This darkness is strong. We've got to act soon."

Pete nodded, sat back down beside her, and stared her in the face. "God is stronger."

She nodded, wiping the tears away with the sleeve of her blouse.

His phone was fully charged. *Good.* "Do you have your mobile phone handy?"

She smiled. "At my age, I don't care to own one."

"Right." He opened the directory and began dialing.

Beside him, Jasmine closed her eyes, bowed her head and began praying silently.

***

Seth (or Jason as he'd asked to be called), escorted Maxine along the narrow, bare-lightbulb-lit hallway. She was being pulled along quickly, urgently.

Her arm throbbed where he held her. His grip was like iron and she felt her fingers tingle with poor circulation. But she didn't dare ask him to let go.

She believed him when he'd told her he wasn't Seth because her husband would never treat her this way. Her husband loved her, but there was no love here.

She didn't know if this was a clone of her husband, or if Seth was somehow possessed. Although demon possession seemed unlikely since Christians cannot be possessed by demons. All she knew for sure was this wolf in sheep's clothing wasn't who he appeared to be.

She feared this stranger. It was the same fear she'd experienced more than two years ago when masked men terrorized her at church.

The police never found out who those men were, the thought dawned on her then.

Terror dripped into her like drops of water from a leaky faucet, increasing her puddle of terror drop by drop. *If this was the man who'd had no qualms with firing a gun at Pastor Pete, then there's no limit to what he might do now.*

"What do you want with me?" she forced the question. Her voice was a shrill staccato.

After a pause, "It's not you that we want. It's the value you represent."

Well, that didn't help explain anything.

"You're just a worm on a hook to us, valuable only to the extent that you draw in the big fish." He paused before adding, "You're a smart girl, I'm sure you've figured out by now who the big fish is."

"I really don't know." She wondered if it was wise to admit this to him.

The man chuckled coldly. "Your husband hasn't told you anything has he?"

So, this is about Seth. *What trouble is he in?* She wasn't angry at him, at least not yet, just deeply worried.

Jason scoffed. "I don't blame Seth. How can a guy tell people he hangs with that he once almost murdered them. Especially if you end up later marrying one of the would-be victims."

Maxine physically felt the color leave her face. *He's lying,* she was 99% certain. *Then again, Seth was secretive of his past.*

"Don't believe me?" he asked.

She didn't answer. She wouldn't answer such a question. She couldn't.

"Hey, believe what you want – whatever gets you to sleep at night." He paused, "But I was there. I know the truth."

They stopped moving along the hallway. Jason pulled her close, staring her in the eyes. "Your face gives you away. You don't believe me."

Maxine began to sob.

"You don't have to believe. But it's still the truth. Deep down I think you know that."

They began moving again. *Will this hallway never end?* She thought as she sobbed.

"You were there too."

"What?" the shock of that statement pulled the question from her.

He grinned. "I remember you. Who wouldn't remember a pretty face like yours? I wonder if Seth saw you that night too? Maybe it was love at first sight? Maybe that's why he didn't kill you like he was supposed to!" he shouted. "Maybe that's why he ran from Zion's Hill, leaving me to fend for myself!"

Vomit stung the back of Maxine's throat. She swallowed hard.

It was Seth. That night, it was Seth. Her mind went to that night. She remembered gunmen wearing ski masks – two of them.

It was Seth. Why had he kept this from her?

"It's a shame you married such a coward. I mean, he's supposed to shoot you, can't do it, and then turns around and marries you without even having the guts to come clean first?" He took a deep breath. "Honestly, I'm embarrassed that we're related."

He glanced at his wristwatch. "We're behind schedule."

He picked up the pace. She went along with him.

She had no choice.

***

Seth continued toward the main room and went over his options. He needed a plan.

Certainly, he couldn't do what Jason was demanding. He knew the truth and would never rejoin the Kinship.

He could run away. But what would that mean for Maxine? A little over two years ago, the Kinship sent him and Jason to put bullets into Christians. They wouldn't suffer a second thought about killing Maxine now if it was in their interest to do so.

He could get help from the police. But how many of those were secretly Kinship sympathizers? Plus, he felt certain they'd kill Maxine before ever surrendering to authorities.

Despite the constant light created by those bare bulbs, Seth felt immersed in darkness. His hope wavered. He needed light at the end of this tunnel, but could find none.

With every stride down the hallway, his future felt bleaker. *Poor Maxine.*

He regretted not telling her the truth at the beginning. She didn't deserve what was happening to her. And it could have all been avoided if he'd only been truthful from the start.

Shame enveloped him. *It's all because of me.*

God, save my wife. Protect her now. I am sorry for my part in this. I don't care what happens to me, just save my wife.

His feet felt heavy, as the guilt piled on. Inexplicably, scripture came to mind.

Yea, though I walk through the valley of the shadow of death, I will fear no evil…

But he did fear it. He feared it very much.

Jesus, give me strength.

***

Cain sat on the bloodstained floor. His eyes were closed as his meditation completed.

He opened his eyes and stared into the gloom of the great meeting room. His face was full of disappointment.

He'd been meditating in hopes that the Spirits would speak to him. But as usual these days, they remained unresponsive to his calls.

Now though, he heard a noise. Somebody was nearing the end of the hallway. Their footsteps echoed into the great room, bouncing off the walls and reverberating into nothingness.

He stood up, waiting. Whoever it was, their footsteps were loud and fast and growing louder with every second.

He watched the entrance with anticipation. *It's time.* Whoever it was, their entrance would push the agenda along. He wanted the agenda to move because the faster it moved, the faster he could take care of his little problem of the twins.

The bare bulbs shined light into the great room. Within that light, two shadows emerged.

"Jason?" Cain called.

"Yes," Jason answered. "And I've brought the wife."

Cain approached and regarded Maxine. *I can see why Seth fell for her.* She was young and attractive with large brown eyes, a petite frame, and thick black hair.

Cain saw beyond her beauty. She was a bargaining chip, and failing that, a sacrifice to the Spirits. Either way, she held value.

They entered further into the room, beyond the light of the hallway and Cain began slowly circling the duo like a hungry shark. He reached out, grazing the back of his hand against the soft flesh of her cheek.

She pulled away from his touch. Cain smiled. This was just the reaction he hoped for because her repulsion could make her more manipulatable, more useful to the cause.

Cain reached for her again. "There's no reason to be afraid," he lied.

This time, she didn't pull away as he touched her cheek. Her breath came in short bursts as she whimpered.

He moved his hand down to the side of her neck, still with the back of his hand. Her pulse beat through his hand – a strong beat.

Good. A strong pulse means better bloodletting if it comes to that, if she must be used as a sacrifice.

Cain's fingers lingered momentarily over her jugular before letting it fall. "I don't believe you understand your value here." His voice was smooth as silk.

He continued to circle, deliberately pushing between Jason and her – separating them as a predator separates the injured from the herd.

Jason stood his ground, but only for a moment. *Good. You must learn your place here.* Cain narrowed his eyes at Jason as the man stood down. Then, he turned to his prey – the woman. "You're a prize to be had for sure."

Her eyes darted about.

"Sure, you can try to run. Nobody's holding you here. But, if you run, where will you run to?"

Her focus reverted to Cain.

"And even if you could escape, which you can't, doing so would only endanger your husband."

The anguish in her eyes made him giddy with pleasure.

"You don't want to risk that do you?"

He didn't need to check her pulse again. He could see her jugular vein throbbing with every beat of her heart.

Cain turned to Jason. "She sure is a prize, isn't she?"

Jason nodded. It irked him that Cain still ran the show. The twitch in his left eyebrow was the giveaway. *That's right,* Cain thought. *I'm going to win this little competition. And when I do, you'll wish you'd never been born.*

"It's time," Cain said to Jason.

Jason nodded.

"Secure the bait," Cain ordered. Then he leaned toward the wife, "that's you," he whispered.

"No. Please," she begged as Jason secured his hold on her and began dragging her away.

Cain flipped a nearby switch and a spotlight luminated a great stone table in the center of the room.

"Let me go!" she shrieked as they approached the table. She began to thrash, but Jason was more than capable. In seconds he had her down upon it.

Cain watched all this with rising glee. With the bait set, Seth would come. And once the brothers are together, it'll just be a matter of time before a moment presents itself. *I'll kill them both.*

He anticipated the surprise Seth and Jason would have the moment he took their lives.

I'll slaughter them both. Then what will become of the precious prophecy?

As usual, the Spirits remained silent.

***

The stone table was ancient, or so Jason had been told. It certainly looked old.

Maxine's body quivered as he held her, pulling her closer to the table. Earlier, she thrashed around like a wounded snake, but as they drew nearer to the table, her fighting subsided.

"Please, don't do this."

Her voice contained resignation, which was a good thing. Everything would work better if the sacrifice was complacent.

He could feel the terror wafting off her. It was almost physical. He could almost see it.

But of course, you're frightened.

Everyone fears the stone table. It was impossible not to fear it. Many had been pulled to it screaming, clawing, and eventually dying.

Yes, you're right to fear it.

He liked it when they screamed and clawed because those victims were more entertaining. Entertainment value aside though, this event today would not disappoint. Of this, he felt certain.

Her panicked voice made him smile. "You don't have to do this."

"I'm afraid I do. It's nothing personal. I just need you to get your husband's attention." Jason didn't mention that if that failed, they'd slaughter her on the stone table as a sacrifice to the Spirits.

He laid her down on the monolith of a table. She didn't struggle. That was good.

He ran his fingers along the many carved runes which indented the table's surface. From there, he caressed the red-stained canals. These were for channeling the flow of blood. It made it easier to collect it for Kinship rituals.

As much as he enjoyed seeing blood flow, he hoped the table would remain dry today. It would be much better if his brother would simply join him and fulfill the prophecy. Sacrificing his brother's wife would only be a last resort.

She trembled as he tied her to the table with reddish-brown ropes. They weren't originally that color, but over the course of use, the stains had set.

"Please stop," she pleaded.

There was no hope in her voice, Jason noticed. *Good.*

She began to sob.

***

Maxine prayed silently as her abductors tied her to the table. She prayed without words. She prayed for Seth. She even prayed for those who held her. She prayed for strength to endure. She prayed for God's will to be done.

Even as terror built up within her, she prayed.

Her terror overwhelmed her. She began to scream.

Yet, her prayers never ceased.

***

Seth stopped running as a blood-curdling scream came to him from somewhere far down the hallway. *Maxine!* He started running again, now with renewed fervor.

Above him, the line of bare bulbs flew past with such speed, they blurred his vision. He flew along the hallway and new stretches of it came into view as he rounded its consistent curvature.

Maxine's screams ceased and Seth's blood chilled from its absence. His heart pounded. His lungs heaved. His footfalls came heavy with excursion.

If you've harmed her in any way... Seth had no ending to that sentence. What could he possibly do in retribution for harming his wife. Nothing, no matter how horrible could serve as equal trade.

She screamed once more and his mind went mad with what might be happening there in the great room. He knew of the stone table. He knew what it was used for. In his short tenure with the Kinship, his brother had told him everything about it.

Shut up, he told himself. He couldn't think such things. He wouldn't think such things.

Still, bad thoughts circumvented his firewall. It couldn't be helped. He remembered blood flowing in that room. He remembered sacrificial knives slicing flesh. He remembered the horrors of being in the presence of the Kinship, Cain, the Spirits.

Those memories haunted him ferociously as he ran the hallway. *Shut up,* he told those memories. But the more he tried to shove them out of his mind, the more they seeped in.

He pushed forward with all he had. It was all he could do. *If I get there in time, maybe I can stop whatever they're doing to her.*

If I get there in time...

He didn't like that choice of words. He had to get there in time. There could be no "if".

Another thought hit him like a load of lead. *This is all your fault. If you hadn't kept your secrets, Maxine would be safe and sound.*

"No!" he shouted.

All your fault, his brain repeated.

All your fault.

Maxine's screams continued. They were louder now. He was closer.

All your fault!

"Maxine, I'm coming!"

All your fault!!!

***

The sanctuary was nearly full. Almost every member of Zion's Hill had come.

Pastor Pete stood before them. He was at the front of the sanctuary where the floor rose. From this vantage point, he could see them all.

There wasn't a smile among them. Then again, they all knew the seriousness of the message Jasmine had conveyed. *Something dark is coming against this church.*

Some of them had been here the last time such a prophecy was given. No doubt the memories from that night still haunted them. Those who weren't there heard about it from those who had been present on that awful night.

Pete began with prayer. "Thank you, God, for your mercy and perpetual protection." he said as the congregation bowed their heads in concentration. "We ask for your presence as we conduct this meeting. Guide us, Lord. Show us the way. Enlighten us regarding this time of darkness that threatens your children here at Zion's Hill. Amen."

Those in the seats looked up and unfolded their hands. There wasn't a dry eye to be seen.

Jasmine stood up from her place in the front row and shuffled up to where he stood. He handed her the microphone and stepped aside.

"Oh, sweet Jesus," she started. "We come to you in this time of distress. Something dark has made a stand against your church." She paused. "And although we don't know exactly what that is, we know from whence it comes."

The sanctuary was eerily silent except for Jasmine's staccato voice. Pete focused on her words. "It comes straight from Hell," she continued. "It is Satan himself who dares stand against the sons and daughters of God almighty!"

Pete grew concerned. Jasmine's appearance was frightening. There was strength in that old woman. He'd never seen such fury. Her eyes flashed. Her parchment-thin skin flushed rose. Here lips trembled with every word she uttered.

Her voice held such venom, such passion. It was righteous rage, and it was contagious. Pete felt it and he could see that those in the congregation felt it too.

"Satan has singled out three from the herd. He has asked God's permission to sift them like wheat."

The ensuing silence was broken by a combined gasp from those who listened.

"And God has granted said permission!"

"What are their names?" Pete needed to know. "Who are they?"

"I don't know." Jasmine's statement came down like a final curtain. "I only know what I'm told."

"What can you tell us?" Pete's voice sounded so small next to the power in Jasmine's.

"One is here," she proclaimed. "The other two are absent."

The congregation of Zion's Hill began to murmur. "Who is it? Is it you? Is it I? Surely, it's not me."

"Who is absent?" Jasmine asked.

"Where's Mike Black?" Someone asked.

"I'm here," Mike replied.

"Did anyone see Louise Darnell?" came another.

"Present," replied Louise.

Pete took back the microphone. "Quiet please. Quiet. We can only figure this out if it's done orderly."

The assembly died down. Pete picked up the church directory. "Looks like it's time for an old-fashioned roll call."

He opened the directory. "Adamson, Jeff."

"Here."

"Adkins, Carol."

"Over here."

"Baens, Billy."

"Present."

This is going to take some time, Pete thought as he called "Caylor, Benjamin".

"I am here."

And down the list he went.

***

Cain felt the electricity of the moment as he held the blade of his sacrificial knife close to the woman's face. She saw it and her eyes widened as she continued screaming.

She struggled against the ropes as he moved that blade back and forth across her line of vision. He found her fear most satisfying.

He leaned down so that he was right next to her ear. "Stop screaming."

She didn't obey.

He saw the panic in her – heard it in her shrieks. He loved her terror. Still, her screaming needed to stop, for his own sanity. *You have got to shut up!*

He touched the blade to her throat, not the sharp edge, he didn't want to slit her throat accidentally. Of course, she couldn't see what side of the knife he was using. "Calm down, or I will be forced to calm you down, and you don't want that – trust me, you don't want that at all."

He could see she was trying to get a grip, swallowing her screams back down as they tried to pop out. After a minute or so, her noises had reduced to sobs and whimpers.

"That's better," Cain whispered to her. "It's true. Silence is golden."

He looked into her brown eyes. They were pretty eyes, full of terror. Perhaps that was part of the beauty in them.

Cain caressed her neck with the knife's dull side. He enjoyed her reaction of wheezes, the result of trying hard to obey him – to keep her panic in check.

Where is Seth? he wondered as he stood up and took a step back from the stone table.

He looked toward the entrance of the hallway, but those bare bulbs revealed nothing new. The hallway was vacant.

You'd better show soon.

If he didn't show, the Spirits would demand blood. He looked at the woman on the table. He would sacrifice her if required. *But it would be a shame to close those beautiful eyes forever.*

"What do you want with me?"

So, you have some courage after all, he thought as he looked down at her. "I am really not in the mood for answering questions. I hope you'll understand."

And with that, he retrieved a roll of duct tape from under the table. He pulled a length from the roll and separated it with a pull from his teeth.

"You don't have to do this," she begged.

He grinned at her. "I'm afraid that I do." He pressed the tape over her mouth.

Her panic began anew, but her screams were muffled by the tape. She was right, he didn't have to do that. But it was better this way. It put an end to conversation and that was good because conversation might breed sympathy, and sympathy for this woman was out of the question. She was crucial to this mission. Her role was either bait, or sacrifice. Regardless of which one she became, there could be no room for sympathy.

"Where is your brother!" Cain turned on Jason. His patience was growing short.

"He'll show."

Jason responded too calmly for Cain's liking. "He'd better," he snapped while thinking *it's easier to kill you both if you're together.*

He looked back at the woman. She was breathing through her nose hard enough to cover the duct tape with her snot.

She stared at him, pleading with those eyes to let her go. *No dear, I can't do that.*

If it came to sacrifice, he'd keep those eyes for himself. They were so pretty, so brown, so full of terror. He loved them.

Will it be prophecy or sacrifice?

It all hinged on Seth.

"Kill the spotlight," he ordered Jason.

And an instant later, the room dived into darkness.

***

Seth sprinted into the large meeting room. Going from the brightness of the hallway to the gloom of the room stole his sight.

He slowed to a stop, trying to see, needing to see. Blindness and adrenaline assaulted him simultaneously.

He spun in circles. *They could attack from any direction, at any moment, and I won't even know it's coming until it's too late.*

Seth tried to control his breathing because his breathes were so loud. He needed silence to locate his opposition.

From where he stood, the hallway entrance looked like the gaping maw of some serpent of the deep, the kind that entices prey with bioluminescence.

He turned from the light. His adversary wouldn't be back there. If he knew them, and he was fairly certain he did, they'd be in the dark. "Hello?" he called.

Nobody answered. But he did hear a noise – muffled cries. *Maxine?*

***

Cain put an arm around Jason and pulled him close. With a whisper in his ear, he said, "He showed up after all."

Seth stood between the hallway and them. His shadow stretched long and dark before him. So far, Cain didn't think the man saw them.

Maybe I could kill them both now?

Cain shook his head. *No. I want it to look like an accident and I want witnesses to verify that it was.*

Have patience, he said to himself. *Your moment will come. Have patience.*

***

Seth's eyes were adjusting. He could make out shapes. Two figures stood in the distance. Beside them was... *The stone table.*

There was somebody on the table, struggling against bindings. "Maxine!" he shouted.

She muffled a cry in response.

He looked at the dark figures. "I've come."

Neither of the figures responded.

"I've come just as you asked."

Still nothing. Seth took two steps toward them, trying hard to keep from shaking. Now that he'd stopped running, the adrenaline was building up, exasperating his fear and making him edgy. *Courage over fear,* he said to himself. *Courage over fear.*

He tried not to look at the table. He tried not to look at the one on it. He suspected terror would take over if he did because he knew about the table. He knew its purpose – its ghastly purpose.

He took another step closer, keeping his eyes on the standing figures. His thoughts went to Maxine. Even if he didn't look at her, he couldn't help but think of what might happen to his wife. A shudder escaped him.

No sudden moves, he told himself. *Smooth and easy. Just keep moving smooth and easy.*

"I've done everything you've asked," Seth said. "Now, let her go."

"I don't think so," Cain's voice echoed throughout the room. "You haven't done everything."

It was worth a shot, Seth said to himself.

He looked down. His eyes had adjusted fully now. He was standing on stains he'd left with Jason last time he was here. It reminded him blood spilled freely in this space. *God, save my wife.*

"Looks like we've come full circle," Jason's voice rang out, as if he could read his brother's thoughts. "Right back to where we started."

Seth didn't respond.

"Can I ask you a question, brother?" Jason sneered. "Why wasn't I invited to your wedding?"

Silence from Seth. Inside, he wanted to scream, but he remained silent.

"Did my invite get lost in the mail perhaps?"

"Enough." Cain's voice boomed. "I'm glad you decided to come."

"Like I had a choice." Seth spat.

"Of course, you had a choice!" Cain retorted. "There's always a choice!"

"Not this time." Seth decided to keep the dialog going for as long as he could. Maybe, in the meantime, he could figure out some sort of plan out of this mess.

"Wrong!" Cain boomed. "People are a species endowed with free will, are they not?"

Seth edged closer. He needed to ensure Maxine was okay.

"Isn't that what your religion teaches?" Cain continued with bite.

Seth took another step. "That's close enough," Jason spat.

Seth stopped.

"You still haven't answered my question Seth," Cain hissed. "Does your region preach free will or not?"

"Yes."

Cain laughed coldly. "So, you admit it was your choice to leave us. It was your choice to disallow the prophecy from being fulfilled!"

"Yes."

Cain moved in fast, to within a foot of Seth. He held the knife, turning it so the blade reflected trace rays of the hallway's light.

Seth's heart quickened at the sight of that knife.

"Ah," exclaimed Cain. "You recognize the knife. I can tell."

Seth nodded as memories of sliced flesh and mixed blood entered his mind. He looked down at the stains on the floor – stains from blood once his.

"Then, you know its purpose."

"Blood sacrifice." Seth whispered – his face contorted with bitterness.

"You are correct," Cain said, smiling. "But blood sacrifice can be avoided today. Seth, today, sacrifice can be exchanged for your pledge of loyalty to the Kinship, to the Spirits, and to me."

That kind of Loyalty, Seth thought, *is the one thing I can't give.*

His eyes drifted to his wife. She'd been crying, but now only the occasional whimper came from her. The sight of the tape over her mouth and the ropes binding her to the table broke his heart.

Stay strong. Don't let the situation crush your spirit, Seth, he said to himself. *Stay strong.*

Cain's voice bellowed, "What do you say? Loyalty, or sacrifice?"

Seth said nothing.

"Make the right choices," Jason hissed, putting his hand on Maxine's head, stroking her hair lightly. "Nobody has to die today, if you do the right thing."

A fresh wave of sobs came from Maxine.

Stay strong. Jesus, give me strength.

Cain stared at Seth. With every moment of Seth's silence, his expression grew increasingly sour. Jason was still monologuing, but it was only background noise to Seth – a drone of noise without meaning or purpose.

This is all my fault. If I'd only been truthful from the beginning, then Maxine would be safe now.

Jason's voice rambled on and on.

I abandoned Amanda. I can't abandon Maxine.

Cain's booming voice simultaneously stopped Jason's speech and Seth's thoughts. "Enough of this. You know who you are – to whom you belong. You're blood mixed with that of your brother's. You belong here. Your loyalty is with us."

Seth looked at Cain. The man's face told the real story. *She dies if you decline my offer,* it said.

Cain spoke quieter now. "It's time to come home and fulfill the prophecy."

Who I am is not who I was, Seth thought to himself. That statement had been in his mind for years, but here and now, it held water more than ever.

"Decide," Jason shouted, his hand remaining on Maxine's head.

"The Spirits demand it." Cain's stare deepened.

Seth took a deep breath and said the only thing he could. "You don't understand what you're dealing with. These Kinship spirits, they're not who they say they are. They're demons, not spirits, and they don't have your interest in mind."

There. He said it.

Cain stared at him, unblinking. "Zion's Hill has filled your head with lies. Would you rather believe them than reunite with your brother?"

Seth looked past Cain, to his brother. "You're smarter than this, Jason. You're just being used here. Even if you're given power, it won't be yours. You'll be at the mercy of the demons who gave it to you."

"Zion's Hill has brainwashed you," Jason replied in anger.

Seth mourned his brother inside. *How can he not see it?* Then again, he himself was ignorant at one time too. "I've seen what the Spirits are firsthand. The night I ran away, they showed their true colors. And if you don't stop following them, they'll eventually show those colors to you too."

"How did you see these true colors?" Cain wanted to know.

"The night I ran away, they came for me in the river. But God showed me who they really were. He also showed who he was. He is my shepherd. He saved me from the enemy. I'm his."

"You saw what you wanted to see – nothing more." Cain's rage was evident in every syllable he spat out of his mouth.

"If you'll just..."

"Enough of this," Cain cut him off. "You have a decision to make. What do we do with your wife, and what do we do with you? Reunite with your brother or watch as we sacrifice your wife to our spirits.

Cain backed away from Seth, back toward the stone table – back to Maxine. "If your wife dies, her blood is on your head, Seth. The choice is yours."

Seth opened his mouth, but no words came. Part of him would do anything to save his wife. But, how could he deny Jesus, the one who saved him from all this.

The great room suddenly felt much smaller. He hadn't noticed until then, the Kinship was filing in from the hallway. The crowd now formed a crude circle around him, Cain, Jason, and Maxine.

Also, above in the dark recesses, he swore he saw movement. *The Spirits?*

Fear enveloped him as the crowd moved in close. He was surrounded. There could be no escape.

***

Everything's falling into place, Cain thought. The brothers were together. The Kinship was present. He held his knife. Now he only needed the right moment to kill them both, make it look like an accident, or self-defense, or something, and make sure plenty of witnesses saw it that way.

It needed to be done before the prophecy would be fulfilled. Fortunately, Seth seemed dead set on not reuniting. If that was the case, then the prophecy would remain unfulfilled.

Even still, he wanted to kill the brothers. If he didn't, they might reunite somewhere down the road. *I can't let that happen.*

He stood there, looking at the Kinship. They all watched expectedly.

They had come right on schedule. Yesterday, he'd put out the summons. All were to come to the great room at this time. *And it's all working out. The brothers are here and distracted by the one on the stone table. The witnesses are present. I'm armed. Yes, the pieces are coming together nicely.*

Now, it's just a waiting game.

***

Maxine had trouble thinking. Terror was her main emotion. It overwhelmed her thoughts, jumbled them together and cluttered her mind.

God help me, was her only coherent thought. *God, please help me.*

Now, a crowd had arrived, adding to her confusion. She looked at them. They didn't look friendly. Her terror spiked.

The crowd was an eclectic bunch. Men, women, even a few children were present. The only thing in common was the darkness which seemed to cover them from above.

When she looked at the ceiling. She swore she could see shapes moving in the darkness, flittering about. Those unidentified things piled her fear deeper.

She closed her eyes. *This is all just in my imagination,* she told herself. But when she opened them, everyone still surrounded her and those mysterious shapes continued to dart about like, but not quite like, bats.

One of those in the crowd had grown particularly close to her. She watched as he slipped in and out of the rest in order to get closer. She stared at him. His face was unreadable. Yet, something about him held familiarity. *Do I know him?*

The one called Cain spoke. "I assume that you remember your true family, Seth."

"This isn't my family," Seth answered with a tremor.

"In your own depraved way, you speak the truth," Cain retorted. "We are more than family. We are everything. Don't you remember the day we took you in, the day we adopted you? Remember the blood that was shed. Don't you recall the connection made here in this very room? Or has it been too long for you to remember what you owe us."

With that, Cain stopped talking. The ensuing silence was almost painful to hear. Maxine whimpered through her taped mouth. That was the only noise.

Cain shattered the quiet. "Surely you remember. Don't you realize that you and your brother's blood still cries out from the floor where it fell and dried?"

What did that mean? Maxine thought. *She was so confused, but one thing seemed true in all this. Her husband had been keeping secrets.*

Frightfully horrifying secrets.

***

Pastor Pete felt like they'd accomplished something. In reality it wasn't much. They'd simply figured out who was absent. It was Maxine and Seth. *But who was the third one that Jasmine had indicated?* He looked into the many faces of those in the seats before him. *It could be any one of these.*

Jasmine had only said two were absent and one was here. *Who was the third that Satan had received permission to sift like wheat?* He had no clue.

"Oh Lord!" Jasmine hollered. "Sweet Jesus, the enemy is trying to destroy those two!"

"Where are they now?" Pete needed to know.

"They are fighting the enemy."

"But where?"

"They are fighting Satan where Satan has his stronghold!"

"Where!" Pete shouted.

"I don't know!" Jasmine screamed back. "It has not been revealed!"

Immediately, Pete dove back into what he knew. He began to lead the prayer. "Dear Jesus, give our brother and sister the strength to remain faithful as they fight the enemy where he has his stronghold. Do not allow the enemy's flaming arrows to harm them."

And the people said, "Amen."

Cast your anxiety on God was what the Bible taught and what Seth was trying hard to do. But with all the pressure of the situation, he was finding that task difficult.

My God, or my wife . . . it was too much.

He could never just watch as the Kinship slaughtered his wife like a fattened calf. He also couldn't abandon the God he knew would never abandon him.

Maybe they're bluffing. He doubted it. He knew them well enough to know what they were capable of.

The crowd around him was large. The Kinship had grown since he'd last been here. They were everywhere, surrounding him like a plague of locus.

Above, he was sure the Spirits were there. He could sense their presence. It was the same feeling he'd felt that night in the river.

He looked at Jason. *Maybe he'll have sympathy for me. After all, I am family.*

He killed his own mother, he argued with himself.

His knees wobbled as that thought hit him like a ton of bricks.

***

Just like old times, Jason thought as he stared at his knee-wobbling brother.

I never let my feelings run the show. He knew he was the stronger of them. He'd proven his strength time and time again, from his willingness to kill Christians to his unwillingness to crumble under rejection and time spent in the inner room.

What have you done to show your strength? he wondered about Seth. *You run away from your fights and hide behind the apron strings of Zion's Hill?*

Jason glared at his brother. You are *weak – useless.*

Well, he corrected himself. *Not completely useless.*

Jason needed him to fulfill the prophecy. *But once that's done, I'll toss you aside like so much refuse.*

And then I'll go after Cain!

***

Maxine kept her eyes on the odd one. He was very near to her now, having squeezed through many bodies to emerge right by her side.

Who are you? she wanted to know. He was so familiar. Yet, she was certain she'd never met him before.

The man was tall with fair skin. He had youthful eyes, but his face looked older, like one who'd lived a hard life. He wore faded jeans and an equally faded t-shirt that had once been red, but was now almost pink. Over that shirt, he wore an unbuttoned olive-green jacket.

What is it? There was something about him, something just beyond her grasp.

She stared into those eyes of his. They had the look of one trying to hide something – like a kid who'd stolen dessert before supper and didn't want anyone to find out.

Speaking of somebody hiding something. Seth had become quite a question mark. *Who are you really?* An additional thought came to her, *and are you worth sticking around for?*

The odd man was standing near her head now, his hands resting on the edge of the stone table. He stared down at her with those youthful, covert eyes, and just watched.

"Now that we're all here," Cain's voice brought her from her thoughts. "It's time to reunite the brothers. It's time for prophecy to be fulfilled."

The crowd murmured their approval.

"Seth," Jason shouted over the murmurs. "It is time to finish what was started last time you were here."

She could see Seth step forward. The crowd parted, very reminiscent of a wild west showdown. The murmurs stopped. Above her, the strange shadows halted. Even the air felt stiff with anticipation.

"No, brother," Seth responded. "I follow a higher power now. I follow the one true God..."

Seth was still talking, but Maxine couldn't make it out. The crowd had begun murmuring once more. They were louder now, angrier, and mixed in were hisses and boos.

Cain held up his hands, attempting to silence the crowd. After a minute, they complied.

"Your god?" Cain shouted. "Where is your god?"

Seth didn't answer.

"Why doesn't your god show himself?"

Again. No answer.

"Why doesn't he come and rescue you and your wife? Is he asleep? Do you need to wake him up? Maybe he's taking a trip and forgot his cell phone?"

The crowd laughed at that. Again, Cain silenced it with a raising of his hands. "We all know you deserve to be deserted by your god. After all the secrets you've been hiding from Zion's Hill, you deserve to be abandoned don't you."

Silence from Seth.

"But what about your wife? Does she deserve this? You can free her just by reuniting with your brother."

And still, Seth remained silent.

Cain chuffed. "Where is this god of truth?" Cain shouted. "Surely, if he cared for you, he'd rescue you now."

Maxine looked at Seth. He looked frightened beyond all measure. Yet, he stood his ground, planting his feet firmly. Silently, she prayed for his safety.

"Hello?" Cain shouted. "Seth's god? Are you there? Are you real? If you are real, show yourself, I'll bow down and worship you."

A dropped pin would have sounded like a nuclear explosion at that moment. The silence was absolute.

Cain poised himself, looking up. The Kinship stood frozen, waiting. Even Seth stopped trembling for a moment.

After a few seconds, Cain lowered his gaze. "Well, it looks like we have the answer about your so-called god," he said triumphantly.

The crowd began to move once more as did the shadows near the ceiling. Maxine kept praying.

"Come closer," Cain uttered through a sadistic grin. "If you dare."

Seth didn't move.

"Come closer, man of a fake god!"

Seth remained where he was.

Cain let out a huff. "Get him over here!"

The crowd moved in and Maxine lost sight of Seth. A moment later, he emerged from the sea of people. They forced him to his knees in front of Cain.

Maxine screamed, but her tape-muffled voice was overwhelmed by the cheering crowd.

***

Cain mulled over his options. Whether Seth joined them or not, he'd need to kill them. Also, regardless of Seth's decision, Maxine would also need to die.

Simple enough.

He had them all here. He had his knife. With all the Kinship surrounding them, it shouldn't be too hard to create a distraction.

Timing is everything.

He needed to do it quickly, when everyone's attention is somewhere else. Then, when they notice what he's done, he can claim self-defense.

Just wait for the right time, he said to himself. *And be ready always,* he added.

***

Because of the crowd, the key players in this little vignette were now very close to each other. Seth knelt within a few feet of Maxine.

She looked at him. He looked back. The fear in her eyes tore him apart. *This is all my fault.*

He was getting sick and tired of that broken-record message. Yet, it was true. It was all his fault.

"I'm sorry," he said to her.

She didn't even try to be heard through the tape covering her mouth. She nodded though as tears streamed down her cheeks.

"You're sorry?" Cain scoffed. "I bet you are."

Seth kept eye contact with his wife. "I never meant for any of this to happen."

"But it has happened," Cain's voice was almost a growl. "And it is all your fault."

"I know it is," Seth said with resignation.

"Do you think your apology means anything?" Cain pointed at Maxine with a jab of the knife blade, "To her, your apology doesn't mean squat."

Seth nodded. "I know."

Maxine shook her head.

"The only thing you can do now that matters to her is to reunite with your brother. If that happens, I promise, she'll be released unharmed. If not," he added, "Well, you don't want that."

Seth broke his stare with Maxine and looked down at the ground. The weight of the situation was pressing him into a state of despair. "God help me!" he cried.

"Hold up," Cain sneered. "Let's see if his god comes to help." After a few seconds, he laughed. "Nope. Looks like you're on your own."

Nearly every Kinship member began to laugh. All except one.

This guy was right next to Maxine and only a few feet away from him. He'd seen this guy before. *But where? When?*

The man leaned down and whispered something in Maxine's ear. She nodded.

***

"Stay calm," the man whispered. Things are about to get real. So, just stay calm."

Maxine nodded. She wasn't sure if she could trust this guy. Then again, she didn't have a lot of choice.

Cain was creating quite a distraction, dancing around like a fool. She didn't think anyone even noticed the man's whisper.

"Maybe if I do this dance, it'll conjure your god," Cain mocked. "After all, you need all the help you can get."

The Kinship laughed even harder.

"Enough!" the man shouted as he drew a handgun from a pocket inside his jacket.

An expression of shock covered everyone's faces as their attention turned from Cain to the gun which was pointed directly at Cain.

"Everyone, stay still," the man shouted. "And I mean, don't even breath hard, or good old Cain gets open-heart surgery the hard way."

Maxine could tell by Cain's expression that this was completely unexpected. She tried to stay calm as the man suggested. But the tension, combined with her restrained condition, created a panic. It took all she had to stay calm.

The silence was oppressive. Everything was still, even the shadows on the ceiling no longer moved.

A clicking sound shattered the silence. It was the sound of the man's weapon as he pulled back the hammer.

Cain raised his hands, gripping the knife in one. "What are you doing?" He said with a voice too calm for the situation. "Just what in the world do you think you're doing?"

The man didn't answer.

***

Cain hid his initial confusion. He didn't like being caught off guard.

His confusion morphed into rage within seconds. "You're making a big mistake, friend."

The man just shrugged.

***

Maxine struggled to make sense of what was transpiring. She felt like her brain's circuitry was about to short out. And still she wondered, *where do I know this guy from?*

"Cut the sacrifice loose Cain!" the man ordered.

"You're making a serious mistake," Cain reiterated. "Here's a counteroffer, put the gun down, and maybe we'll let you live."

The man shook his head. "I wasn't born yesterday, and I've been a part of this group long enough to know you'll never let me walk out of here alive if I put down this gun. This gun is the only reason I'm not dead already."

Cain nodded. "So, what happens when you start shooting and run out of ammo? You can't kill us all."

The man smiled. "I only need one bullet to kill you though."

Cain crossed his arms and narrowed his eyes. That threat obviously made him on edge.

"I'll ask again, cut the woman loose."

Cain didn't move.

"My trigger finger is feeling mighty itchy, Cain."

Cain grunted and began moving toward the stone table.

"Nice, easy movements. Don't do anything fast, or it'll be the last thing you do." The man sounded confident, but Maxine was close enough to see the sweat soaking through his faded red shirt around the collar.

"Cain continued closer. "It's not me you should worry about. You're an enemy of the Spirits now. They'll hunt you down, and when they find you, you'll wish you'd never been born."

"Shut up!" he shouted. "Cut her loose now!"

Maxine looked beyond the main characters in this scene. The Kinship stood clear of the showdown. No doubt none of them wanted to catch a stray bullet. Above her, the shadows flittered about once more, angrily.

"Why do you want to free this woman so badly?"

The man didn't respond.

"Why do you want to release the one selected for sacrifice?"

"I don't owe you an explanation!"

Cain smiled, but Maxine could see sweat coming from him as well. "You're a dead man. You know this, right?"

The man stood his ground. "Do as you're told. Cut her loose."

"Apparently, I'm not the one giving the orders anymore," Cain grumbled. He moved right up beside Maxine.

The man took a step back to say beyond the reach of the knife. "Cut her loose, but be careful. If you so much as nick her, you'll regret it."

Keeping his eyes on the man, Cain leaned over Maxine. By feel, he found the ropes and sliced them through.

He was so close that Maxine could feel the heat wafting from his body. He smelled sour with perspiration. His pursed lips conveyed intense rage.

He stood up, still holding the blade. "Now what?"

The man didn't respond. Maxine had the feeling he hadn't planned it out this far.

"Do you think we're going to just let you waltz out of here?" Cain taunted.

"I am the one with the gun," the man responded.

Maxine rolled off the stone table and stood on aching legs. Her wrists and ankles hurt from where the rope chaffed her skin.

"Get behind me," the man said to her.

Maxine complied.

"How far do you think you'll get?" Cain uttered with a murderous look.

"You too," the man said, nodding his head to Seth. "Join us if you want to live."

Cain piped in. "Sure, Seth. Take your chances with him. He's clearly got it all together."

Seth moved slowly, cautiously.

Once Seth was beside Maxine, the man said to Cain, "Now, drop the knife."

"You'd like that wouldn't you." Cain took a step closer, shifting the knife from one hand to the other.

"Drop the knife!" he repeated with a roar.

Cain didn't respond. His eyes had that crazy look. His grinning face was the face of insanity.

"Drop it!"

The man backed away from Cain. Seth and Maxine backed up with him – a close-knit trio. "Stay back!" he yelled to the Kinship members who blocked their path. "Or you'll be the first to die!"

Maxine didn't know if the man was bluffing. Regardless, the ploy worked. The Kinship parted like the Red Sea before Moses.

Cain pressed forward, knife extended. "You think you're so tough," Cain spat. "Here I am bringing a knife to a gun fight and winning."

"Stay where you are, Cain!" The man's statement had authority, but his voice conveyed the opposite.

"Or what?"

The man didn't answer.

"That's what I thought."

Behind them, the crowd continued to part as they backed away from Cain. They angled their escape toward the hallway entrance.

They were moving away faster now because Cain was pressing harder from the front. "Cowards!" he shouted as he waved his knife.

The man jabbed his gun at Cain. "Stop coming at us!"

Cain didn't stop.

"Don't be stupid, Cain. Gun beats knife every time."

Maxine caught movement above, out of her peripheral vision. She glanced up. The shadows were very active now, like a brewing storm.

"Every time?" Cain struggled. "Are you sure? Do you want to bet? Would you bet your life?"

The man didn't answer.

Maxine was overwhelmed. The surrounding crowd, the shifting shadows, this mystery would-be rescuer, the knife and the man who wielded it, she felt like reality was slipping away.

Cain suddenly lunged at the man.

The gun fired. The knife dropped. Cain fell to his knees, clasping his hands over his chest. When he pulled them away a second later, they were dripping with blood.

He looked up – his face pale, his lips quivering. Blood spurted from the hole in his chest.

He fell forward and more blood spurted out the exit wound in his back.

Time seemed to stop. The crowd, Cain, Seth, the stranger, Maxine – everyone and everything was still.

Maxine stared at the twitching body. Cain looked up for a moment. His eyes rolled in his head. Then, his head fell back to the concrete floor. His body went limp and the spurting blood no longer spurted but trickled.

She could hear him gasping, gurgling, trying to catch a breath. And then she couldn't.

Cain was dead.

CHAPTER 7

Pastor Pete's led Zion's Hill in prayer when a shriek interrupted everything. He looked up, startled.

The death-rattle scream came from Jasmine. She looked ghastly, standing ridged as a pole. Her skin paled as her lungs emptied.

She inhaled again, and shrieked again, trembling like a leaf about to fall from the tree. Everyone in the church stared at her with looks of shock on their faces.

Finally, she spoke, her trembling voice on the verge of incoherency. "Now don't go and stop praying, pastor," she said. "That's one of your spiritual gifts, so use it as I use mine."

But Pete didn't resume. How could he with her bazar behavior stealing his attention?

She looked straight at him. "Keep praying, Pastor. And while you do, follow me. All of you, follow me to where God's spirit leads us. Keep on praying. Follow me."

Jasmine shuffled to the main aisle. Nobody else moved a muscle.

"Follow me now!"

Pete forced his legs to move. He followed and others followed behind him. He resumed praying, using the best voice he could find, which wasn't much, but it was all he could muster.

Jasmine led the crowd down the main aisle of the sanctuary, past the lobby, and out the front door of Zion's Hill Church. Night had fallen.

"Jesus, give us strength as you lead us out this night," he said.

And the people said, "Amen."

The air felt unnaturally humid as they progressed further and further from the church. It felt heavy, almost to the point of weighing him down as he walked along.

Jasmine led them down 42nd street. The streetlights were on, making an almost inaudible buzzing sound.

The street was curiously vacant. It was a weekday evening, but still, there should have been somebody out there, but there was none besides them.

"Jesus be with us," Pete shouted. "Lead us!"

"Amen," Zion's Hill responded.

"Jesus, guide us!"

"Amen."

"Jesus, protect us!"

A coldness enveloped him as Pete led the prayer. It was as if a thick blanket of ice covered him. He'd experienced such heaviness before, back on the night of the masked gunmen.

Battle lines are being drawn. The thought came of its own accord. *Lines are being scratched in the dirt, and not by mortals. By the Devil himself.*

But, we're not alone in this fight, he said to himself.

"We pray the blood of Jesus over us. Lord, create a space around us that the enemy cannot penetrate. We pray in the name of Jesus, all demons, all who are fallen, they must flee at the sound of Jesus' mighty name."

He felt the heaviness lift some. It didn't leave, but it grew less. *The gates of Hell will not overcome us.*

"Jesus, march before us. Lead your army ahead."

And the people said, "Amen."

***

Jason stared in disbelief at Cain's lifeless body. All along, he'd been considering how to do the deed himself. And now, it had been done for him. *Isn't that convenient?*

BOUND BY BLOOD

Cain's corpse was still with the exception of the occasional twitch. *Looks like the life stolen in sacrifice was your own, Cain.* The thought made him smile.

The body was surrounded in a pool of blood which had stopped expanding because the heart had stopped pumping it out.

He looked toward the ceiling. The shadows of the Spirits were there. They hid in the darker recesses, but Jason sensed their presence. "Cain's blood poured out for you Kindred spirits," he shouted, raising his hands toward them.

The shadows lit with emerald-green orbs. "Behold, the eyes of the Spirits."

The Kinship looked up. A few of them gasped. A few of them fainted. They all stared with eyes like saucers.

Jason turned toward the Kinship. "If the Spirits wish me to be the new Hight Priest, show us a sign."

He waited. This was a do or die moment. The Kinship watched. *Come on. I've waited so long. Don't abandon your servant now!*

A noise. All turned to Cain's corpse. If flopped once, twice, a third time. Cain drew a raspy breath, extending one hand, dragging it through the blood pool. Then, nothing.

"A sign has been given." Jason yelled.

He had no idea if it was truly a sign, but getting what you want is 99% being confident. Plus, the smear of blood from Cain's clawing hand appeared to make the letter "J".

He pointed to the blood smear. "J," the Spirits have spoken.

"Hail Jason, High Priest," someone in the crowd called out. Others joined in. Soon, all were shouting the slogan.

"Hail Jason, High Priest!"

***

Maxine ripped the tape from her mouth. Its removal worked better than wax. Despite the pain of involuntary hair removal, she remained silent. She dared not make a sound because strange things were afoot, dark things.

She witnessed Cain's death. She witnessed the Seth lookalike claim leadership. She saw the strange reanimation of the dead. Now, reality hit her. *I'm in the middle of a hostile crowd with only myself, my husband and a stranger with a gun for defense.*

The man with the gun now aimed it at the one who looked like Seth. The one who everyone called Jason. "Back away," he said.

Jason stood straight. "Who are you?"

"Just let us go," the man answered.

"You look like one of us, but you're in league with them. Why?"

Maxine wondered the same question.

"Cain decreed that all should come today unarmed. He didn't want any mistakes by a trigger-happy crowd. Yet, you came armed. Why?"

"You're stalling," he answered. "Let us go."

"You're the only one here with a firearm. So, you're running the show," Jason's voice sounded genuine, but Maxine wondered if it covered deception. "Go ahead, leave."

They began edging toward the hallway. The man kept his aim trained on Jason. All the others kept their distance.

"Who are you?" Jason asked again.

"Call me Jacobson."

Maxine realized in an instant why the man was familiar. *The jacket!*

***

"Pray for Maxine and Seth," Jasmine's voice carried as she led Zion's Hill down the sidewalk. "Pray for their safety. Pray that God's protection rests on them!"

Pete added in at the top of his lungs, "Please cover your servants Seth and Maxine! Keep them safe from all that the enemy has planned for them! Rescue them! Deliver them!"

Jasmine shouted. "And pray for the one in our midst that Satan has asked to sift as wheat! Pray that this one will remain strong in the Lord! Pray that this one will resist the enemy when their time comes!"

"Yes, Lord!" Pete shouted.

And all the people said, "Amen."

"Oh Lord, we pray confusion into the enemy's camp!" Jasmine yelled. "Pray that the light of salvation would be seen in the ranks of the enemy this night!"

Jasmine left the sidewalk and began walking right down the middle of the street. Pete and the others followed without objection. The street was strangely vacant. *Supernaturally vacant,* Pete thought. *As if the battlefield had been cleared and prepared for battle,* and his adrenaline surged accordingly.

An old hymn came to mind. "Onward Christian soldiers, marching as to war. With the cross of Jesus, going on before," he sang.

And Zion's Hill joined in. The march to war had begun.

***

Cain's dead.

That statement rolled over and over in Seth's mind. It seemed unbelievable. Then again, wasn't everything?

Their rescuer was the man Seth gave his Jacobson jacket to – the drunk from the streets. *It's so obvious!* Yet, he hadn't recognized him until he said 'call me Jacobson'.

"Okay, Jacobson," Jason hissed. "You're the one with the gun, so I guess you're calling the shots. So, what's your plan of getting out of here alive? Honestly, I don't think the odds are in your favor."

Jacobson steadied his gun at Jason. "I don't know if we'll get out alive, but I do know if we don't, I'm taking you with me."

Jason didn't move. "If you shoot me, all these," he said indicating the crowd, "will tear you apart with their bare hands."

"The way I see it, we're dead either way," he cocked the hammer on his gun.

Seth stepped out from behind Jacobson and stood in the line of fire.

"What are you doing? Jacobson demanded. "I need to end this now!"

"I can't move," Seth answered with a loud whisper. "This is my brother."

"It's him or us!" Jacobson spat.

Seth stood with the gun to his back and Jason at his front. He stared at his brother. *Please, just let us go!*

Jacobson's voice came clear and cold, "Get out of the way!"

***

Why risk your life like that, Jason wondered as he stared down his renegade brother. *Such sentimental feelings are one of the reasons why you're so weak.*

Regardless of his brother's folly, the situation had grown too risky. It needed to be defused.

And soon…

***

"For the last time, get out of the way!"

"I can't," Seth answered. His own voice seemed far away from his body, as if it wasn't he who spoke. "If you read the Bible you found in my jacket, you know this isn't the road you want to take."

The silence from Jacobson spoke volumes.

"Thou shalt not kill," Seth said. "And, love your enemies."

"It doesn't count if it's self-defense."

"Is that what this is? Self-defense? You're the only one with a gun." Seth added, "Vengeance is mine, sayeth the Lord."

"Fine. Get back behind me."

"I'll take you at your word," Seth answered as he slinked back to his place beside Maxine.

"Your brother must love you very much," Jacobson said, still pointing the weapon at Jason. "Now, let us go and nobody gets shot. How does that sound?"

Seth felt clammy and realized just how drenched his cloths were. The smell of his own sweat was overpowering, but he didn't care much. He only wanted to survive the next hour.

Together, Maxine, Seth and Jacobson backed away from Jason. The crowd parted as they drew nearer to the hallway's entrance.

Seth's heart pounded and vomit stung the back of his throat. He swallowed hard to keep it down.

Above them, the shadows danced. All around them, the Kinship seethed. In front of them, Jason stood, motionless.

Their shadows grew shorter and sharper as they neared the bare-bulb hallway. *I can't believe they're letting us go.* Finally, they arrived at the entrance.

Jacobson boomed, "The first to try following us will be the first to die. Got it?"

No one said a word.

"No one follows!" he shrieked.

Seth glanced at the ceiling. *What about them? Will they follow?*

Fear not, for I am with you. Those were words Jesus spoke. He'd read it in his Bible.

Despite that, he feared greatly. He couldn't help it.

Above, the shadows swirled and raged. Seeing them only added to his terror and he didn't need any help in that area.

"Don't follow us!" Jacobson shouted as they turned and fled down the hallway.

And the curving hall hid them from those in the main room.

***

"After them!" Jason commanded the instant they were out of view.

For a moment, nobody moved. *Cowards!*

Not that he could blame them much. Nobody was armed except for those three escapees. Still, he couldn't just let them waltz out of here after making such a fool of him.

You should have shot me when you had the chance. Weakness is for fools. I'll not show any when I find you!

All the Kinship looked at him. None pursued those in the hallway. *Stupid cowards!*

He kicked Cain's body hard enough for the blood to splatter across the floor. "He's dead! I'm your leader now! By the Spirits, you'll obey."

The rafters shook. Above, the Spirits became like a tempest. That got the Kinship moving. *Good. They understand I'm the ordained leader.*

With a thunderous cry, the hoard of Kinship members stampeded the hallway.

Finally, Jason thought as he entered the hallway with them.

He made sure to stay in the middle of the crowd. *No sense in taking a bullet when so many others are more expendable. I'm the High priest after all.*

"Avenge Cain's death!" he shouted. "The one with the gun is fair game! Just don't harm my brother or his wife! They have a higher purpose!"

He hoped all heard him. *The prophecy must be fulfilled. It can still happen.* But he'll need his brother alive. Plus, Maxine could still prove valuable in coaxing reunion from Seth.

Jason wondered how much of a lead they had. If they could catch up before they got out of the building, then all would be well. Sheer numbers would overwhelm them.

How much of a lead? That was Jason's question.

***

Jasmine staggered. Pete grabbed her, steadied her.

"What's wrong?" he asked.

"I don't know."

For a moment, the world seemed to tip on its side and then spin. It only lasted a moment before passing.

Now, everything seemed normal, except it wasn't. Something significant had happened. *Something to Maxine and Seth?* She didn't know. God hadn't revealed it.

"Are you okay?"

She nodded and continued leading Zion's Hill down the street. *Something's happening to Maxine and Seth.*

The cold hand of fear touched her. She hated that she feared. Jesus commanded his followers to fear not. But she couldn't help it.

Despite her fear, she marched on, and Zion's Hill followed.

***

The hallway was an acoustic nightmare. The sound of every footstep, every gasp, every whimper, echoed and amplified throughout the hall. Because if this, it was impossible to tell how far behind their pursuers were. This lack of knowledge irked Jacobson.

Why do I do things like this?

Jacobson never actually did this exact thing before. But he was impulsive. And now, his latest impulse meant risk to his very life.

But it's the right thing to do. The man had given him a jacket when he was in need. That act of kindness was huge. Nobody in the Kinship, his supposed friends, had ever done something so nice for him.

Because of that specific act, Jacobson decided to start a fresh life which began by taking the name on the jacket as his own. Also, he vowed to stop drinking, which he did then and there.

White-knuckling it may not be the best approach, but it was the one he took – the impulsive option.

Without alcohol, things sometimes seemed ugly. but so far, he managed to stay clean. Every day seemed like an accomplishment.

Part of his self-created program of betterment meant paying back debts. It was something he took seriously – something he'd vowed to do at any cost. Now though, as he ran for his life, he realized some debts had a hefty price tag.

In true impulsive fashion, he'd shown up with his gun hidden inside the jacket. Knowing he was the only one armed gave him confidence. But that was the extent of his planning. *Just bring a gun and everything will fall into place.* At the time such impulsive planning seemed to hold water. Now though, the whole idea seemed ludicrous.

As for the Bible he'd found in the jacket's pocket, he read some of it. He didn't read it often for fear of it being discovered.

Throw it away, he'd often told himself. For some reason, he never did.

Jacobson's anxiety multiplied as he ran. Part of him thought about turning back. Perhaps, he could beg for forgiveness.

No. The Kinship didn't forgive. They punished. And punishment for this crime would be a slow and painful death.

He allowed the man and his wife to lead the way down the hallway. This was safer. All the Kinship had been required to come to the main room. They were all behind them. As he was the one with the gun, it made sense that he brought up the rear.

You're making a huge blunder.

Hearing that voice raised gooseflesh on his skin.

Such a blunder will not be forgiven.

He realized the Spirits were speaking to him. They'd never spoken to him before. He wasn't high priest. Yet, he knew the sound of their voices as they spoke in his head.

Do you think you'll just be allowed to leave?

Jacobson tried to ignore them.

You murdered our priest!

They were almost to the exit. Just one more bend in the hallway and they'd be there. "Hurry!" he shouted to the others. "We're almost out!"

TREASON! You are guilty of treason against the Kinship, and more importantly, against us, the Spirits who took you in!

Jacobson tried blocking them out, but they only screamed louder in his mind.

We condemn you.

"Leave me be," Jacobson whispered.

No! they answered. That one-word reply reverberated in his brain over and over like an eternal echo.

"There!" the woman shouted. "The exit!"

Seth slammed into the door ahead of the others and pulled it open. A rush of air hit Jacobson, chilling him.

Seth and his wife exited the building, their bodies a contrast to the surrounding darkness of night.

Jacobson approached the door. His legs felt strangely heavy. He forced them forward. He was only a few steps from escape.

"Come on!" she screamed.

Jacobson grabbed hold of the door frame. He tried to pull himself through.

Something grabbed him, flung him back. His fingers stung as he lost hold of the frame.

He landed on his butt, sliding away from the door. *Oh no!*

The woman tried to come back for him, but the Seth held her back. Then the door slammed shut.

Overhead, one of the bare bulbs flickered and buzzed. Then a second, then all of them began to flicker. The strobe light effect disoriented him as he staggered to his feet.

Where's the gun? He must have dropped it when he fell.

Looks like you didn't quite make it did you? the Spirits sang in his head.

The lights brightened and dimmed with their words. *I bet you could use a drink about now, huh.*

Jacobson found the gun and picked it up. "Shut up!" he said waving the weapon.

But they didn't stop.

He ran to the door and began pounding on it with all he had.

***

Seth shuddered as he inhaled the air outside. It seemed impossible, certainly not something he ever predicted. *I should be dead right now.*

How he came to be here, alive and breathing, was a miracle in itself. Plus, Maxine was with him.

He grabbed her by the upper arm. "We need to get out of here." *My brother could be just on the other side of that door!*

He started going, but she dug in her heals. "No! We need to help the guy wearing your jacket."

"What we need," Seth countered, "Is to put some distance between us and that this place!" *Hurry! Time is running out!*

Maxine didn't yield. "We can't just leave him."

Seth tried pulling her, but Maxine wouldn't move.

"Not after what he did for us!" she added.

Seth could hear pounding. It was coming from the door. *Jacobson?* Or, it might be the Kinship. Either way, opening that door was a huge risk.

"Seth," Maxine said quieting her voice. "I don't know what you're mixed-up in. But, I'm a pretty good judge of character, and I know that whatever you did, you're not the sort to just abandon somebody in need – not when doing so means somebody could die."

Seth gritted his teeth. "Geez!" he grunted as he ran to the door.

He could feel the latch scrape along the strike plate of the door frame as he turned the knob back and forth. So, it wasn't locked. The door just wouldn't open.

Whoever was on the other side was frantic. The pounding was incessant.

He could hear muffled screams. It sounded like Jacobson. *Or is it all a ploy to get me to open the door?*

Seth let go of the knob. It was turning of its own accord with panicky shakes and turns. *Someone really wants out. Or, somebody really wants me back in.*

"Come on! Hurry!" Maxine shouted. "Open the door!"

"It's stuck!" Seth yelled, grabbing the knob once more.

"We can't just leave him here!"

"We have no choice. We've got to go!"

She looked at him, then at the door. The pounding continued more frantic now, coming in quicker harder pounds.

He grabbed her arm and began to drag her away. "We can't just leave him in there," she sobbed. But this time, she didn't resist.

"We can't just leave him in there."

***

Tears streamed down Jacobson's cheeks. His heart raced. His breathing was erratic. Panic was taking over.

His hand hurt from pounding the door so he resorted to using the handle of his gun. He hit it hard enough to put little divots in the steel. But in the end, nothing changed.

The Spirits chimed in, *We told you, did we not?*

"Shut up!" Jacobson screamed.

We told you there would be no escaping – not for a traitor like you. Not for Cain's murderer.

Jacobson blocked out the voices as best he could. But it was hard being they were in his head.

With a groan, he turned away from the door and faced the hallway. "I won't go without a fight," he mumbled.

Looking down that corridor was like staring down the open mouth of sleeping alligator. Sooner or later, that alligator is going to wake up, and when it does, that mouth is going to shut and kill whatever was stupid enough to be there.

Noise came to him from down the hallway. He heard his pursuers. He heard their curses. He heard their footsteps. He prepared for the attack. "I won't go down without a fight!"

Jacobson backed up against the door. The coolness of that steel permeated through his jacket and shirt, icing his shoulder blades.

He wiped away the tears and raised his gun, leveling it at the hallway's emptiness. *It won't be empty soon enough.*

He prepared to fire at whatever came around the bend first. *Take out as many as you can,* he thought to himself. *Go out in a blaze of glory.*

You treacherous pig! The Spirits grunted.

Jacobson let out a whine. "Stop it! Leave me alone!"

He planted his feet and steadied his weapon. He could hear their footsteps. The Kinship was coming fast. Any second he'd empty his gun and watch them fall.

How many bullets do you still have in there? Hmm?

"I won't go down without a fight," he hissed. "Mark my words."

Oh, we hear you, the voices came to him with sickening sweetness, speaking in unison as if from one mind.

Let's see, you killed Cain in cold blood. That took a bullet. Did you shoot off any more? Think – think – think – think, you stupid pig!

Jacobson's hands shook. He willed them to steady. He couldn't afford to throw away a single shot.

The Spirits taunted, *It doesn't really matter how many rounds are left now does it? It doesn't matter if you have one or eight. It's fair to say, there's more of them than you have bullets. Don't you agree?"*

Jacobson knew he didn't have eight bullets left. That would have been a full cylinder, and he knew he'd fired at least one already, maybe even more. It was all such a blur.

"I'll take out as many as I can before I die." He spoke through gritted teeth.

You know we're right, you stupid pig! the Spirits spat. *You can't kill em all!*

Jacobson forced his hands to steady. He could feel the Spirits' presence. It was a greasy feeling, a disturbing feeling. "I won't enter Hell alone."

They chuckled at that. *That's what we were hoping to hear.*

Jacobson guessed that the Spirits did not possess the ability to read thoughts. If they did, they'd know he had a hidden card to play.

It was a long shot, improbable but not impossible.

The sounds of the approaching enemy grew louder. He prepared himself for the battle to come.

***

"Don't harm my brother or his wife!" Jason shouted as the Kinship stampeded down the narrow hallway. Above him, the bare bulbs flickered from the vibrations of many feet running toward one goal. Ahead, the bulbs began to flicker like strobe lights.

On he ran, letting his stampede of sheep lead the way. *Because why should I take a bullet when I have this herd of sacrificial sheep at my disposal.*

A grin covered his face. *I'm coming for you brother, and I'm bringing the Spirits with me!*

***

Maxine stopped once more. She looked back toward the building. They'd only made it twenty yards.

"If you're thinking of going back, it's out of the question," Seth uttered.

But Maxine had already turned back.

"Ah, nuts! You are crazy!" But he followed her back to the door anyway.

The door was silent now. The banging had ceased.

"What's the plan here, Maxine?" Seth needed to know.

Maxine didn't respond.

"These people, they're known as the Kinship. They will kill you given the chance. Let's not give them that chance." Seth added, "Jacobson's probably already dead."

Maxine began to sob. She closed her eyes and leaned against the door. "Please God," she wailed. "Where are you?"

***

The narrow hallway amplified the stampeding Kinship. The lights continued to flicker and strobe. Jacobson felt like he would puke any moment.

He turned back toward the door. It was time to play his hidden card. *I won't let them take me alive.* He jammed the gun's muzzle against the door's knob and pulled the trigger.

The report left his ears ringing. Half the knob was missing where the slug screamed through it.

He slammed against the door, but it still wouldn't open. He touched the damaged knob. It scalded his fingers, but he was unable to unlatch the door.

He angled the gun's barrel into the exposed latching mechanism and fired again.

Now only a gaping hole existed where the knob once was. Yet, the door still wouldn't budge.

Having trouble? The Spirits laughed. *Keep shooting if you must, but we don't think you'll get that door open.*

Anxiety drove him. He fired again and again. Fragments of steel flew from the door. A piece of shrapnel shattered the nearest bulb. But the door remained closed.

He played his card but lost the poker match. Still, he had a final hand to play.

He pressed the gun against his temple and pulled the trigger. But the chamber was empty. He pulled it again. The hammer came down, but no bullets remained.

Having problems? the Spirits taunted. *You stupid pig. Who told you that you could end this on your own terms and avoid your due punishment?*

"Shut up!" Jacobson shouted as he continued pulling the trigger, desperate for death to take him away.

He slammed into the door. It didn't budge, but he did see something he didn't notice previously – something near the bottom of the door, revealed in the strobing light of the remaining bare bulbs. He looked closer. It was an additional lock, a brass heavy-duty barrel sliding lock.

Unbelievable! He reached down and tried to slide the barrel into the unlocked position, but it wouldn't move and his last bit of hope dissolved into hopelessness.

Did you think we would make it that easy? They began laughing.

"Shut up!" he screamed.

But the Spirits didn't seem to care.

***

Maxine trembled. She was beyond terrified. She held her hands over her ears and squinted her eyes shut.

She felt Seth grab her. He pulled her off to one side of the door.

She opened her eyes. The door's knob was gone. In its place was a gaping hole. Through the hole, strobe lights flashed.

Then, more bullets flew through the door, creating punctures through the steel. *If Seth hadn't moved me...* she couldn't finish that thought.

She let out the most bazaar sound. It was almost a scream, but so filled with sorrow – so filled with lament. It just came out, as if of its own volition.

"Shut up!"

Maxine jumped. That voice, from the other side of the door, sounded so rage filled. Yet, she recognized it. *He was alive? He was alive!*

"Shut up! Shut up! Shut up!" Jacobson seemed to be in the midst of a vicious argument.

His voice sounded desperate. Despite the risk, Maxine ran back to the door and began to pull.

***

"Shut up! Shut up! Shut up!" Jacobson shrieked. He didn't like the sound of his own voice. It was shrill – insane even.

But the Spirits didn't shut up. *Shooting a door? Well, that's pretty stupid. You really are a stupid pig. Don't you know that we're the ones holding the door shut? Bullets can't harm us you know. Stupid, stupid, so very stupid.*

Jacobson began to sob. It was very stupid to use all his ammo on a door. He should have stopped after seeing that the first bullet did nothing to unlock the exit. Now he was trapped and unarmed.

Do you want to know what the stupidest part was? Do you want to know?

Jacobson provided no response.

You didn't even leave a bullet for yourself. If you'd have left just one bullet, then you could've taken the easy way out.

Jacobson leaned into the door. He pressed his head against it, closed his eyes and waited for the end.

His brain conjured ideas about what the Kinship might do to him. All of them were terrifying.

You killed their priest, he said to himself. *Mercy won't be given.*

And all the while, the Spirits continued to harass him. *You are about the stupidest we've ever encountered. Stupid – stupid – stupid!*

***

Maxine grasped the door and pulled. She knew Jacobson was still alive. She'd heard him.

It would not budge. Seth pulled with her. No luck.

"Dear Jesus, help me!" she cried.

***

Jacobson opened his eyes. "Dear Jesus, help me," a woman's voice said.

The woman sounded close, perhaps just on the other side of the door.

The Spirits grew louder. *We'll put you on a spit and roast you over the fire, you stupid pig!*

The sound of stampeding feet was now close enough to feel. It vibrated the floor, the door, and his bones. Overhead, the bare bulbs swayed on their wires as they continued to flash on and off.

Despite all the disruptions though, he focused on the woman's words. *Dear Jesus, help me.*

Stupid pig! Stupid pig! Let us in! The Spirits shrieked in his brain as if trying to distract him from those words spoken from the other side of the door. *Not by the hairs of our chinny chin chin,* they taunted.

He mulled over the words, *Dear Jesus, help me.*

Then we'll huff and we'll puff, and we will blow you to Hell! the Spirits shrieked.

"Dear Jesus, help me!" Saying it out loud was like letting go of a 50-pound weight.

With those words, the brass heavy-duty barrel slide lock disengaged. The steel door flew open.

He stumbled into the night, tripping over two people. He hopped up and ran. The other two ran with him.

The night was silent except for his panicked breathing, the footfalls of those running with him, and the screaming memories of what he'd endured.

Am I dreaming? Did I really escape?

The absence of the Spirits' voices confirmed he had.

***

When the door burst open, Maxine fell hard. The man came down on her, stumbling over her, scrambling to remain upright.

Adrenaline masked all pain though. Seth grabbed her. The next thing she knew, they were running for their lives.

Jacobson was white as a sheet. Despite the fresh night air, she could smell him. He stank of perspiration.

Behind them, she heard a sound, like the clanking of metal against metal. "Go! Go! Go!" She screamed.

And they went, went, went.

***

"There they are!" the one who'd flung open the exit door hard enough to bang it against the side of the building shouted.

"Where!" Jason screamed.

This was a detriment to not leading the pack. Yet, he'd heard shots fired just moments prior and wasn't about to take prime cross-hairs position.

"There!" the front-runner replied.

And he took off into the night. Others followed.

Jason followed the Kinship into the outside. It was dark. He saw no sign of his brother or the others.

The bullet-ridden doorway indicated that Jacobson had spent all or nearly all his ammo. The hallway's bulbs had stopped flickering. The light filtered out the doorway, but was insufficient to see clues as to which direction the trio had run.

He followed those who were in pursuit. But the trail soon went cold. This was an old part of the city, ripe with alleys, and buildings that prevents one from seeing around corners until you rounded it yourself.

Jason stopped and all the Kinship stopped with him. "Fan out in all directions. We'll find them."

Deep down he wasn't so sure. The escapees had a sizeable lead and unless they were stupid enough to be hiding somewhere nearby, they wouldn't likely be discovered.

This way.

The Spirits spoke in his mind. Their voices rang so clear, clearer than ever before. Even though the voices were internal. It sounded like they were standing off to the left.

"This way!" Jason shouted.

Most of the Kinship were still in hearing distance and rallied to their leader.

"This way!" he said again.

And they followed.

***

Seth led with Maxine and Jacobson right on his heels. He had no plan other than to put distance between them and the enemy.

Where to from here? They knew where he lived. The police were out of the question.

So where?

Another issue: *How do I come clean with Maxine?* He just knew he had to.

And, will she forgive me?

That question chilled him.

***

They have a gun. Jason found it hard to keep that in mind because he was fairly certain they had no bullets. But, fairly certain and completely certain are two entirely different things.

He didn't know if Jacobson had more ammo in his jacket or just what was in the gun's cylinder. Regardless, he acted shrewdly keeping some of his minions ahead of him as a firewall of sorts.

The Spirits continued directing him, and he in turn directed the Kinship. *After them!* he ordered. *This way! Quickly!*

He needed his brother for prophecy fulfillment. He needed Maxine as leverage. He wasn't sure what to do with Jacobson. *Torture? Absolutely. Death? Eventually.*

The end of Jacobson would be long in coming and only arrive when the man's body was so desensitized to pain that he was no longer capable of feeling it. *And that's a promise*, he said to himself.

Take a Left at the next corner. Run! Faster! They must not escape! the Spirits shrieked in his head.

Jason looked up into the night. The shadows he'd seen earlier near the rafters of the main room now soared above. He saw the stars flicker as they passed overhead.

This way!

"This way!" Jason relayed.

And the Kinship obeyed.

***

Maxine slowed down. She thought she heard something. The other two slowed to match pace.

"We've got to keep moving," Jacobson said.

She cocked her head, "Do you hear that?"

Both Jacobson and Seth listened. The street was strangely vacant of cars, of pedestrians, even of stray dogs and cats.

"This way!" came a shout from behind them. It sounded like Seth's voice, but Maxine knew better.

She stared back, but buildings hid them from her. Above though, she saw a darkness hide the moon and stars. *The shadows from the ceiling!*

"Run!" Seth shouted.

They ran for their lives. Maxine glanced behind only once and what she saw terrified her to her core.

The sodium-vapor lights which lined the street were being swallowed one by one as the darkness descended and approached.

There's no way to escape, Maxine thought as her hope dissolved.

Still, she had to try.

***

"There they are!"

Jason pushed through the Kinship all the way to the front. His excitement outweighed any risk of being a target. He rounded a corner and caught sight of them.

They were very noticeable, spotlighted by the streetlamps. Sticking out like sore thumbs.

In contrast, the Kinship was in darkness. He looked at the streetlights overhead. They were nothing but sickly glows.

He was happy the Spirits had descended to their level. *United, we'll win.*

Go after them! the Spirits shrieked in his brain.

The escapees were running away. "Get them!" Jason shouted, leading the charge.

The thrill of the hunt intoxicated him and he charged like a bull in the arena.

Quickly! There they are!

"Brother!" Jason shouted between inhalations. "You can't outrun the Spirits! They're bigger than both of us!"

They didn't stop running. Jason hadn't really expected that they would. *Oh well. We'll have you one way or the other. The prophecy must be fulfilled.*

BOUND BY BLOOD

***

Seth heard his brother. He did not stop.

Fear not, for I am with you. Those words from his Bible were spoken by Jesus.

Despite that mantra playing over and over in his mind, he feared greatly. *What will happen to me if they catch me? What will happen to this guy who risked his life to save mine. And what will happen to my wife?*

He glanced back as he fled. They were nearly upon him, and with them – the darkness of Hell. It was deep and absolute, blocking out the streetlights as it advanced.

Fear not, for I am with you. He recited. *Fear not.*

Yet his fear lingered and multiplied.

***

Don't let them get away! the Spirits boomed inside of Jason's mind.

Jason shuddered. The force of those voices unnerved him.

I can't fail them, he announced to himself. *I won't fail them.*

The Spirits didn't accept failure. Failures ended up in the inner room, or worse. *I won't fail. No matter what, I won't fail.*

Being High Priest didn't exempt him. *Look what happened to Cain.*

The memory was fresh: Cain lying in a pool of his own blood – dead.

I won't let that happen to me.

Soon, the Spirits said to him. *Soon, you will have what you desire.*

"Unimaginable power," Jason uttered.

Yes.

"I will rule this city!"

Yes!

"The world?"

Yes! And more.

Jason ran with renewed vigor.

And the darkness went with him.

***

Jacobson was lagging. *I should've turned my life around earlier.* His body wasn't trained for this.

His lungs chugged like hot bellows. His heart pounded like a steam engine about to blow. Every gasp of air rattled his ribs. *If I can just get away.*

A second thought followed: *Is that possible?*

He'd double-crossed the Kinship. *Nobody ever survived for long after doing that.*

Showing mercy wasn't in the Kinship's repertoire. Such a concept was foreign to them, not possible in fact.

There will be no mercy – no forgiveness.

Deep down, he didn't want their forgiveness. *I did what had to be done – what was right.*

He was glad he'd done what he did. It was the first time in a long time he'd taken the high road on anything. *And of course, you had to start with something that would end badly.*

Jacobson kept chugging along because the alternative wasn't attractive.

Not in the least.

***

Pastor Pete marched on with Jasmine at his side.

That woman amazed him. *When I'm her age, I expect to be sitting in a Barcalounger doing crossword puzzles to stay sharp, not marching to war.*

She didn't even seem winded. Plus, the look of determination in her eyes put fear in Pete's heart, and he was on the same side. *I can't imagine what the enemy will think when they come face to face with her.*

Her appearance could only be the result of the Holy Spirit dwelling within her. There was simply no other explanation.

***

Pain bolted through Maxine's body with every stride. She was becoming desensitized to the adrenaline surging in her veins. She needed more, but her body couldn't comply.

I've got to keep going, she thought, knowing that determination only went so far.

Her left leg hurt the worst. She injured it when Jacobson fell on her when the door finally gave way. Now, it felt like a hot blade was stabbing into her thigh with every step she took.

She heard noises from behind – evil noises. She didn't look back.

Above her everything dimmed. The darkness was overtaking them.

The light from the streetlamps was sickly at best. The darkness blotted out the sky. It blotted out her hope.

How many seconds before the darkness swallows us up? Ten? Twenty?

Despite her pain, she pushed forward. At least for now.

***

Jason ignored his exhaustion. Every step invigorated him because every step was one step closer to his goal. Plus, the Spirits had his back, descending from above, overcoming the enemy.

Behind him, the Kinship kept pace. He could hear them running along. He wondered if Cain ever tired of this commitment they had to their leader. *I never will. That is for sure.*

My reign as Priest will last forever, he said to himself. *As long as the prophecy is fulfilled.*

He pondered that thought a moment.

And it will be.

***

Jasmine knew it was a miracle she hadn't toppled from exhaustion. At her age, it could happen by just getting up in the morning.

God is strengthening me.

She kept pace with Pastor Pete. Behind, Zion's Hill followed.

But there was something more also. She couldn't see it but sensed it. *The Army of God goes with us.*

The street was long and straight. They marched down its center. There was no traffic. There were no pedestrians. The battlefield was clear and ready for its purpose.

The scene reminded her of old westerns where the showdown was about to begin between the good guys and the villains.

She looked at her watch. It was nearly midnight. *The Devil's high noon.*

Jasmine squinted, trying to see what was happening down the street. Something WAS happening.

Something moved down there. She couldn't tell what it was at first, just movement. As it approached though, she realized what it was. *Darkness.*

It drew nearer, enveloping the streetlights one by one – consuming the buildings, the street and everything else in its path. With every streetlight that disappeared her fear grew. Her prophetic words echoed in her mind. *Something's coming against this church! It's ugly. It's dark, and it comes with great power.*

God, help us.

She continued marching, keeping her eye on that darkness. *I won't fear it.* But her thought lacked confidence.

She drew strength from that which marched with them. *We are not alone.*

Sure, the enemy had its darkness, but the Army of God marched with Zion's Hill. *And with that strength, we will overcome.*

She could feel God's presence. *Thank you, God for not abandoning your servants.*

She knew better than to think otherwise. *The Bible says, I will never leave you nor forsake you.* And she believed it.

Jasmine stared hard. Something moved on the very edge of the darkness, fleeing from it.

There were three figures. "Help!" one of them screamed. *Maxine?*

"It's them!" Pastor Pete shouted.

They're being chased. But she quickly changed her mind. The third person was running with them, not after them.

By the way they staggered and stumbled, it was plain they were exhausted. The darkness was right at their heels. "They need help!" she yelled.

Pete burst into a sprint. In a second, he was with them. "Help!" he screamed as he put his arm around Maxine.

The darkness was overtaking them as four of Zion's Hill ran to Pete's aid. They each took an arm of the other two and together they ran for safety.

The darkness reared up, ready to crash down on the group as they fled.

Jasmine staggered forward without a plan. She only knew they needed help.

What happens when the darkness crashes down? She pushed that thought away, opting instead for prayer.

Please Jesus, don't let the darkness overtake them, she prayed in earnest. *Don't let this darkness overtake us.*

Maxine stumbled and fell. Pete helped her up, but it was obvious she was spent.

"Jesus! Help them!" Jasmine screamed.

Oh God, help them please.

***

Maxine fell, and for a second wasn't sure she'd get back up. Every fiber of her being was exhausted.

Fortunately, Pastor Pete was there, pulling her up – disallowing her to throw in the towel. With his help, she regained her footing.

Ahead, she saw Jasmine and Zion's Hill. But the darkness was descending and she saw them less and less with every passing second.

"Don't give up," Pete shouted in her ear.

She forced her legs to move. She no longer saw Jasmine or the others. They were hidden behind the darkness that separated them.

"There they are! Get them!" Jason's voice echoed.

Hearing him got her moving faster. Jason sounded close, perhaps only feet away, hidden by the darkness.

"Get them!"

She stumbled again and Pete literally picked her up off the ground, running with her like she was a sack of potatoes. Her feet dangled in the air, moving as if she were running, but Pete was doing the grunt work.

"Grab them now!"

"Just a little further!" Jasmine's voice called out.

She stared ahead, seeing silhouettes only. The darkness felt damp and heavy upon her, like a wet blanket. *Please God, help us out of this mess.*

Just beyond the edge of darkness, she heard, "Don't let them escape!"

***

Seth felt the darkness descend and old memories resurrected within him. It was very reminiscent of the feeling of being pulled to the bottom of a dark river by a horde of demons, of experiencing that greasy feeling.

No!

He wouldn't let his past condemn him, not here, not now. Still, that greasy feeling stuck with him.

Would you be helping me now if you knew my past? He wondered about the two men who were helping him. *Probably not.*

"Seth!" Jason sounded close behind. "Give up the fight. It is pointless. Join me. We'll fulfill the prophecy and rule the Kinship together."

Seth didn't answer.

"Come on, brother. This can all be avoided. Just give in to the prophecy."

"I will never do that." Seth found his voice.

Ahead of him, he saw Jasmine and the rest of Zion's Hill. They were fading in and out of view as the darkness tried to hide them. But they were there and that knowledge strengthened Seth.

He forged ahead with all he had left.

***

Jason frowned at his brother's determination. *Why not take the easy way?* It baffled him.

The Spirits spoke in his mind, *Caution, use caution.*

Why? thought Jason. *Wasn't this the point?*

They are many.

This change in the Spirits demeanor puzzled Jason. *They are many, but we are greater!* He responded in thought.

They are many, they said again.

Are you spirits or are you cowards? He thought but dared not think so they could hear.

This was the way with the Spirits. It was just like real conversation. You could think whatever you wanted them to hear, but they weren't mind readers. They couldn't hear what you didn't want them to hear.

Above, the darkness began to churn. *Caution. Use caution.*

He slowed his pace. The Spirits hadn't steered him wrong yet.

He could see Zion's Hill standing ahead of the darkness. They faded in and out with the darkness pressing in, but they were there for sure. Still, they didn't seem like so many that the Kinship couldn't take them.

Plus, surely a battle was to begin. The street was vacant. All was ready for the battle. *Why use caution?* he asked.

The Spirits didn't respond.

Why, he pressed them.

We already told you.

"Why!" he shouted at them.

They are many.

***

Pastor Pete lugged Maxine along. He feared putting her back down. He could see her exhaustion.

The sheer mass of the darkness captivated him. He looked up. It seemed to go on and on forever.

Why haven't they caught us yet?

He had no answer. *Perhaps they're as exhausted as we are.*

The darkness felt physical, pressing down on them. But he endured it, forcing his legs to take steps, making progress toward the light – toward those of Zion's Hill.

Something like a voice called to him from within the darkness. He listened, but the voice didn't come through is ears. It came from within. Yet, it was coming from the darkness.

There were no words with the voice, yet it sounded familiar. He found himself wanting to hear it.

"Do you hear that?" he asked Maxine, hoping she did.

She shook her head.

Peter, the voice said at last.

Hearing that name spoken by that voice caused gooseflesh to erupt on every inch of his skin.

Peter, it came again.

Pete bit his lip. *Maybe the pain will stop the voice.*

But it didn't.

Peter! It called louder now. *Peter!*

To everyone, including his own parents, he was Pete. Only one person ever called him by his full name.

Beth?

The voice stopped.

"Beth!" he called, tears streaming down his face.

No answer.

***

Jacobson clung to the two men helping him from Zion's Hill. *Don't let me go,* he thought. *Because if they catch me...* he couldn't bear to finish that thought. The three of them stumbled forward.

You stupid pig! the Spirits blared in his mind. *Do you really think you can escape?*

Jacobson glared into the darkness. He saw them. He hated them more than anything he'd ever hated.

You can never escape us. You're rogue Kinship. You belong to us.

Those waiting for them faded away as the darkness grew thicker. He felt the weight of it coming down on him – the Spirits crushing his will to live, taking away his hope.

Terror seized him as the darkness pushed in, grabbing at him, slowing him down. His body shivered. Sweat poured from every pore. He felt ill.

"Don't leave me here," he begged the men helping him. "Please."

You pathetic pig – begging for help from the scum of Zion's Hill. You are an embarrassment to the Kinship and to us.

Then let me go! Jacobson mentally shouted.

And the Spirits cursed him.

***

Maxine and Pete neared the darkness' edge. The darkness itself slowed them down, as if it had solidity.

She worried for Pete. The look in his eyes conveyed fear. *He shouted Beth's name. Why?*

Ahead of her, she glimpsed Jasmine through the darkness. Jasmine was shouting. Her words though were absorbed by the darkness.

The enemy had to be close, right on her heels. "Jesus, help us!"

She reached out past the darkness' edge.

Someone grabbed her hand and pulled. She and Pete stumbled out of the darkness.

They were in the midst of Zion's Hill.

Maxine fell to the ground. *Thank you, Jesus!*

***

Jacobson saw Maxine disappear ahead of him. "They made it? They made it!"

The Spirits boomed in his ears. *But you won't.*

He felt the darkness cling to him like the suction-cupped tendrils of a giant squid. If those two others hadn't been helping him, he would have been dragged down and back. But he was being helped!

"You have no hold on me!" he screamed.

The Spirits responded in cursing and threats, but he wasn't listening. *I'll never listen to you again!*

A weight seemed to lift from Jacobson. He began pushing forward with the help of those at his shoulders.

You have no hold on me!

And with that thought, he pushed past the darkness, into the light. He stumbled and fell, but he didn't care.

Instantly, the cursing spirits were silenced. He regained his footing and stumbled through the crowd.

Beside him laid Maxine. She was laughing and praising God. He joined her.

***

Seth saw the others enter the light. *Just a few more paces.*

"What, are you just going to keep running away?" Jason said.

Seth glanced over his shoulder. Jason was only a few feet back. The darkness was thick and it was hard to see, but his shadow stood firm. "Join me, brother! This is our time to shine!"

Seth was done. "No Jason, this is your chance to leave these demons that control you! Come with me to Zion's Hill. Learn about the Good Shepherd and the meaning of His many scars."

The darkness stirred, blowing like an angry tempest. Jason screamed something, but his words were eaten by the gale.

It blew against Seth, and the men helping him. It shoved them out of the darkness.

They stumbled into the crowd of Zion's Hill.

It's over. Seth thought as he looked back into the darkness. He hoped Jason was coming too.

But he wasn't.

***

Jason fumed. He could have grabbed his brother. *I should have grabbed him,* he thought to himself in a way that the Spirits couldn't hear. *I could have made him stay.*

Use caution, the Spirits had said. *They are many.*

And in the end Jason listened and let his brother slip through his fingers.

Jason held the sacrificial knife firmly. He saw the two that were helping Seth, and he could have made quick work of them.

Instead, he listened to the Spirits and let Seth go – again. "How many times will we do this?" he asked in frustration.

Be patient.

"We can still get him!"

They are many.

***

Euphoria overcame Maxine as her church family engulfed her and she praised God for her rescue. With a burst of strength she didn't think she had, she got up from where she was and staggered to Jasmine.

The woman was standing firm on the front line. She faced the darkness with anger in her eyes.

Maxine followed that stare. The darkness swirled and spun before them. It reminded Maxine of the way a small dog bristles the hairs on the back of its neck to appear tougher.

Pete moved to her other side, staring as she was. He was breathing hard, but otherwise seemed unfazed by the display before them.

Jacobson and Seth stood as well. Together, they defied this enemy, this darkness that came against them.

Within the darkness, green orbs appeared – *eyes?* Maxine wondered.

The eyes drew near the edge of the darkness, glaring. They rose up into the sky staring down at them maliciously.

"Do not fear them," Jasmine called out. "Remember, David won over Goliath. Gideon's 300 men beat the Midianites, and a Nazarene carpenter saved the world. So why should you think for a moment that this enemy has any chance against army of the living God?"

The darkness fanned out on either side of the Zion's Hill crowd, surrounding them with darkness. More green eyes peered out here and there.

"Don't let them intimidate you!" Jasmine shouted. "They are nothing."

Maxine saw the silhouettes of those who chased them from the great room. They approached near the edge of the darkness.

"All we want is Seth," came Jason's voice from one of the silhouettes. "Hand him over and the rest of you can live."

"Don't let his threats startle you!" Jasmine retorted.

"All we want is Seth!"

Jasmine roared, "You will not have any in our company!"

Jason answered, "Do you even know who he is? He's the one who came at you wearing a ski mask and gloves. He had intentions of shooting you all. Do you not recognize him?"

Maxine glanced at her husband. His face was pale. Tears trickled down his face. She'd deal with all that baggage later.

She pondered what Jasmine had said of this darkness – *It's ugly. It's dark, and it comes with great power.* This was no time to listen to the darkness, whether it was true or false, she wouldn't listen. She would stand her ground.

The seconds ticked by. The darkness continued to surround Zion's Hill. The green eyes stared and the silhouettes lingered, but nothing else happened, yet.

Despite Maxine's determination, fear crept in and lingered there. She bit her lip to distract her from her growing terror.

She bit hard enough to draw blood. But her terror only festered and grew.

***

The darkness swirled around them. It grew close enough that Pete could have reached out and touched it if he wanted to. The problem was, part of him wanted to.

Beth?

He knew he'd heard her call his name earlier.

He did reach out, letting the tips of his fingers graze the outskirts of the darkness. *Peter,* her voice sounded so clear, so unlike how she sounded in her final days battling cancer.

Peter.

He didn't answer, but neither did he pull his hand from the darkness.

Peter, I've missed you.

Tears stung as they formed. *I've missed you too.*

That was the understatement of the century. Not a day went by that he didn't miss her, yearn for her, asking himself what he'd do if he could just hear her voice one more time.

But now he was.

I love you, Peter.

No. It's not you. It can't be. Pete answered in thought. He knew the Bible's stance. When a person dies, the soul goes to heaven or hell. It never stays behind.

Oh Peter, her voice sounded as if on the verge of crying. *Oh Peter, don't you recognize me? It's me, your wife.*

It can't be you. Pete began to cry.

It is me, Beth.

Pete began arguing his own knowledge. *God can do anything. Couldn't he even let a poor widower hear the voice of his wife one more time?*

And the seed of doubt began to brew inside him.

***

Jasmine glared at the darkness as it hovered over her in black tendrils. It looked like phantom fingers. Yet it didn't come down and grab her.

She stood her ground, knowing that the enemy was trying to instill fear. She would not give it the satisfaction. Silently, she prayed for strength.

Within the darkness she saw movement. Those within approached. They were so close, only the thinnest veil of darkness separated them. One held a knife. Others rallied around him. They all glared with malevolent eyes.

"All we want is him," the one with the knife said as he pointed to Seth.

She shook her head.

The brevity of her answer seemed to stir up the darkness. Above, the green eyes stared down, but she didn't flinch. She continued praying silently.

She heard crying. It was Pastor Pete. Tears rolled down his face.

At first, this confused Jasmine. Then she noticed his hand. It was extended into the darkness.

"No!" she screamed as she pulled his hand out of the mire.

Pete blinked as if waking from a dream. He looked at her. His face immediately relayed embarrassment.

"See," the one with the knife spoke. "He likes it in here. You're all invited to join us, especially you Seth."

"We will stand our ground!" Jasmine shrieked at the darkness and everything within it.

"We will stand our ground!"

***

Jason glared out from that womb-like darkness. *Let them soak that into their stupid brains.*

Even Christians couldn't forgive Seth. Not now that they know the truth. Not now that they realize he tried to murder them.

From his side of the darkness, Zion's Hill virtually glowed under the light of their unveiled streetlamps. Front and center of the limelight stood his brother.

He glared at Seth and anger brewed. *If you think I'll let you rule with me once the prophecy is fulfilled, you have another thing coming.*

He shifted focus to the Kinship traitor called Jacobson. *You will die a slow and painful death. I promise you that my friend.*

Last, he stared at Maxine. *And you! You'll be sacrificed. Even if your husband does everything demanded of him, you'll be sacrificed.*

He clenched his fists as rage engulfed him. *As for Zion's Hill, you will all die. I proclaim it as High Priest.*

Why are they even here? The question about Zion's Hill demanded an answer. Yet, none came. *Who told you to be here at this time – just in time to rescue your beloved members.*

The Spirits said, *use caution.* But he barely heard them. His rage drowned them out.

"You want to fight?" he yelled. "The Kinship does not back down from a battle!"

They are many, the Spirits reiterated.

"Go ahead!" Jason screamed. "Make your move! Throw the first punch, if you dare!"

He waited. Zion's Hill remained still.

"What are you waiting for?"

Not today! They are many! Fight another day!

But Jason was done listening to such rhetoric. "Come on!!!"

Above him, the darkness began to churn. *Stop! They are many!*

Jason walked right up to the edge of the darkness. "Let's end this now!"

He locked stares with the old woman. They were only inches apart. Her eyes glimmered with a strange inner light. They narrowed and he knew she could see him.

He plunged the knife toward her. *I'll gut her like a fish!* But the darkness pushed him back.

He stumbled a step or two, staying upright. *Not today!* the Spirits screamed with such volume he could ignore them no longer.

They are many!

The Kinship gathered around him, lining up against darkness' edge. *Look at them,* Jason thought to the Spirits. *We are many! We are stronger!*

What the Spirits said next shocked Jason greatly.

***

Jasmine watched. *I'll stand my ground.*

She didn't even flinch when the man tried to stab her. His appearance mesmerized her. He looked just like Seth. *But he isn't, is he?*

She knew the answer the moment she asked. *No. This is not Seth, but a trick of Satan.*

She glared at this trick of the enemy. Anger filled her. *How dare you come against God's church!*

The darkness swirled between them, obscuring her sight. Yet, he remained. She could feel it – sense it.

"We will not be moved!" she yelled.

***

Pete wished for Jasmine's confidence. He resolved to stand his ground. *Still, Beth was in there. Somehow, she was there.*

Jasmine stared at the darkness with anger in her eyes. He followed her line of sight. She glared at a figure at the very edge of the darkness, the one holding the knife. On either side of that figure, others emerged. Their sight brought shivers. *I will stand my ground,* he thought followed by, *is Beth with them?*

Part of him wanted to touch the darkness. He wanted to hear his wife's voice again. He yearned for it – needed it.

Yet, he refrained. Jasmine pulled him free of the darkness before. He would not show such weakness again. *But I want you, Beth.*

He knew he should be stronger. *I will be stronger.* He was the church's leader after all.

"Beth?" he whispered. *I know it was you, Beth.*

No answer.

He ached for her. Every fiber in his body ached for her, but he couldn't reach her without touching the darkness, and he couldn't touch the darkness without showing his weakness.

He recalled the facts, *Beth is dead.*

And yet, was she? The voice certainly didn't sound like the voice of a dead woman. She'd sounded very much alive.

It's not right. He knew this. *You can't speak to the dead. That's witchcraft, and God hates witchcraft.*

But was it? He argued with himself. He hadn't done anything akin to witchcraft. His wife called and he listened. That was all.

He wanted to hear her voice again. He needed to hear it again.

Pete stared into the darkness. "Beth," he whispered – hopeful.

Again, no answer.

"What did you say?" Jasmine asked.

"Nothing."

Pete mimicked the resolve in Jasmine's stare. He wanted to be as determined as her. Deep down though, he really just wanted to hear his wife's voice one more time.

...Just one more time.

***

Jason was frustrated. He tried again to move beyond the darkness – to attack the enemy. But the darkness held him back.

It's not the right time, the Spirits said.

Why not? Jason thought the words back.

Do not question us.

But this makes no sense.

Do no question us!

Jason fell back, landing on his butt. He scrambled to his feet. "I'm your high priest!"

Do not test us!

I am the high priest! I am your high priest!

Don't forget who put you in your position! they answered. *Don't forget your place among us.*

Jason rubbed his butt, hoping he hadn't broken his tailbone. *But they're right there. We outnumber them. We can end this now!*

Patience. They are many.

He was getting tired of that statement.

Now's not the time. Your moment will come, and when it does, you will slaughter them and their blood will flow like a river. But not now.

The darkness retreated and Jason was forced back with it. *No! We can take them!*

But the Spirits said no more, and Jason was forced back as the darkness retreated.

He screamed in anger, but had little choice. He went and the Kinship followed.

***

Maxine's legs felt like they were filled with jelly as she stood near Jasmine. She'd never been this exhausted in her life.

Before her, the darkness was retreating. One by one, the streetlights brightened. One by one the stars lit up the sky.

She sideways-glanced at Jasmine and Pastor Pete. They were both intent on the darkness with intensity she'd never seen in a stare before.

Yet, the intensity was different between the two. Jasmine's was hard like stone, filled with anger and determination. Pete's on the other hand was intensely sad, as if he'd lost something of great value – something that he wanted back with all his heart.

Jasmine recited from the Bible in a voice she could barely hear. "The Lord is my shepherd; I shall not want. He maketh me to lie down in green pastures: he leadeth me beside still waters. He restoreth my soul: He leadeth me in paths of righteousness for his name's sake. Yea, though I walk through the valley of the shadow of death, I will fear no evil: for though art with me; thy rod and thy staff, they comfort me. Thou preparest a table before me in the presence of mine enemies: thou annointest my head with oil; my cup runneth over. Surely goodness and mercy shall follow me all the days of my life: and I will dwell in the house of the Lord forever."

Jasmine's words refreshed her like a glass of cold water. She felt stronger, renewed, ready to go on.

The darkness continued retreating. Within it, she saw the silhouettes of those who'd pursued her. Above, she saw the angry green eyes of the Spirits that chased her. But they were leaving now. *Thank you, Lord.*

"Lord!" Jasmine yelled. "Thank you for protecting us. In the name of Jesus, amen."

And all the people said, "Amen."

Maxine heard something else besides Jasmine's voice. She swore she heard the sound of marching troops. The sound was above her.

She looked up, but saw only the night sky.

***

Jason didn't know if his brother could hear him. He screamed anyway. "This isn't over! Do you hear me?"

He was enraged beyond any level of anger ever experienced. *We could end this now! And yet, we're running away like beaten dogs?*

The idea infuriated him. But there seemed nothing he could do about it.

The Spirits made clear their intentions and he tried to mask his anger so they didn't perceive it.

Why are we letting them go? Jason thought once more.

The answer came in the same four words as before. *Do not question us.*

But it made no sense. He saw no weapons and Zion's Hill appeared no more numerous than they. Plus, the Kinship had the Spirits with them. Who did Zion's Hill have? A pretend god? *Why?* he dared ask again.

They are many.

That statement grated on Jason's nerves. He'd heard it too many times.

They are not that many! he answered.

Open your eyes, mortal. The risk of battle is too great. Behold, their forces.

At those words, Jason's eyes were opened. He could see what the Spirits saw.

Jason stumbled back as he beheld the hidden army of Zion's Hill. They surrounded the darkness, pushing it back.

All of them, taller than the Spirits. All of them, armed with swords, shields, bows and arrows, spears and knives. They shone with angelic light so bright Jason couldn't bear to look at them for more than a moment.

Now do you perceive it, mortal?

"Yes," Jason gasped.

Do you see that they are many?

"Yes." Jason loathed the fear evident in his voice. But it couldn't be helped.

He turned from the angels, cursing. *So, there's something to this god of Zion's Hill after all.*

***

Seth shivered as the Kinship retreated. Already, the darkness was a block away. Yet, a coldness remained in his bones.

Between shivers, he praised God for doing nothing short of a miracle. The odds were so stacked against them escaping that to deny God's involvement was sacrilege.

Yet, there was one more miracle for which he prayed. *I've got to come clean.*

The lies of his past had been found out. He would start by explaining to Maxine. He prayed she'd understand why he lied. He hoped she'd understand that his love for her was real.

I'm not who I used to be. Surely, forgiveness is available. Right?

Doubt lingered within. *Would I forgive if the tables were turned?* He couldn't answer for certain.

"Thanks for all you've done," Seth said, turning toward Jacobson.

The other nodded. "I'd call us even."

"What do you mean?"

"You gave me your jacket when I was cold. And, you gave me the drive to dig my way out of the life I'd led up till then."

Tears began forming in Jacobson's eyes and he twisted his long hair around his fingers nervously.

"I've made a lot of mistakes in my life from dropping out of school to drinking too much. I thought the Kinship was the answer to my problems, but being there only seemed to make things worse.

"Lately, I'd been asking for a sign. I'd heard people from Zion's Hill witnessing in the streets. I'd heard about your Jesus. I wanted him to be real, I really did. But I was skeptical. I mean, what kind of God gives eternal life to trash like me? It seemed too good to be true.

"When you found me in the alcove of that building the other day, I was praying to a God I didn't know. I was asking for a sign. I was asking Him to reveal himself.

"Then you showed up with your kindness. Your act gave me hope."

"I quit drinking that day and started making changes in my life.

"So, when I saw you and your wife at the old warehouse, I couldn't resist the opportunity to pay back a debt."

Seth nodded. *If this guy can make a change, then so can I.*

He just hoped everyone would accept the apology for his past. Or, if not everyone, at least Maxine.

CHAPTER 8

Jason sulked as he walked back toward the old warehouse. Every step was a lesson in self-control.

His rage was just below the surface. But it'd do no good to blow a gasket, especially since much of his anger was directed toward the Spirits.

He couldn't let them know how angry he was at them. Like it or not, they were his source of power. Plus, he couldn't really blame them for retreating.

He still cringed at the memory of those celestial warriors. The looks on their faces burned into his mind. He'd never forget them even if he tried.

And he would certainly try.

The anger was because they retreated from a more powerful force. He was angry that they appeared weaker.

We didn't even put up a fight. We just walked away with our tails between our legs like beaten dogs.

For the first time, he realized the Spirits weren't necessarily the most powerful. *All the more reason to recruit his brother and fulfill the prophecy.*

Only then would the Kinship stand a chance against this foe. He hated thinking it: *I need my brother.*

***

All was silent from Seth's perspective as they walked back to Zion's Hill. The darkness was gone, and yet a darkness remained within him because of the task before him.

He hadn't told the truth for a long time. Could he even do it?

I have to do it. People deserve the truth. He thought about it. *Maxine deserves the truth.*

His determination didn't eliminate his dread. Mostly, he worried about the worst-case scenario.

The worst case is almost never the most likely.

Still, even a 1% chance that the church would throw him out and Maxine would divorce him was enough to put him near panic-mode.

They could have me arrested for attempted murder and I'd go to prison.

He thought about that. Prison, he decided wouldn't be any worse. If Maxine left him, he wouldn't care really where he was. Life would suck regardless.

Pastor Pete walked beside him. Seth looked at his pastor, hoping the man had some insight that would be helpful, but Pete appeared too preoccupied.

"It couldn't have been her," Pete mumbled. "It just couldn't have been her."

***

What would Seth tell me, Maxine wondered as she walked beside her husband. *What could he possibly say that would make this all okay?*

He'd never talked about his past. And now she knew why, at least a little.

If he loved her, he'd come clean now, she hoped. *He owes me that much.*

But can I trust him? That question burned in her mind like a red-hot poker.

***

Jacobson's hands trembled. The combination of stress and exhaustion took its toll.

His main thought was, *I really need a drink.*

This was the longest his body had been without alcohol in a long time. It always helped him cope in the past.

No! I'm not that man anymore!

Yet, deep down he knew part of the old man was still there, waiting for him to slip up – waiting for the opportune time to tempt him with a good stiff drink. *It's not if, but when.*

That idea frustrated him because he knew it was true. Sometime, he'd slip up. If not with drinking, then with something. He was trying to turn his life around. *Isn't that what the Bible teaches? How to turn my life around?*

He wasn't sure what the Bible taught. He'd only read snippets here and there. He wanted to read it more but was afraid. If he was caught with such literature in the Kinship's company, it wouldn't end well.

Jacobson clenched his fists so tightly the knuckles turned white, but they still trembled. *Not if, but when.*

There's a light at the end of this tunnel, he tried focusing on the positive. *Where there's a will, there's a way.*

Yet, his trembling didn't stop and that tunnel felt very long. He tried putting himself in a better place. *Look at how far you've come. You're still alive for one thing.*

A smile began in the corners of his mouth. Yes, he was alive. That was something of a feat in itself. It was akin to a seal escaping a hungry polar bear. It happened rarely.

But will I survive the night? That question plagued him. *And if I survive the night, will I survive a week, a month – a year?*

The Kinship was known for being relentless. *They won't let bygones be bygones, that's for sure.*

And even if by some miracle, I escape them, I still have my addictions to fight.

Suddenly, the tunnel felt very long and the light at its end almost nonexistent. *Can I do this?*

Maybe with the help of his new friends he could. But, were they truly his friends? *What if they don't accept me? What if I'm too messed up? What if my past is too dark?*

His grin was gone now. These people were his only line of defense. Without them, he didn't have a chance.

I rescued two of their own. But would that be enough?

He just didn't know.

***

Pastor Pete hit rock bottom. It had been a long slow slide that started the day Beth died, but over the last few hours, it was like falling into a deep hole.

Since Beth's death, he developed a certain expertise regarding the art of holding in one's feelings. He felt he had to hide his sorrow. He was the leader of Zion's Hill. He couldn't let them see his weakness.

But tonight, when he heard Beth's voice, everything changed. *I know it was her.*

He'd know that voice anywhere. *It was her.*

He had no idea why she was there in the darkness, but she was there. The memory of her voice consumed him now. Replaying it in his mind was both wonderful and terrible at the same time.

The absence of her voice now was torture. He wanted to hear it again.

It was you. I know it.

He wanted to hear her. He craved it. He needed it like he needed oxygen to breath.

Oh Beth, he lamented. *My dear Beth.*

***

Jasmine fretted. She sensed fear within the ranks of Zion's Hill. Specifically, she sensed this in Seth, Maxine, the newcomer in the Army jacket, and of all people, her pastor.

She glanced at the one in the jacket. She'd seen his kind before. He was one struggling with the idea of a God that loved so deeply he'd accept you no matter how bad you've been. She prayed he would see the truth soon.

Pete worried her more. Jasmine couldn't explain it, but Pete seemed weighed down as if a small piece of that darkness remained on him, hovering like a hungry hawk with its eye on a helpless fieldmouse.

She prayed hard knowing that everything was in God's hands. Still, she fretted.

She couldn't help it.

**

Do not question us, the Spirits had ordered. That command frustrated Jason.

They were almost back to the old warehouse, but the memory of the surrounding army of angels remained fresh.

We should have engaged them in battle, he said to himself. We aren't weaklings and the Kinship prides itself in never backing down from a fight.

He cringed. *Yet, that's exactly what we did.*

The only logical answer: *They were stronger.*

Jason scowled because that wasn't a good reason not to fight. The Kinship is scrapy. They fight dirty. They do whatever is needed to win even if the enemy appears more powerful.

Yet, we walked away with our tails between our legs.

For the first time, he questioned the power of the Spirits. *Are they afraid of this enemy?*

No. He shoved away such self-defeating thoughts. *Still…*

He guarded his thoughts carefully. The Spirits could not know his doubts. If discovered, the horrors of the inner room would be nothing compared to what they'd do to him.

Once Seth and I join forces, then the prophecy will be fulfilled. Then, there'll be no stopping us.

He began to wonder if that would ever occur. *It must.*

This is the only way.

***

They entered Zion's Hill. The members walked in silence through the lobby and back toward the sanctuary. No one made a sound.

Pete offered use of his office so that Seth and Maxine could have a private moment. "Do you want me present? I am happy to listen," Pete suggested.

Seth shook his head. He needed to do this on his own. Maxine agreed.

Pete nodded and led them to his office. He handed Maxine his cell phone. "Everyone's going to the fellowship hall. Feel free to join us whenever you're ready. Also, if you decide you need me, just call the Fellowship Hall landline. I'll be there to answer." Then he left, closing the door behind him.

As soon as the door closed, Maxine set Pete's phone on the desk. "Tell me everything."

Seth needed a moment. His emotions were high. It was all he could manage not to break down in front of her.

He took a deep breath. What he was about to divulge had been bottled up a long time. If he uncorked it too fast, it might not come out right. *I only have this one shot.*

"Seth," Maxine said, cupping his face in her hands so that he had to look into her eyes. "I married you for better and worse. Tell me the truth now. Please."

He motioned to Pete's desk chair. "You should sit down for this."

She shook her head and folded her arms.

He shrugged. Then, he began telling her everything.

***

Pastor Pete didn't join everyone in the fellowship hall right away. He stood outside his office leaning against the wall with his hands covering his face.

It couldn't have been Beth I heard. Could it?

Part of him wanted it to be Beth. He'd wished for so long to hear her voice again.

No. Something didn't seem right about it. Something definitely wasn't right Biblically about it. Yet, that same part that wanted it to be Beth tried to ignore the Biblical inconsistency.

Was it really you I heard? He hadn't thought of his deceased wife in the present tense for a long time.

He lowered his hands from his face. They were wet with tears.

He walked slowly toward the fellowship hall. He needed the others. Strength was in the numbers, and he needed strengthening.

Yet, he walked slowly, taking the time to process his thoughts. *Beth? Was it really you? Is it really you?*

I miss you so much, Beth.

After her death, Pete had spent a period actually being angry at God. He was a pastor – God's servant. Why would God do this to his servant?

Over time, things got better and his anger mellowed. He'd even apologized to God for his anger. It was uncalled for because God does things beyond our understanding sometimes. But His will must still be done.

Tonight though, when he'd heard that voice, it was like ripping open the wound all over again. *If only I could spend just one more day with you Beth,* he thought. *If only…*

***

Maxine felt numb. The information-dump her husband just piled on her was almost too much to take.

She knew he was being honest. What he said was too bazar to be made up. Plus, recent events collaborated his story.

She didn't know when, but by the time he finished, she was sitting in Pete's office chair. She tried to say something, but words failed her.

Seth ran his fingers through his hair. She could see how much it took from him to share what he was, what he'd done – why he lied.

She leaned forward and pinched the bridge of her nose to release some of the tension. It didn't work.

My husband tried to murder Zion's Hill.

But this wasn't the man she'd married. This was pre-saved Seth. The man she knew would never try to murder anyone. *Right?*

She stared into his face. He stared blankly back.

Those eyes, she thought, *had once been framed by the eye-sockets of a ski mask to hide his identity.*

But that was the old Seth. He's changed.

Was she sure about that? Maxine didn't know.

Fear crept in. *My husband has a secret life where he planned to kill Christians.*

But didn't Saul become Paul? Didn't Nicodemus change from Pharisee to born again believer? Even one of the thieves on the cross repented and was forgiven. If these Bible characters could do it, then why not Seth?

Could she trust her husband? Tears ran down her cheeks because she just didn't know.

***

Pastor Pete was half-way to the fellowship hall when he heard something, a barely audible noise – a tapping sound. It reminded him of somebody typing if they only hit one key every second or two.

He walked cautiously toward it. When he approached the lobby, it grew louder.

What now? What could possibly make this night any weirder?

Tap – tap – tap. Pause. *Tap – tap…*

He looked toward the front windows. The tapping was coming from out there, just beyond the glass. *Tap – tap – tap…*

He walked to the windows, wringing his hands together as if that would erase the terror growing within.

Retreat, a tiny part of him said. *Go to the fellowship hall with the others.*

But he didn't retreat. The tapping continued and he felt drawn to it like a horsefly to a bug zapper.

He stared out the window, but saw only thick white fog. It must have arrived sometime after they got back to Zion's Hill.

He stared hard into the opaque whiteness. The fog, unlike the darkness from earlier, accentuated the streetlamps light, creating an ethereal scene.

Tap – tap – tap…

The sound was close. Pete cocked his head to listen better.

Tap – tap – tap…

Something was lightly hitting the window. He was so close now, almost touching the glass with his nose, staring hard – trying to see. But the fog was so thick.

Tap – tap – tap…

There it is! A single finger was tapping the glass.

Move away, a small voice in his head said.

But instead, he focused in on it, with nothing but the glass separating them. The finger reminded him of somebody.

The fog was so thick. He could see the silhouette of a hand and fingers. Everything beyond that was swallowed up by the fog.

The finger was slender. The nail was manicured and polished.

Pete gasped. The polish was Beth's favorite color.

***

Seth poured everything out – things he held in for so long – things he thought he'd never divulge. Now, he was done speaking and one question remained. Would Maxine forgive him? Could Maxine forgive him?

The silence between them was stifling. *Say something, anything.*

Her face hinted at nothing new. There was sorrow there. There was frustration there. There was even some anger. But this was all present from the beginning.

Seth couldn't stand it any longer. "Please accept my apology. I'm not the man I used to be." He forced the tears back. "Please believe that."

She looked away. "Why didn't you tell me all of this before?"

He had an answer, but didn't say it. It was difficult to put into words.

"Why?" she reiterated.

"Because I was ashamed." His voice cracked as he spoke. "And guilty."

He wished she'd look back his direction. Then maybe she'd see how sincere he truly was.

She did look back, but the tears in her eyes weren't promising.

Seth couldn't stand it. *Just tell me off and let's get it over with.*

***

Beth?

Pastor Pete stared at that tapping finger. The swirling fog and the impossibility of that hand created a dreamlike atmosphere.

It can't be you. You died of cancer. You're in heaven.

Pete's heart broke as he looked at that finger. *It is the right color of polish.*

Not a day went by that he didn't pray memories of Beth would come to him in his dreams. Yet, here she was at the window. He wasn't dreaming.

An answer to prayer?

No. he chastised. *Beth is in heaven with the Lord.*

But God can do anything he wants, thought Pete. *Oh yes, he surely can.*

"Peter."

He cocked his head, listening. It was the same voice as from before – Beth's voice. But now he heard it through his ears, not just in his mind.

"Peter, come with me."

"Come with you where?"

"Come out here, into the fog."

Her finger stopped tapping. It now used a beckoning motion.

"Come out here," the voice cooed.

Pete was torn. To go into the fog felt risky somehow.

"Join me, Peter."

"Is it really you? You died."

"Peter, there's no time for questions. Join me now, or I'll have to leave."

"No," Peter sobbed. "Don't leave."

"Then come."

Slowly, Pete opened the door, and entered the fog.

***

The large refrigerator in the kitchen adjoining the fellowship hall was filled with sandwich fixings. Also, there were loaves of bread.

This was in preparation for Sandwich Sunday, which was only a few days away. Sandwich Sunday was an annual tradition at Zion's Hill. Essentially, it was a soup and sandwich potluck where members brought homemade soup and the sandwiches were provided through church donations.

After the night Zion's Hill had, the vote was to dig into the sandwiches early. So, they ate.

Jasmine nibbled at her bologna on white bread with mustard and cheddar. She glanced at the clock. *What's keeping Pastor?* With every second her edginess increased.

It only takes a minute or two to get from Pete's office to the fellowship hall. By her estimate, he should have been here by now.

Maybe I missed him somehow. She looked over the crowd. They all sat at tables eating sandwiches and talking about the strange happenings from earlier. But no Pastor.

That's when she noticed Jacobson. He wasn't at a table. He stood off in the corner leaning against the wall, eating slowly from a sandwich he held in one hand. In the other, he held an open Bible.

"As I'm sure you can tell, we love to eat around here," she said as she approached him.

Jacobson looked up from the book. There were tears in his eyes. "This book says I can still be saved."

Jasmine smiled. "If you put your faith in Jesus. If you believe he has the power to erase your sins, then yes."

"Even after all the things I've done…"

She interrupted him. "We've all done things that separate us from God. That's why God came to us. That's why God died and rose. He did this so that we can call on his name and be saved despite our sins."

"But how…"

"Have you seen Pastor Pete?" she asked.

He glanced around and then shrugged. "I haven't seen him."

Jasmine sighed. "Well, I'm going to go looking."

"I'll go with you."

She nodded and together they left the fellowship hall.

***

Jason felt sick with frustration. Once back at the warehouse, he went directly to Cain's private quarters, which were now his by default.

He shut the door behind, locked the door and took a deep breath. The smell of Cain still lingered here and Jason found it disgusting. When time allowed, he'd have the place aired out and cleaned. Now though, more pressing matters took center stage.

He needed to plan a funeral full of pomp and circumstance. Kinship royalty like Cain should not be buried flippantly after all.

Jason smiled. After all the scheming he'd done to rid himself of Cain, it was done for him. *Funny how those things work out sometimes.*

He'd already given orders for the body to be removed from the main room and his blood cleaned from the floor. He also decreed a period of mourning.

Of course, he'd mourn with them and the Kinship would buy his performance. *They have no reason not to. It wasn't me that killed him.*

Jacobson would be the one taking the bullet for that one, which was another thing that worked out well because the man deserved death. Jason didn't care that the man killed Cain, but he'd ruined his chance to fulfill the prophecy. *And that is unforgivable.*

He beheld his new digs. The room catered to a minimalist's mindset.

There was a desk-sized wooden table against the left wall with a basic wooden chair beside it. At the far wall stood a dresser, and beside it was a bookshelf stuffed with books and instruments of witchcraft. To the right was a twin-sized bed mattress on a box spring. And that was pretty much it.

Jason approached the table. He pulled out the chair and sat down.

Sitting open on the table, was a journal. The page was filled with tiny handwritten script. This was Cain's standard writing style. Even the margins were filled. At the top of the page was yesterday's date – Cain's last entry.

***

I have implored the Spirits. I have begged. I have cut myself many times as a blood sacrifice to show my devotion, but I cannot trust that the outcome will be positive. I cannot shake the feeling that something is about to happen – something bad.

I feel that whatever the bad thing is that's about to happen, it has something to do with the twins.

The Spirits have foretold that the joining of these brothers will fulfill the prophecy and create a bond of power, which should be a good thing. Yet, I sense disaster in it.

I don't know details and if the Spirits know, they've chosen to remain silent on the topic. I will continue asking. I will continue to beg, meditate and cut myself as blood sacrifice. Perhaps they will acknowledge my deeds and will divulge what I need to know.

Until then, I will stay vigilant.
In the service of the Spirits,
Cain, High Priest of the Kinship

***

Jason laughed out loud. *If he'd only known.*

***

Jasmine almost didn't notice Pastor Pete. He stood outside, surrounded by a thick, white fog. Although he was only a few feet from the window, the fog reduced him to a ghostly silhouette.

He appeared to be engaged in conversation. But whoever he spoke with was hidden in the haze.

"Pastor?" Jasmine called.

He didn't respond.

She tapped on the glass.

Still, no response.

Jacobson did an open-palmed slap on the glass. Jasmine flinched. But Pete remained entranced.

Jacobson's hand remained pressed to the window. "It's the Spirits," he hissed. "I can feel them."

"They're not just spirits," Jasmine corrected. "They are demons."

"Whatever you want to call them – they're out there, hiding in that fog."

"This enemy is not of flesh and blood." Jasmine uttered.

Jacobson pulled back his hand and wiped it on his jeans as if it had been exposed to the plague.

"Don't be afraid. Just trust in Jesus," she said.

Jasmine grabbed the handle on the front door.

"Stop," Jacobson hissed. "Please. Don't."

His breaths were hard and raspy. His eyes conveyed terror.

"Just trust in Jesus," she said again.

His voice trembled. "Please don't open the door."

"I have to get Pete back."

Trust in Jesus, she said to herself even as her own fears emerged. *Trust in Jesus.*

***

Jason sat at the table staring at the journal which he'd just closed. He'd read a few additional entries. It was quite revealing.

He learned that Cain didn't want the prophecy fulfilled. It was all just an act. He read about how he planned to kill him. *Well, that backfired badly. Didn't it Cain?*

He rose from the table and approached the door. That journal reinvigorated him. *I need a plan. The prophecy must come to fruition.*

He smiled as he pulled the door to leave, but it wouldn't open. He pulled harder, his smile turning sour almost immediately.

Nothing changed. The door was stuck.

It wasn't locked. It simply wouldn't open.

He let go of the knob and backed away from the door. Something wasn't right.

His heartrate increased as flashbacks of being confined to the inner room flooded his memories. Sweat shined on his skin and dampened his clothing, and a whimper involuntarily escaped his lips.

Then, he felt it. The Spirits were here in the room. Their presence felt different than ever before. It felt like a chord tightening around his neck one twist at a time.

Jason reached out to loosen the chord, but of course there was nothing there. Still, the pressure remained.

***

"Oh Peter, I've missed you so much."

Pete held his wife. He didn't understand how it was possible, but she was here in his arms. He didn't say a word because speaking might corrupt it somehow and he wanted that moment to last forever.

"Come with me, Peter."

Pete looked her in the eyes. He'd forgotten how beautiful they were – green with flecks of brown.

He stared at her face. She was even more beautiful than he remembered. Or, maybe his memories had just faded with time.

"You're gorgeous," he whispered.

"Come." Her voice held a sense of urgency. "Come with me now."

"Where?" Pete wanted to know.

"Does it matter where as long as we're together? Just come."

Pete hesitated and glanced around. The fog swirled, disorienting him – clouding his thoughts, if that made sense. Nothing felt real. *Maybe I'm only dreaming.*

No, he argued with himself. He would not indulge such an idea. This was real, and if it wasn't, he wanted it to be. He needed it to be.

Beth pulled away. Her face took on a forlorn expression. "Why the hesitation? Come with me now."

"I…" he couldn't finish the sentence. The fog made it so hard to think straight.

"Don't you miss me?"

"Yes," was a huge understatement.

"Then come with me."

He wanted to. He really did, but that small voice in his head still protested.

"There's not much time. You must come now, or not at all."

Or not at all? Those four words silenced any opposition in his mind.

She guided him away from the window. After only a handful of steps, he looked back. The fog completely hid the church.

Out here in this ethereal haze, it felt like the world was gone. All that existed was them, and that was enough.

He stopped and listened. *A scraping noise?* It could have been the door to Zion's Hill opening. It always scraped the sidewalk when it opened. Or, it could have been his imagination.

"Don't stop. Come with me now," Beth said, tugging gently on his hand.

He started walking and she smiled. "That's it. Come with me."

Together, they walked deeper into the fog. His mind stayed cloudy – his thoughts slow. But he didn't care. He felt happy, happier than he'd been for a long time.

Beth held his hand tight and picked up the pace. He ran along with joy in his step.

She laughed. It was contagious.

He laughed too.

***

Jasmine opened the door of Zion's Hill. The scraping sound it made was loud in comparison to the silence of night. She opened it just a crack, paused and listened.

Pete was nowhere to be seen. He might still be nearby. It was impossible to know with this fog obscuring everything.

For a second, she thought she heard something. *Laugher?* If it was real, it was gone now.

She opened the door further and leaned out. The fog swirled around her as she penetrated it.

"Pastor? Are you out there?"

The fog drifted into the lobby through the open doorway in wisps and swirls.

"Pete?"

Silence.

"Pete?" she called again.

Somebody screamed from behind. Jasmine spun around. What she saw chilled the blood in her veins.

Jacobson writhed on the floor. His eyes rolled so only red-veined whites were showing. The fog which drifted in hung over him as if he were dry ice. He never stopped shrieking.

"What's wrong?"

Jacobson's eye unrolled and stared at her. He scurried back crab-walk-style until he hit the nearest wall. Even against the wall, he didn't stop his scurrying motions. And he never stopped screaming.

Jasmine closed the door and the mist dissipated. Jacobson's screams morphed into gasps. But that look of terror remained in his eyes. They kept searching the room, frantically searching.

He curled up, crying like a baby. "I'm sorry, Ms. Jasmine," he said. "I want to trust in Jesus, but those spirits are in the fog. When they came in, I lost faith."

"Not spirits. Demons," she corrected once more. "It's okay," she said as soothingly as possible. "Do your best to put your trust in Jesus. Your faith is new now, but it will grow over time. Just do your best to put your life in his hands."

He nodded and began to sob louder.

She put her hand on his shoulder. "Stand firm."

"I'll try."

***

Pete heard a scream. His head cleared. He looked back.

"No time for that," Beth said. She pulled on his hand. "Come with me now."

The fog pressed in. The scream faded away.

He felt Beth's cold hand on his cheek, guiding his focus back to her. He turned forward. Beth looked sad.

"What's wrong?"

"Why are you so distracted?" she pouted. "We can't move forward together if you keep looking back."

"I'm sorry," Pete answered sincerely. "I thought I heard a man screaming."

He saw happiness in her eyes once more. "I'm just glad you're with me now."

"What about the screaming?"

"Just give me your attention and all that will fade away."

"But…"

She whined, "I haven't been with you in so long. Don't you love me? Can't you give me your full attention?"

He nodded. "You're the only thing that matters to me."

She giggled. "That's what I want to hear, Peter."

She pulled him deeper into the fog as his thoughts grew cloudy once more.

***

Jacobson felt better the moment that door closed because with that action, the mist dissipated. He felt the presence of the Spirits in that fog. No, the presence of demons. For Jasmine was correct. He realized this now.

They were pure evil.

***

Maxine and Seth bolted from the Pastor Pete's office. Somebody was screaming bloody murder.

They stood in the hallway, cocking their heads – trying to hear. But by then, the screaming stopped.

Seth pointed down the hallway, toward the lobby. "It came from this way."

He took off down the hallway and Maxine followed. *What poor timing,* she thought to herself. They hadn't said all there was to say about, well about everything. She didn't like leaving things unfinished.

They found Jasmine and Jacobson in the lobby. She had her hand on his shoulder. He was crying like a baby and trembling. His eyes looked wild and his stare darted about like he was tracking the flight pattern of an angry wasp.

"I'm sorry, I'm sorry, I am so sorry," Jacobson blubbered.

"What's going on?" Seth asked.

Jasmine just shook her head.

"The Spirits were here." Jacobson's voice was barely audible – nothing more than a whisper. "They came in when the door was opened. They spoke to me."

"Not spirits..."

Jacobson interrupted. "I know – I know, demons."

"What did they tell you?" Maxine asked.

"They don't always speak in words. What they told me was beyond words. They communicated their anger at my defection. They promised me a world of pain and death."

Seth nodded.

Based on what he'd told Maxine, Seth understood more than this man could know about how the demons operate.

Movement caught her eye. Swirling fog danced just outside the window.

"When did this move in?"

"Don't know," Jasmine answered. "Sometime after we got back here. When I opened the door, some of it drifted in. That's when Jacobson started freaking out."

Maxine got down on the floor and hugged Jacobson fiercely. "You're safe now. The demons are liars, and whatever they said isn't true. Put your faith in Christ and Christ alone. He never lies or forsakes his followers."

Jacobson nodded. She could feel his heartrate as she held him. It was a pounding pulse, but calming with every second.

"Pastor Pete went out into that fog, and I don't think he was alone."

Jasmine's statement scared her. *Why would he go out there?*

She let go of Jacobson and stood beside her husband. A shiver escaped her as she looked into that unnatural haze.

"I'll go get him."

Seth's words drove terror into her. "No. Don't go out there. It's not safe." There was so much more she needed to say to him about what he'd told her. He couldn't leave now.

He looked at her, his eyes kind. "I'm the reason they're attacking this church anyway."

"No!" Maxine's voice cracked with emotion. "I won't lose you again!"

"I have to go," he said. "The Kinship won't stop until they have me. It's the only way to end this."

"Then I'm going with you."

Seth shook his head. "It's too dangerous."

"We're both going, or none of us will go," she answered. *This isn't debatable.*

Seth took a step away from her and toward the door. "I'm the only one they need."

"They'll kill you!" Maxine's voice was no more than a hiss. It was all she could muster.

"Not as long as I have value to them. Not as long as they think I'm key to the prophecy being fulfilled."

Maxine grabbed his hand and held it tight. "I'm not letting you go!"

He looked at her with a frustrated expression bordering on painful. "Why should we both be at risk?"

He tried to shake his hand free, but she wouldn't comply. After a moment, his frustrated face morphed into one of resignation.

With a sigh, he opened the door. They exited together.

And the fog engulfed them.

***

I should stop them.

Yet, she did nothing. Jasmine felt uneasy watching them exit. *That fog is evil.*

I should have stopped them, she thought as they disappeared into the mist.

She worried for them. She also worried about Pastor Pete.

"I should have gone with them," Jacobson muttered between sobs.

Jasmine shook her head. "You're in no condition."

"It's what I deserve," he retorted.

"Listen," she said. "God doesn't care what you've done. He's all about who you are now and who you put your faith in."

"That's the problem," Jacobson mumbled. "I don't know who to put my faith in." He looked out at the fog. "When that door opened and the fog came in, I heard those voices. I can't put into words what they said exactly, but they told me essentially that the god of Zion's Hill would never want me because I'm worthless – just a homeless alcoholic."

"Lies!" Jasmine answered. "We're all worthless in that way. We all have a past. We're all sinners. But that's not who we are now because God does want us. He sent Jesus to die for our sins. If we put our hope in that, then he forgives us. We are new creations because he first loved us. Do you understand?"

Jacobson didn't answer.

Jasmine sighed. "Do you still have that Bible with you?"

He shook his head. "I dropped it when the doors opened."

Jasmine saw it sitting on the floor beside him. She picked it up and opened it.

"Do you know what Jesus calls the Devil in John 8:44?" she said as she flipped through the pages until she came to the spot she was looking for.

"No." Jacobson mumbled.

"It's written right here. Jesus calls him the 'Father of Lies'. There's no truth in him."

Jasmine paused to let that sink in. "These so-called spirits are the devil's minions. They lie just like their leader, the Devil."

Jacobson looked up at her and wiped tears from his face with the sleeve of his jacket.

"Can you believe that simple fact? Can you believe the Devil and his demons lie?"

He nodded.

"Can I get an Amen?"

"Amen," he answered.

"So," she continued. "If you believe that these demons are liars, then you shouldn't believe anything they say to you."

With effort, Jacobson got up. He was no longer sobbing. "I don't know what to believe anymore, but I'll think over what you've said."

She nodded. "Think hard on it because time may be short. You'll want the right decision before it's too late."

He nodded again. "We should go tell those in the fellowship hall what's happening."

"I suppose we should."

He started toward the fellowship hall, but the instant he turned his back, Jasmine opened the front door.

He turned back toward her as the door scraped open. "I'm going after Seth, Maxine and Pastor. They may be in danger."

She exited and closed the door before the fog could drift in. Going alone wasn't optimal, but Jacobson was in no condition to go with her, and every second delay meant those she needed to find might wander farther away.

She looked back after two steps. The window was hazy. Jacobson stared out at her, a frantic look on his face.

She took two more steps and he disappeared from sight.

***

Jason worked the knob with both hands. The knob turned freely, but the door remained shut.

The Spirits were here. He felt them. It wasn't a pleasant feeling.

He called, pounding on the door. "Is anyone out there?" he hoped. *Anyone at all?*

"We're here."

Jason spun around. Never before had the Spirits spoken audibly. They were somewhere in the room, unseen.

His mind went crazy with worry. *What are your intentions?* he thought, careful to guard his thoughts so they couldn't perceive it.

One hand continued to work the knob. The other was clenched in a tight fist. His eyes roamed the room. *Show yourselves.*

"Why are you so frantic to leave," they asked in playful banter.

Jason let go of the knob. "How is it I can hear you so clearly?"

"You're in the room of the high priest. This place is sacred, a holy of holies, where we are more powerful."

Shadows emerged from the corners of the room. The darkness it created was like that which went with him earlier that night.

The shadows coalesced into four separate figures.

Jason gasped. He'd never seen the Spirits so plainly – so close.

They appeared vaguely human. Although they were much bigger, stretching from floor to ceiling. On top rested a head-like sphere. Below the spheres, dark shafts of shadow draped all the way down to where they darkened the ground like the hems of long cloaks.

"What do you want with me?" he dared ask.

The air grew colder. His skin pocked with gooseflesh. Jason folded his arms to stay warm.

"Come nearer, High Priest. It does not do to lurk in doorways. Come."

Jason stepped away from the door and the four shadowy forms took positions around him. He saw now their emerald-green eyes staring down at him.

These were his gods. *So why am I so afraid?* He didn't like being surrounded by them, unable to keep his eye on them all at once. *But why should they bother me? Am I not their priest? Are they not my gods?*

Power and unpredictability. That's why he feared them.

"What do you want?" he asked again.

The shadows remained silent. The air was so cold now that it actually felt hot on his skin, as if it were burning him.

They leaned over, staring down at him as if he were a lab rat in some experiment. They observed him, their green eyes wide and bright.

He struggled to catch a breath. The air felt stagnant and thin.

They leaned further. He could see them in more detail now.

Their green-glowing eyes were set deep in their sockets. Their facial features were varying shades of shadow. When he looked closely, he noticed their skin had a certain raisin quality, wrinkled and shiny.

He couldn't judge their mood by their faces. But their intense study of him made him squirm. He found it impossible to maintain eye contact.

He looked down. "Pease, speak to me."

It was now very cold. His breath was visible. His body shivered.

"Please," Jason begged. "Speak to me, your loyal priest."

Their silence took its toll. The urge to run and hide was strong. But where could he run?

Confusion set in. *Why the fear?* It made no sense. These were the Kinship Spirits – his spirits, benevolent benefactors, not cruel masters. Yet, fear festered and grew within him.

He dared ask the question burning in his mind. "Why didn't we engage the enemy in battle?"

The Spirits didn't respond. Their emerald eyes just stared.

Despite feeling intimidated, Jason pushed the subject. "We should have fought."

"They were many," they answered with a hint of anger.

Jason's breath was an icy cloud as he spoke. "But we are the Kinship. We have you. We are powerful."

That statement brought a thought. *How powerful is the enemy? We retreated. Can they be more powerful?* No. He would not entertain such nonsense.

The Spirits darkened. Their eyes glowed intensely from their deep sockets. "We pick our fights carefully. We will pick our enemies apart, separate the weak from the herd. Even now, that mission is in process."

Jason wondered what this meant. "What mission?"

"Do not question us."

Jason hunched down. They leaned over him further. The weight of their presence was intense.

I'm the High Priest. "What mission!" *I need to know.*

The air became so cold, snow began to fall from the Spirits above, onto the frosty floor. Jason shivered, rubbing his extremities and stomping to keep his blood flowing.

I will not be intimidated by you. "Answer me!" he shouted. "I have the right to know these things!"

An arctic wind blew. The Spirits' cloaks flapped. Jason's blond hair whipped about as his teeth chattered uncontrollably.

He'd replaced his fear with anger. "What mission?" he screamed at them.

"Enough!" The Spirits shrieked as they came down on him like a tidal wave.

Jason screamed! His fear returned like a rampant virus infiltrating every cell in his body.

He collapsed to the floor – shrieking. They piled on him. The pressure was unbearable, the pain – excruciating.

It felt like a thousand needles were stabbing into him all at once. Jason screamed until his lungs were empty.

Then all went black.

***

"Just a little bit further, Peter."

Beth's hold was firm on Pete's hand, her pull persistent. Every so often, she'd turn to look at him, pleading with her eyes for him to continue following.

To Pete, it all felt like a dream, one glorious dream. *If it is a dream, I don't ever want to wake up.*

The fog pressed in close as they pushed their way through it like an icebreaker plowing through pack ice. It swirled as they passed through, its whiteness reflecting the streetlamps above.

His thoughts remained foggy, as if he'd had too much to drink. Yet, he knew enough to know he was sober.

"Where are we going?" Pete inquired.

She glanced back and smiled. "Away."

"Away? Away from where?" He didn't understand.

"Away to be together, just you and me," she sing-songed.

Pete struggled to remember how Beth used to speak. He never remembered her using a sing-songy voice before. "Just you and me? Alone?"

"Don't you want to be alone with me?" Her voice, although still sing-songy, took on a melancholy tone. "Don't you want that?"

"More than anything," Pete answered without hesitation.

"Then, come."

They continued onward. She seemed to have a destination in mind. But where? Pete couldn't fathom. Still, he was happy. He was with Beth, and that was all that mattered.

Beth appeared radiant under the glow of the streetlamps and the luminescent haze. Her hair flowed as one would see it in slow motion. *I must be dreaming.*

The thought of waking up upset him. *I don't want to.* He wanted this to last. Yet, deep within the core of his brain, a thought persisted: *Beth is dead.*

"Shut up," he mumbled to that thought.

"Hmm?" Beth turned back, looking at him quizzically.

"Nothing," Pete answered quickly. "Just talking to myself."

"And what does yourself have to say to you?" she asked with a playful chuckle.

You're dead, he dared not, could not say. "Nothing," he answered instead. He changed the subject. "How much further are we going?"

She held his hand in both of hers, stroking his fingers as if his hand were a kitten. "We're almost there, Peter."

She started moving faster, pulling him along with greater urgency.

"What's the hurry?"

She didn't answer.

Deep inside, that thought persisted. *Beth is dead.*

***

"Yea, though I walk through the valley of the shadow of death, I will fear no evil: for thou art with me; thy rod and they staff they comfort me," Jasmine recited as she pushed through the mist. She clung to those words with all her heart, soul, and mind.

The fog reduced her visibility to a few feet. It swirled around her, creating a mild vertigo effect. So, she walked heavily on her cane to retain balance.

"Pastor!" she called. "Pastor Pete!"

No answer came.

The ethereal environment was like a dreamscape. The sodium-vapor streetlamps 20 feet above her, cast everything into whiteness. Yet, it was a light which did little good. The fog hid everything beyond an arm's reach.

"Yea, though I walk through the valley of the shadow of death, I will fear no evil: for thou art with me; thy rod and they staff they comfort me."

She kept reciting that over and over. If she could just keep those words in mind, she'd retain some measure of peace in this place.

Then, she fell.

Her foot met nothing but air. She must have stepped off a curb.

The impact of her fall was brutal on her old bones. Jasmine screamed as she hit the ground, pain reverberating through her body.

She didn't move. Fear of what might be, kept her still. *Broken bones? Internal injuries?*

Her body felt wet. She was in the gutter on the edge of the street. It hadn't been raining, but she was lying partially in a large pothole where moisture had gathered. Fortunately, the street was vacant.

She moved slowly at first, pushing through the pain. But, as far as she could tell, nothing was broken. *I'm going to have one horrid bruise tomorrow though.*

Jasmine started searching for her cane. She needed it to get up.

"Yea, though I walk through the valley of the shadow of death, I will fear no evil: for thou art with me; thy rod and thy staff they comfort me."

But Jasmine did fear. She feared for Seth. She feared for Maxine. She feared for Pastor Pete. *Where is that cane?*

"Yea, though I walk through the valley of the shadow of death, I will fear no evil: for thou art with me; thy rod and thy staff they comfort me." Her voice cracked with tension.

"Pete!" she yelled. "Where are you!"

She crawled along the curb, looking for her lost cane. The fog pressed down on her ominously, reminding her that an enemy lurked.

Jasmine knew for some time that an enemy stronghold was here in this city. But she never knew the strength it possessed or its intent to destroy Zion's Hill specifically.

"Yea, though I walk through…"

Jasmine stopped talking. She didn't move a muscle.

She cocked her head, trying to hear the sound she thought she heard. *Footsteps.*

"Pastor Pete?" she hoped. It came out as only a whisper.

The fog behind her grew brighter. She began crawling away from it. Her terror growing with every stride she made.

She glanced back. The light was closer now. She tried to use the curb to get upright, but it wasn't tall enough for the task. *Where's that cane?* She searched for it, but had no luck.

The phantom light was nearly upon her. She crawled from it, her knees burning as they scrapped against the rough asphalt.

"Jesus help me!" she hissed.

Something grabbed her. She whimpered and struggled against it, but it was far stronger.

The light blinded her as it shone right in her face. She was manhandled out of the gutter. "Let me go!"

She was on the sidewalk now, being held up by strong hands. The light flickered about, reflecting the fog as it swirled around them.

"Calm down!" It was Jacobson. He was holding a flashlight in one hand and had her cane looped around his arm. The other hand was on Jasmine.

"You scared me something awful." She sounded meek. "Why did you follow me?" *You shouldn't have followed me.*

He smiled weakly. "I'm learning you're worth fighting for. Also, I found this flashlight in a drawer near the candy display in the lobby which makes me a little braver."

What he said wasn't conveyed in his action, Jasmine noticed. His body trembled. His voice was shaky. Maybe he was trying to be brave.

He looked around him. "They are here. I can feel their presence."

"Resist them with prayer," Jasmine answered.

"They're telling me things without words – horrible things."

"Trust in Jesus," she said as she took her cane from him.

"I want to."

"You must. It's the only way to rid yourself of these demons."

Jasmine put her hands on him. "Jesus, release this man from the grip of demons. Please Lord, help him with his unbelief. Increase his faith."

Jacobson continued to tremble. Under his breath, he mumbled, "Amen."

***

Seth and Maxine walked side by side. The city's streetlamps shined down on them, accentuating the fog as if it were made of floating bits of fine crystal.

The fog was disorienting and Seth kept his eye on the sidewalk for point of reference. With every step, it swirled around them like blobs in a lava lamp.

I can't believe I'm going back. He'd spent so much time staying away, and here he was going toward the Kinship twice in a 24-hour period. *But I've got to. It's the only way past this.*

He glanced at Maxine. She was also keeping her focus on the sidewalk.

Why did you insist on coming along. I should have not allowed it.

Deep down, he knew he had no say in the matter. She was an independent woman. She'd go where she wanted.

Did this mean she forgave him? He hoped so. He prayed so.

Seth changed focus. *Why did Pete go out here?*

The possible answer? *He has secrets of his own.*

No. Seth argued with himself. *Not Pete. It's inconceivable.*

Yet the very fact that he conceived it meant it was possible. *Was it? Could even Pete succumb to temptation?*

Seth knew what the Bible said. "All have sinned and fall short of the glory of God." And that includes Pete. *Even Pete?*

"Maxine?" The name fell from his lips almost of its own accord.

She stopped walking and looked at him. "What?"

"I know I should have told you everything way back at the beginning. I hope you know I love you more than words can say. I hope you know I never meant to hurt you. I hope…"

She interrupted. "Yes, you should have told me all of this long ago. Yes, you should have been honest from the beginning."

He looked down, trying to hold the tears back.

"But I understand why you felt pressured to keep this hidden. I know you did it to protect me, to keep me from hurt."

He shook his head. He was done living lies. "No. I did it out of shame about what I used to be. It did it out of fear that I wouldn't be accepted based on what I was. I did it out of guilt – I considered killing you! I considered killing everyone at Zion's Hill."

"But you didn't," she replied. "Because that's not the kind of man you are."

He stared at his feet. He couldn't look at her. He'd break down if he did. "You deserve better."

"For better or for worse. That's what I vowed when Pete married us." Maxine paused. "I stood before God and man and said those words. I meant them. I still mean them."

"I'm so sorry for everything." He wiped the tears away with the back of his hand.

"You don't need to be ashamed, or feel guilty, or afraid. I forgive you."

He looked at her. In that otherworldly fog, she looked radiant. Her eyes were wet. She managed a small smile. That was all it took for Seth to start sobbing.

They embraced. They cried. The tears ran hot from them both.

"I love you," he blubbered.

"I love you too."

Together, they continued toward the stronghold of demons, toward the place where they would confront the enemy once and for all.

***

Jason twitched as consciousness returned. *Don't open your eyes,* he said to himself.

The horror he'd endured was more than he ever imagined possible. The Spirits' discipline was merciless. But now it was done. He could move on.

Every fiber of his body hurt. Yet, it was better than earlier. The pain was now more of a general aching – one that affected every muscle, every nerve, every sinew.

Fear kept his eyes closed. He was afraid of what he'd see if he opened them. What new horror would the Spirits have for him?

Still, he had to open them sometime. In fact, delaying the inevitable may incite more punishment. Cringing, he opened his eyes.

He saw nothing, only absolute darkness.

Immediately, his breathing quickened. *What new hell is this?*

Jason stayed still. Without sight, he wasn't sure what to do next.

He gathered his courage. "Hello?"

His own voice echoed back. But that was the only response.

He sat up. Feeling his immediate surroundings.

He was on some sort of platform. His fingers ran along the edges. It was about the size of a twin-sized bed. Its surface was rough and cold as if carved from rough-hewn granite.

He swung his legs over the edge and his feet touched what felt like solid ground. He stood up, staying close to the table because it was his only point of reference.

"Hello?" he called again.

And again, his own voice echoed back. But nothing more.

Time felt irrelevant here. A couple of times, he thought he heard a sound. But by the time he listened, it was gone. Perhaps, it never was. He couldn't tell.

"Hello?"

A silent, barely perceptible breeze blew by him. It was cold. His skin prickled as it blew by him.

Where am I? he desperately wanted to know. *And where are the Spirits?*

Why did they punish me? The moment that thought entered his mind, he knew the answer. *Because I questioned their authority.*

He was High Priest, but they were in charge. "I'll do as told from now on," he called into the emptiness. Once again, his echoes were the only reply.

"I've learned my place among you."

Even more than the Spirits, he feared the enemy. He remembered that angelic army surrounding him on the street. He remembered retreating. *If the Spirits fear them, they must be worthy of being feared.*

But the Spirits had a plan. They said they'd pick apart the Zion's Hill herd one by one.

I'm with them 100%. "Is anyone here?" He felt so alone.

The breeze ceased. In its absence, a collective voice grew. "We are all here."

Jason trembled and grabbed the table for balance.

"We've been here all along."

"I know my place. I will serve you wholeheartedly."

"We know you will."

"Where am I?" Jason dared ask.

"You are exactly where we want you to be."

The breeze returned suddenly, but now it was a full-blown gale. It whipped his cloths so hard it stung.

"Why are you doing this to me?" he shouted over the whistling of the wind.

"Be still," the Spirits chastised.

The wind ceased, leaving Jason shivering in its wake. *Even the wind obeys them.* He felt foolish that he'd ever questioned their authority.

Gathering his courage, Jason declared. "I am your High Priest."

They said nothing.

"Give me another chance," he begged. "I know I can bring my brother into the Kinship. I know I can do this."

The Spirits remained silent.

"The prophecy can still be fulfilled. Together, we will be more than the sum of our parts, and all to your glory, oh spirits of the Kinship."

"Do you think we need to be glorified?" they asked with a sneer.

Jason began to shake. This wasn't going well. If the Spirits decided he was no longer needed, then he worried what would become of him. *More pain?* He shuddered at that thought. "Please, have mercy on me."

"Mercy?" the voices came.

"Please," Jason begged.

"Mercy is for the weak. Are you weak?"

Before Jason could answer, a wall of pain slammed him. He screamed out, but the darkness muffled him like a wet blanket, cutting off his air.

Unconsciousness slipped in once more and he welcomed it. *Anything to escape the pain. Anything.*

***

The fog thickened as Beth guided Pete further along. It was thick enough to be felt as he passed through it. It felt like wet cotton on his skin.

"Come along, Peter," Beth sing-songed. "It's not much further now."

"Where are we going?"

She ignored his question. "Not much further."

She held his hand tight, pulling him along.

He looked at it. The fingernail polish was her shade. Yet, something was amiss.

What is it? What's isn't right? But his thoughts were so cloudy, as if the surrounding fog had infiltrated his mind.

I first heard you coming from the enemy's darkness. Was that right? He was having a hard time remembering. *I think that's right.*

"We're almost here. Just a little bit further."

And if that's correct, then this isn't Beth. Is that correct? He slowed down as his thoughts coalesced.

"Don't stop. She pulled him along – forcing him onward."

This isn't Beth. It cannot be her. Beth is dead.

The realization hit him and his head began to clear. *If you're not Beth. Then who are you?*

Facts began to materialize. He missed his wife very much. He privately obsessed in the hope that he could spend just one more moment with her. But what was happening now was not an answer to prayer. *You're not Beth.*

He tried to pull away, but her grip tightened.

"Just a little further." Her voice lost some of its playfulness.

"Let me go!" Pete shouted, trying to pry her fingers away from his hand.

He broke off one of her nails. It fell from her hand, no longer looking polished and beautiful.

"Just a little further!"

Her voice was no longer calm – no longer sweet. *This isn't my wife!*

She glared at him with intense rage. Then, the disguise melted away, revealing what Pete already knew.

"You're not Beth!" he screamed.

Its hand held his like a vice. He struggled against it, but it would not relinquish him.

Pete stared in horror as the last vestiges of disguise fell away. What remained was hideous.

It glared at him with empty skull sockets. What had once been Beth's porcelain skin was now rotten and smelled of decay. Her face, now skeletal hissed at him through a mouth of exposed teeth. The scant amount of flesh remaining hung from her jowls like catfish bait on a hook.

He gagged. The thing smelled of the grave.

Despite the lack of flesh, he couldn't pull his hand free. It had him like a steel trap. Even when he used his other hand to pry away its fingers, they wouldn't budge.

The Beth impostor laughed at him. "It's just a little further Peter. Just a little further!"

The hand which held him was no longer a hand at all. The polished nails were gone. It their place, were evil-looking claws. The hand itself, nothing but a gnarled talon.

Pete screamed as those claws dug into his palm. "Come on Love. We're almost there."

An emerald-green glow lit up the fog as those skull sockets shined bright. "We're here," it hissed.

A beaten-up steel door appeared in the fog. The knob hung loose.

"We're here, my love," it guffawed with a skullish grin.

It opened the door and pulled Pete into the building. The ceiling was lit with a single row of bare bulbs. The hallway seemed to go into infinity.

Pete flailed his free arm, clawing at the corridor's walls, doing anything he could to get away, but he was caught like a bear in a steel trap.

Behind him, the door shut. "We're here, Love."

Panic racked Pete. Everything began to spin as his grip on reality slipped away.

***

Maxine grabbed hold of that lose knob and opened the battered-steel door. *I can't believe we're actually going in – again!*

The bare-bulb hallway appeared like the gaping maw of some giant serpent. They entered.

She pulled the door shut behind her. "At least we'll keep the fog out."

Seth nodded.

Maxine squinted under the glare of the bulbs. Ahead, the hallway wound its way into the warehouse. She thought it looked more like the gapping esophagus of a giant serpent. *And we're the mice.*

She glanced at Seth, and despite the situation, smiled. *Forgiveness is good medicine.*

She was far from perfect. Her past also held things she was ashamed of. Everyone at Zion's Hill, she was discovering, fit into that mold. *That's why we all need Jesus. And if Jesus can forgive me, I can forgive my husband.*

They progressed further down the bare-bulb hallway. Strangely, her fear was overcome by contentment. *If we die today, I can't think of a better place and time.*

She took his hand. Together, they moved deeper into the serpent's maw.

***

Jason moaned. Every inch of his body felt like he'd been used as a human pin cushion.

He opened his eyes. The Spirits were nowhere to be seen. He was on the floor of Cain's old room.

He tried to get up but his muscles spasmed. He groaned as pain traveled the length of his body. In that moment, the Spirits spoke.

You've failed, they said in his thoughts, *you have not convinced your brother to join us. But we have given you a gift. Seth is in the warehouse at this exact moment. We have brought him here to give you another chance. Now, take him. Force him to join the Kinship and the prophecy will yet be fulfilled.*

With their last words, Jason's pain reduced to a mild ache. Still, he didn't get up.

Part of him wanted to just run away. But, where could he go that the Spirits wouldn't find him. He was their slave. They owned him lock, stock, and barrel.

I'll do what I must, he thought, hoping the Spirits could hear his thoughts. *I'll make Seth join me. I'll force the prophecy. I'll do anything to satisfy you – anything to avoid your wrath.*

Good, they replied. *Very good. And to help, we've added additional weapons to your arsenal.*

Intrigued, Jason wondered, *what weapons.*

We've lured the Pastor of Zion's Hill here. He walks the bare-bulb hallway as we speak.

You lured him?

We did.

How? Jason assumed the pastor's faith would be too strong for such trickery.

We've watched him for so long, and we've learned his weakness. We remember his wife always called him 'Peter'. We took note of that years ago. We also see how much he misses her now. So, we put those facts together and caught him like a fish on a hook.

Jason didn't know what all that meant. But, having the pastor here could provide valuable leverage if used correctly.

Also, the wife is back. She's with your brother right now. They walk the bare-bulb hallway together.

Seth will join me, or he'll watch them die.

Good, the Spirits said with one voice.

***

What was I thinking going out into this fog?

The flashlight was dimming. The battery was running low. Jacobson sensed the Spirits within the mist and it resurrected old fears within him. They wanted him. If they got him – well, he couldn't dwell on such things because the fact was, he did go into the fog and there was no going back.

Plus, I have a choice to make.

Jasmine had said to put your trust in Jesus. *But I've been burned before.*

Christianity seemed too good to be true. *Just put your faith in Jesus and repent?* It seemed too easy.

He'd learned early on in life that there's no such thing as a free lunch. There's always a catch.

Jasmine had been persistently urgent. It made sense. They were in a very dangerous situation. He may not have the chance to mull things over for long. *Can I choose after I die?*

He'd spoken with enough well-meaning Christians over the years to know the answer to that question. *But I've been burned before.*

He looked at the old woman. Jasmine was determined. He saw it in her walk. He saw it in her face. He even heard it in the tapping of her cane. If she feared, she didn't show it.

He wanted her courage. *Did that come with believing in Jesus?*

One thing was certain, he'd never allow the Kinship to take him alive. *So, I'd better commit one way or the other. Jesus, or no Jesus, that's the question.*

I've been burned before.

The flashlight flickered out. He wacked it against the palm of his hand, but nothing changed.

"Batteries dead?"

He nodded. The light from the streetlamps luminated the fog enough to see. Still, his security crutch was gone. He kept hold of the flashlight though. It might prove handy as a weapon.

They moved through the fog and it swirled around them as they pushed through it. The only sound was the rhythmic tapping of Jasmine's cane.

"I've done so many things wrong. I don't think they can be just wiped away."

Jasmine laughed. "I can't choose for you. I can only tell my story. I've done a lot of bad things too. But I've been forgiven of them all."

They walked in silence for a minute. *I want it to be true.*

"I can't promise the demons won't continue to target you if you choose Jesus, but I can tell you that you won't be alone in the fight. Jesus promises never to leave you alone. He'll fight for you if you put your trust in Him."

He thought hard on it. *I really want this to be true.*

Jasmine's cane kept the beat as she started singing. "Amazing grace, how sweet the sound, that saved a wretch like me. I once was lost, but now am found, was blind but now I see."

Jacobson knew the tune, but he'd never listened to the words.

"There are more verses," she said, looking at him. "But you get the gist.

Jacobson tried to talk, but the lump in his throat prevented it.

***

Shame and terror. This was a feelings combination Pete wasn't accustomed to. *I should have been stronger. I shouldn't have let down my guard.*

Why didn't I see it years ago. His obsession with wanting to see Beth one more time started the day she died and consistently grew every moment since. He knew even then, it wasn't smart to dwell on such things. But at the time, he didn't care.

He felt entitled to his feelings. And that sense of entitlement only fed his desires.

And now look what it's gotten me.

The demon dragged Pete along a long and winding hallway. Above him, a string of bare bulbs cast hard light and sharp shadows.

He struggled to get loose, but its grip was solid. "Where are you taking me?"

The demon didn't answer.

Blood dripped from where its talons pierced his palm. With every tug, the pain festered.

"Just a little further, Peter," the thing taunted. Its voice was no longer Beth's, its tone no longer coaxing.

The stench of decay filled the hallway, wafting from the meat hanging from the creature's bones. "Not much further!"

Pete gagged as the steamy odor entered him, burning his nostrils. He struggled to break free, but it was futile.

They moved faster now. "We're almost there! Just a little further, Peter!"

The bulbs above them flashed as they passed by, the wire on which they swung, swayed gently as if by some unseen force.

"Let me go!"

It laughed sadistically. "Not a chance."

Pete jogged to keep pace. The thing bounded along, using its free hand to grasp the wall and pull itself forward.

Pete stumbled and fell, but the creature dragged him by his pierced hand. The pain was incredible.

The demon laughed and yanked Pete back to his feet. "Don't stop now, not when we're so close to the end."

To the end? Pete's last vestige of hope plummeted with that statement of finality. The shame and guilt avalanched onto him, crushing his spirit.

I've sinned, he thought bitterly. *And now, I'm reaping the consequences.*

"Just a bit further, Peter! Just a bit further!"

***

Jason entered the great meeting room. He brought Amanda with him. She'd struggled some as he pulled her from the inner room, but it wasn't much of a fight. She was still quite heavily drugged.

He'd put a strip of duct tape over her mouth and zip-tied her hands behind her back for good measure. Drugged or not, he didn't need any surprises.

She whimpered as he tightened her ties, which made him smile. *You made me miserable for years. Ain't payback grand?*

He jostled her to the center of the main room. Above him, the shadows spun and shifted.

Jason stared up at them in distain. *I'll be your high priest yet, he thought privately so they couldn't detect it. When the prophecy comes to fruition, then you'll see my true power. Then, you'll see who's in charge!*

He held a fully loaded Glock 19. He'd found it under the pillow on Cain's bed. He jabbed it into Amanda's ribs. She moaned. His smile widened. *This is going to be fun.*

Sheathed on his belt, the sacrificial knife dangled. *Blood sacrifice will surely be required. How much? Well, that's up to you brother.*

There was certainly no shortage of sacrifices to be made. *How many will die?* He already had the first one bound and gagged. Plus, others were on the way: the pastor, Maxine, maybe even more.

I'll leave Maxine for last. She was the most valuable. He'd only kill her if the others failed to stir Seth to action.

Amanda quietly moaned. Otherwise, the space was silent as the grave. He jabbed the gun into her back to keep her from slouching. "Good posture is important, Mother."

She mumbled something, but the duct tape kept it from being understood. Not that he cared. He'd been done listening to her for years now.

Unlike last time, there was no Kinship gathering. Instead, he'd ordered them all to stay in their quarters.

He deemed it a time of mourning for the loss of Cain. In reality, he didn't want them here because of the last fiasco. He didn't want another Jacobson situation. He couldn't afford another Jacobson situation.

He glanced up at the shifting shadows. *Seth had better show.*

He'll show, they answered.

He'd better.

Do not question us!

My apologies. He couldn't withstand another bout of pain.

*But when this is over…*he thought so they couldn't hear. *I'll inflict some pain of my own.*

Jason watched the rectangle of light which denoted the entrance to the main room. The bare bulbs cast its light into the darkness until the darkness overtook it.

"Where are you, brother? I won't wait forever."

And Amanda whimpered.

***

The thing that wasn't Beth, that didn't even look like her any more, yanked Pete away from the light of the hallway and into a great and dark cavernous space. The sudden absence of light played havoc with his eye. He stumbled in under the momentum of the one who pulled him, skidding to the concrete floor upon his hands and knees.

He landed hard, his pierced hand stinging as the demon relinquished its hold. Pete flipped to his back, but the demon was nowhere to be seen.

He stumbled to his feet, spinning in a panic. *Where was it?* Here, the monster could be anywhere, lurking in the darkness, waiting to pounce.

Pete caught movement above him. He looked up. The ceiling was high and dark. *Are my eyes playing tricks?* he wondered. It looked like the darkness itself moved up there, flowing to the currents of unseen air movement. *It must be a trick of lighting.* Then again, he'd experienced so much over the last few hours that before tonight, would have been deemed impossible.

His hand was warm and wet. The blood oozed from the wound and ran down his fingers. Already, the flow was slowing as his blood coagulated.

His eyes adjusted to the dimness. Two figures stood in the center of the room. It was too dark to identify them, but he could tell they were looking in his direction.

"Hello?" his voice sounded weak.

The figures remained unmoving.

He took a tentative step toward them. "Hello?" he called again.

"Don't come any closer!"

Pete stopped dead in his tracks.

"Stay where you are!"

The voice was Seth's. And yet, it wasn't. This voice held venom, which was a quality Seth's did not possess.

The figures drew closer. As they approached, Pete could see one of them was bound, gagged, and being led by the other. The other was the spitting image of Seth.

"Turn around," the Seth-lookalike blurted.

Pete didn't obey. He was mesmerized by the man's appearance – so identical to Seth. And yet, this wasn't Seth. It couldn't be.

The man pointed a gun at Pete. "I said turn around."

Pete turned around. Then he heard the distinctive buzz of zip-ties being tightened and felt their pressure against his wrists.

The man dug his finger into Pete's pierced hand. "What have you been into, Pastor?"

Pete didn't answer. He was too busy managing the pain in his hand. "Please stop," he gasped.

"Already begging for mercy?" he chuckled. "That's disappointing. I thought the leader of Zion's Hill would be tougher."

He did stop, leaving Pete to regain composure. For that, Pete was thankful.

"Turn around."

Pete did as told. The man stared him down. His eyes flared with anger and hatred.

This definitely wasn't Seth.

So, who was he?

***

Seth wanted to cry and laugh at the same time. *She forgives me?* It was almost beyond belief. *Maxine forgives me.*

He felt a weight lift from him, one that had been pulling him down for a long time. *I'm free. Finally, I'm free. No more guilt. No more shame. I'm free!*

He praised God for matching him up with such a woman to be his wife. It amazed him.

Despite the relief, fear still existed. *We're not out of the woods yet.*

They walked down the hallway. The bare bulbs swayed above them. The air itself felt ominous.

Despite being forgiven, he still felt responsible for the situation. He looked at Maxine. *I can't live with myself if harm comes to you because of this mess. I'll sacrifice myself before I'll let anything happen to you.*

He made up his mind. *Life for a life. I'll die for you, love.*

***

Jasmine was tired. This was a lot of exercise for a woman her age. Still, she plodded on.

She glanced at Jacobson out of the corner of her eye as they walked along. She had no clue as to where to go, but Jacobson knew. "They're all at the Kinship warehouse."

You worry me, she thought about him. *You're so young in your faith – like an infant, like a preemie.* She frowned. *You're not ready for this kind of test.*

The fog seemed thicker the further they marched. It swirled around them seductively. She felt it trying to infiltrate her mind. For a second, she felt the fog get in – cloud her mind and distort her thoughts.

No! I won't let it! And she continued with Amazing Grace.

"Twas grace that taught my heart to fear, and grace my fears relieved. How precious did that grace appear, the hour I first believed."

She stopped singing. She knew the words, but just didn't feel like singing any more. *It's this stupid fog.*

"Why'd you stop singing?" Jacobson asked.

"I – I'm not sure."

"Please keep it up. I like the words."

And, so she did. "Through many dangers, toils, and snares, I have already come. This grace that brought me safe thus far, and grace will lead me home.

"When we've been here ten thousand years, bright, shining as the sun. We've no less days to sing God's praise than when we first begun.

"Amazing grace how sweet the sound that saved a wretch like me. I once was lost, but now am found, was blind but now I see."

She finished just as a mangled steel door became visible through the fog.

"We're here," Jacobson said those words as if he'd just found out he had a terminal illness.

Jasmine leaned on her cane and reached for the door. The knob was dangling loose, but it still worked. She turned the knob and the door opened.

"I like what you sang," he said.

Jasmine smiled and nodded. *I hope the words sunk in.*

They entered a long hallway. Above them, bare bulbs swayed on a single wire.

Jacobson stopped only a few steps in. Fear was evident on his face.

Jasmine worried. "Are you alright?"

He looked at her for a moment before nodding. "Just keep singing that song and I'll be okay."

She started singing the song again. Together, they progressed down the hallway.

And Jacobson started to sing along.

***

The singing helped. Jacobson told the truth when he said liked the words. They helped preoccupy him – overpowering the self-destructive voice of his own thoughts.

You're walking to your own funeral, he thought. *And it's not going to be pretty.*

It seemed crazy he was actually walking back to the place where he was almost killed just hours before. "Keep singing," he said. "Sing it loud."

He sang along as best he could. It helped alleviate his stress. It was nice to hear those words and sing along. *I might even be starting to believe them.*

He almost didn't come in with her. The terror he felt nearly paralyzed him. But those words, they were sticking – giving him strength. *Plus, I can't just let this old lady cane-walk in here and die by herself, let alone the others.*

Out of the frying pan and into the fire, he thought. But that thought barely registered over the words "I once was lost, but now am found, was blind but now I see," which he sang along to now, better than before.

This is suicide. "'Twas grace that taught my heart to fear, and grace my fears relieved. How precious did that grace appear, the hour I first believed."

We're all dead. "Through many dangers, toils, and snares, I have already come. This grace that brought me safe thus far, and grace will lead me home."

He no longer heard his self-condemning thoughts. "When we've been here ten thousand years, bright, shining as the sun.

We've no less days to sing God's praise than when we first begun."

He sang now with gusto. "Amazing grace how sweet the sound that saved a wretch like me. I once was lost, but now am found, was blind but now I see."

I believe. And an unexpected joy entered him.

But I've been burned before, he countered meekly.

No. He was done with this inner debate. *Jesus is the real deal.*

"Keep singing!"

And, so they did.

***

Seth and Maxine picked up the pace and the bare bulbs passed by like lights on a subway. Time was of the essence.

Maxine had trouble keeping up. She noticed a change in Seth. He ran determined, almost angry. She could hear his breathing. It came hard, full of rage.

He's finally confronting his past.

That thought both frightened and comforted her. Only by confronting his past, he could break its hold on him. But, would doing this end badly?

She knew where the hallway ended and memories of her own past resurrected within her – memories of being locked in a room with an unconscious woman – memories of being bound to a stone table.

She forced those memories away. *This is a past I must relive because it's the past my husband has to confront and conquer.*

There really was no other choice.

***

Quick footsteps echoed from the hallway, filling the great room – stomp, stomp, stomp…

Jason planted his feet and leveled his Glock at the entrance.

The Spirits spoke within him. *Don't shoot. Wait and see who it is. You mustn't kill your only chance at redemption. You mustn't slaughter your brother.*

"Don't worry," he replied to them.

He guarded his thoughts so they couldn't read them. *My only chance at redemption. No one ever accused you of not having a sense of humor.*

He glanced toward the stone table where both Amanda and the pastor had been bound. His sacrifices looked terrified. *Good.*

Do this right, and all will go well with you. You shall reign with your brother and the prophecy will ring true. You will have power greater than any priest ever.

Jason mumbled, "I won't fail."

What good is power if I am a slave to the Spirits? He knew they couldn't hear these thoughts. *I'll take back what's mine once the prophecy is fulfilled. Then, you can take your turn being the slave.*

If the Spirits read those thoughts, he'd be toast. But Jason knew how to keep his mind his.

Be patient, priest. They told him. *Do this well, and you will be given the power due you.*

He aimed his Glock. He would not fail them. He would not be their whipping boy.

Failure was simply not an option.

***

Amanda felt lousy. Jason gave her only enough drugs to keep functioning. She supposed that was merciful. Addicts like her couldn't just go cold turkey, the shock of doing so was potentially fatal.

She lay there, strapped to the table, a strip of tape over her mouth. Beside her was a strange man, also bound, taped, and afraid.

What's the plan here, son? she wondered.

Was this it? She hadn't been a good mother. Now, would that infraction mean death at the hands of one of her boys? She shuddered to think.

She watched him level his gun at the hallway entrance. This wasn't behavior normal to sane people.

His state of mind concerned her. He kept mumbling things as if he were having a conversation. But no one else was in the room.

If the voices in his head tell him to kill me, it'll be all over. She wasn't a praying woman and didn't know how to go about it, but if she believed in a god, she would have started asking for help.

The darkness in the rafters above swirled and shifted. She watched it do this. *Was this evidence of a god? Should I pray to them?* She didn't know.

The man beside her struggled with his bindings. He was also watching the ceiling-shadows with fearful eyes.

Jason began to mumble. "I'll not shoot my brother. He is my only hope. I'll not shoot my brother."

She closed her eyes to it all. *I need a fix.*

***

They passed the last bare bulb and entered a world of darkness.

The sudden change was disorienting. Seth stared hard, trying to see.

He barely made out the shape of the stone table, probably because he knew where it was in the room already. He sensed movement on it. *A sacrifice?*

"Hello, brother! Jason's voice boomed. "Welcome home!"

Seth's eyes adjusted and a figure emerged from the darkness. Residual light from the hallway reflected off what the figure held. *A gun?*

Jason spat, "Don't you have words for me, brother? I said welcome home."

Seth answered, "This is not my home," in a voice he wished sounded tougher.

"It will be. You know as well as I that the prophecy says we must join together."

"I thought I was clear before. I will not follow the Spirits. I follow Christ and Christ alone..."

Gunfire interrupted him, leaving Seth's ears ringing. He dropped to the ground to minimize himself as a target.

The first thing he determined was that he wasn't hit. But, if not him - *Maxine!*

"Maxine! Dear God, no!"

***

Jacobson froze and both of them stopped singing. "That sounded like gunfire."

"How much further?" Jasmine wanted to know.

"Not much."

They looked at each other. For the first time, he saw weariness in Jasmine. "What's the plan," he asked.

She shrugged and continued down the hallway. "I trust God. He'll provide a plan in his time."

"So, no plan."

She glanced in his direction. "None other than to trust in God."

"Is that enough?"

"It's always been enough for me."

They continued onward. Jacobson wished she'd start singing again. But, the time for singing was over.

***

Seth looked behind him, terrified at what he might see.

Maxine was lying on the ground. She didn't move. *Jesus, please! Not Maxine!*

Her body twitched. Then, she lifted her head. *Thank God!* She appeared uninjured.

Jason's voice rang out. "Now that I have your undivided attention, we have some things to discuss. So, get up off the ground so I can talk to you brother to brother."

Seth got up. His legs felt shaky.

"If I fire this gun again, somebody's going to die. Do you understand me?"

"Yes." Seth felt so small – so helpless and his voice showed it.

"What was that brother? I can't hear you."

"Yes!"

"Good." Jason walked to the stone table. "I believe you know my guests."

Seth eyes had adjusted to the dimness of the room. He could tell two people were tied to the table. He suspected one of them to be Pastor Pete. The other though, he had no idea.

"Maybe this will help." Jason flipped a light switch and a spotlight blazed up the table.

Jason gasped. One of them was indeed Pete. The other one seemed an impossibility "Amanda?"

His mom was gagged. Yet, when he said her name, she groaned and struggled. Beside her, Pete lay still, his eyes fixated on the ceiling.

Seth looked up just long enough to see the swirling shadows. *The Kinship demons.*

Seth felt hot with rage. "You told me Mom was dead."

"Did I?"

"You told me you killed her!" he shouted.

Jason chuckled. "Just a little white lie, don't hold it against me, brother. Of course, things might still end up with me killing her. It's really up to you."

Seth looked at Amanda. It was strange seeing her alive after accepting the fact that she was dead.

"You know the prophecy."

Seth nodded.

"Say it."

"Say what?"

"Tell me the prophecy."

Seth spoke. "If we join together, much power will be given."

"I'm glad you remember. I was starting to think you'd forgotten. Why else would you have made everything so difficult?"

"It doesn't have to be this way," Seth said in a rally of courage. "You don't have to do what the demons tell you to do. You can…"

"This old story again?" Jason blurted. "I'm growing tired of hearing it, Seth! I hold all the cards. That means you'll do as I say. Now, join me."

"I can't," Seth said shakily.

The venom in Jason's voice was potent. "Those pigs at Zion's Hill have filled your head with lies. What's it going to take for you to realize that?"

"They're not lies."

"Will Mom have to die for real?"

"Jason, just listen."

"Will your pastor need to die?"

"Please!"

"Will your beloved Maxine, will she need to die?"

Seth stopped talking. His heart felt like it was going to explode. *Not Maxine. Not any of them. Please God, help us.*

"They are lies," Jason spat. "Those stupid Christians filled you with them. The Spirits are demons. The Kinship is evil. Jesus is Lord, yada, yada, yada."

"Jason please, just listen to me."

"No," Jason cut in. "You listen. I will do what has to be done to fulfill the prophecy. You will join me or people you care about will start dying. It's that simple."

Bile stung the back of Seth's throat. This wasn't going as he'd hoped.

"Do you really want to be responsible for all of this death? I'll start with good old Ma. She's so pickled it won't matter much if she dies. What's one less deadbeat parent in the world?

"Then, if you still won't see reason, I'll slice and dice your pastor. It'll be slow and painful. He needs to suffer for the lies he's filled your head with.

"After all of that, if you still insist on being a stubborn moron, then I'll turn on your precious wife. She'll suffer the most, I promise."

"No," Seth said, defeated.

"Hey, I don't want anyone to die personally. I'm leaving the ball in your court."

Seth said nothing. Shock was setting in.

"I'm losing patience, brother."

***

Jasmine and Jacobson slipped into the great room unnoticed. They stayed in the shadows while all others were distracted by the strange dialog between brothers.

Jasmine moved slowly, making sure her cane didn't tap. Silence was key.

She'd heard enough of the conversation to get the gist. Seth had to renounce his faith in Jesus, or people were going to start dying.

They slinked along the room's perimeter where the shadows were deepest. Here, the spotlight on the table worked to their advantage, creating a focal point in high contrast to the darkness in which they hid.

"Jason," Seth said. "I know you feel trapped. I was once in your shoes too. You feel enslaved."

Above, Jasmine noticed the shadows stirring. It increased with every word Seth spoke.

"I follow them," Jason retorted. "They hold the key to real power."

"At what cost?" Seth replied. "At the cost of these lives? At the cost of your own life?"

"Shut up!"

Seth didn't shut up. "There was a time when I wanted to believe the Spirits had my best interest at heart too. But I was wrong. You're wrong. They're just greedy demons who want to own you."

"You'll see how wrong you are," Jason hissed. "Once we've joined forces and received the power foretold by the prophecy, then you'll see."

Seth's voice calmed. "They've hurt you, haven't they?"

"Shut up!"

"They tried to do the same to me in the river."

"I said shut up!"

Jasmine and Jacobson froze where they stood. They were roughly halfway between the hallway entrance and the stone table.

Jason unsheathed the knife hanging from his belt. He waved about a gun in his other.

Jasmine needed to act before the situation fell apart, and it would need to be done under the radar.

Jason smiled and leveled the gun directly at Maxine where she lay on the floor.

"No!" Maxine wailed.

"Please," Seth pleaded. "Don't do this."

Maxine's sobs echoed throughout the room.

"It's your call brother. It's not necessary for anyone to die, especially your wife. Just say the word. Just tell me you'll abandon your god of Zion's Hill and join me."

Jasmine started moving again. There wasn't much time to defuse the situation. She motioned to Jacobson, hoping her gestures were enough for him to understand the plan.

Jacobson nodded and snuck up to the table. He was in the spotlight, but all parties were distracted. None took notice.

Jasmine remained in the nearby shadows – watching.

He pulled out his pocketknife and began cutting the prisoners free.

The ones on the table reacted, but stayed quiet.

Jasmine felt weak. Her knees quaked. The stress was overwhelming.

She wondered what they were bound with because Jacobson seemed to be struggling to saw through whatever held them. In her mind, the sound of his blade cutting through whatever it was, was louder than thunder. Yet, nobody seemed to notice them.

She glanced up. The shadows were going crazy.

Come on. Come on. Let's go. Jasmine leaned heavily on her cane – her knuckles white where they wrapped around its handle.

"What's it going to be Seth?" Jason shouted. "Will you join me, or would you prefer to watch your wife die?"

Sweat dripped down Jasmine's brow. She wiped it dry with her sleeve. *Hurry up!*

She watched in horror as Jason took two steps nearer to Maxine. She shook like a leaf on the floor before him.

Jason took aim. "Make a decision, man!"

Jasmine looked back at the table. It was empty! Jacobson and the others were slinking in the shadows back toward her.

Now the hard part began.

***

"Brother, I've made it so easy for you to make the right choice," Jason yelled. "We both know you'll eventually decide to join me. It might as well be without bloodshed. What do you say?"

Seth didn't say anything.

Don't push things too far, he said to himself. *I need him to hit rock bottom so he'll join me. I don't need him having a complete breakdown.*

"Look," he said in a friendlier tone. "This is the best for both of us, and you know it. I don't want anyone to die. You don't want anyone to die. Join me. It's a win/win."

Tears ran down Seth's cheeks. "Jason," he said with little more than a whisper. "These Spirits, as you call them, will destroy you. Whether I join or not, they'll absolutely destroy you."

"I've been obeying them for years!" Jason paused for emphasis. "I've only grown stronger. That's what they do for you!"

"But, in the end, you'll be destroyed. Your soul will burn in hell for all eternity," he choked back a sob. "I don't want that to happen to you brother. It doesn't have to be that way, but you have to leave the Kinship and follow Jesus."

Lies, the Spirits said in his brain.

Jason glanced up. The shadows had become quite still, like the calm before a storm.

Your brother won't relinquish his faith without blood sacrifice.

Jason took aim and pulled the trigger.

***

Jacobson heard a shot and his terror mounted. They ran down the bare-bulb hallway much slower than he wished.

Jasmine just wasn't fast at her age. And the woman was coming down from something. He wasn't sure what she was on, but his own experience told him something was in her system.

Pete helped steady the woman, encouraging her along. "Don't give up. We'll get to safety, if you don't give up."

She nodded and continued with them.

He struggled with abandoning Seth and Maxine back in the main room. But it seemed prudent to get as many to safety as possible. With the dialog between Seth and Jason, it was a perfect opportunity to sneak out the ones on the table.

Please God, keep the others safe. Protect them. Save them. The concept of praying to God was new to him. It felt a bit awkward and a little too easy. He did it nonetheless.

***

The shot rang loud in her ears, but Maxine felt no pain. *Is this the way it is with being shot?* Maybe her body was in shock.

It took time to realize she hadn't been shot at all. *But it was point blank. How did he miss?*

She'd planted her face against the concrete floor and closed her eyes in terror. Now, she dared open them and looked up.

The gun's barrel smoked. But it wasn't pointed at her.

Jason was looking at the stone table. A gouge sliced into its surface where the bullet had ricocheted. The table itself was empty.

Seth pulled her up and she bolted toward the hallway's entrance. She expected any moment to feel the searing pain of a bullet piercing her back. But it never came.

She entered the bare-bulb hallway and kept running. Only then did she realize she was alone.

Seth!

***

At the last moment, Jason remembered his initiative to keep Maxine alive as a last resort sacrifice. With one fluid motion, he changed the Glock's trajectory. He knew right where the table was. He pulled the trigger without even looking.

That proved to be a mistake. He realized that now as he looked. *Where are they?*

At first, he thought his mind was playing tricks. He squinted his eyes shut and reopened them. The table was indeed vacant.

When he turned back, Maxine was gone. He heard her footsteps fade away as they echoed to him from the hallway.

Well, that's just great. And then a follow-up thought. *The Spirits won't be pleased.*

***

How did we not notice? The Spirits scolded themselves.

They'd been so focused on their slave and his strategy to get Seth to join, that they hadn't noticed the sneakers.

They snuck in right under our noses. They stole away those on the stone table without us noticing.

They decided to place blame on the slave. Blame was a great distractor after all. It would keep Jason from realizing how limited their power actually was.

***

Jason assumed he was alone, that all had escaped – again! So, it came as a complete surprise when Seth flew from the shadows and plowed into him.

The gun fired, but Seth had redirected the arm which held the Glock. The bullet shot upward, past the swirling shadows.

Seth took him down like a pro-team linebacker. He hit the concrete hard. Seth landed on top. The impact sent the Glock skittering away into the shadows.

Stars danced before his eyes as the back of his head connected with the floor. He heard a cracking sound, like the sound of a homerun being hit. He struggled to remain conscious.

Jason's vision blurred. He saw his brother's expression, more sorrowful than enraged.

He tried to buck him off, but Seth had the higher ground. Plus, Jason's strength was waning as the knock to his head took its toll.

He tried cursing his brother, but wasn't sure the words made sense, or that they even came out at all.

He wasn't sure if the shadows descended over him, or if all light simply vanished. Regardless, everything went black.

***

Oh no!
Seth didn't mean to hit his brother's head so hard on the floor. Everything occurred spontaneously, without plan.

He got off Jason and stood up. The man lay still as death.
No! No! No!
He leaned down, checking for a pulse. He found one. *Thank you, Jesus.*

As he touched Jason's jugular vein, Jason twitched. Above him, the shadows raged like a whirlwind.

Seth fled the room, entered the bare-bulb hallway, and ran for his life.

I should have taken his gun.
But it was too late now. There would be no going back.

***

Get up! The Spirits screamed in his head. *Your brother is getting away!*

Jason opened his eyes. A raging headache blurred his vision.

He stumbled to his feet. The room felt like it existed on a rough sea.

He took a few steps and tripped, falling to his knees. *Get up!* The Spirits screamed.

Jason moaned. Their shrieks pained his head even more.

He touched the back of his head. *Man, that's tender.*

Get up!

He got up. Already his vision was clearing – his legs, strengthening.

Quickly – after them!

His legs were cold. He looked down. His pants were damp and smelled of urine.

Go! Now!

Jason located his Glock in a shadowy corner. Then, he turned and gave chase.

He entered the hallway, keeping near to the wall for balance support. Under the bare-bulb light, his head felt like it would explode.

His stomach lurched. He stopped, bent over, and vomited.

They're getting away, the Spirits urged him on.

His vomit smelled like death. He wiped it from his chin and looked back.

He could see the entrance to the main room. Here, the Spirits materialized.

Their green eyes glowed with rage. Their long forms, the darkest of shadow.

Get them! They shrieked in his mind.

He turned and ran after the escaping prisoners. There was no room for failure this time.

The Spirits wouldn't allow it.

BOUND BY BLOOD

***

Seth swore the hallway was longer now than before. He rounded curve after curve, expecting to see that battered steel door. Yet, every curve only revealed more hallway and more lightbulbs.

Why didn't I grab the gun? His incompetence frustrated him. *Now, I'm unarmed and left behind a weapon for my enemy to use against me.*

He stopped his thoughts right there. Even after all that Jason had done, this was the first time he labeled him an enemy.

He's my brother, he thought to himself. He sighed. *He can be both.*

Seth preferred to think of the days before they were enemies. His brother was his protector when they were kids. His brother was the one to encourage him to leave Amanda. His brother was the one who tracked him down on the streets.

How can he be my enemy?

He knew why. The demons owned Jason. And as long as that remained true, he could only be Jason's enemy.

Guilt was there. *Why did I get a second chance? Why did the Good Shepherd save me and not my brother? Why am I allowed a wonderful wife like Maxine? And a supportive church family? Why?*

He was so deep in thought that he almost ran over Jasmine. She, Jacobson, Amanda, and Pete were fleeing, but at a slower pace. Maxine was also there, having caught up to the slower moving group.

Maxine screamed.

"It's me."

"Prove it!"

"I just told you my secrets in Pete's office."

She let down her guard. "You look so much alike."

They progressed down the hallway, but the speed was infuriating to Seth. They were only as fast as their slowest members, and Amanda and Jasmine were not capable of going fast.

"Hello, Mom," he said without knowing why.

She didn't answer, but her pupils told the story. She was on something.

He thought, *Story of her life.*

"Just leave me here," Jasmine gasped as she leaned against the wall.

"You know we can't," Seth answered without hesitation. "We're all getting out of here, or nobody does."

Jacobson and Maxine supported Amanda. He and Pete helped Jasmine.

They continued on.

***

Jason stumbled, fell, and got back up. His head pounded with every stride, every stumble, every fall. He needed time to recover, but time was something he didn't have.

At least I have the Glock. That was something in his favor.

The Spirits hadn't stopped at the entrance to the hallway. They ran with him, dimming the bare-bulbs as they went.

Failure is not an option, they shouted at him.

I won't. But inside he worried that it was possible.

If he failed, then what? How would the Spirits react? What punishment would they deal out?

He pushed those thoughts from him. *I won't fail!*

***

"There it is!" Jacobson said. "The exit!"

Bad memories bombarded him. The last time he was here at this door, things got a bit hairy.

But that was then. He believed in a new God now. He had a new master. *I won't go back to the Spirits – I won't.*

They're not spirits. They're demons. It was time he started calling them by their true name.

Do you hear me? he thought. *You have no control over me because you're just demons, and I follow Jesus now!*

Feeling empowered, he grabbed the door and pulled. It opened freely and his newly found faith increased.

They exited and stood outside. The fog was still here, thick and swirling. But Jacobson feared it no more. *I trust Jesus!*

"Where's Seth," Maxine's voice sounded frantic.

Jacobson turned back to the door. But it was closed.

He tried the knob, but it didn't work. The door remained closed with Seth presumably on its far side.

And just like that, doubt and fear grew once more.

***

Seth made up his mind. Once the others were out. He shut the door, latching it with the heavy-duty barrel slide lock that he saw low on the door.

"How do you like that, Jason!" he shouted. *I've just taken away all your bargaining chips.*

"What are you doing?" Maxine shouted from the door's far side. The door shook as she pounded on it.

"Saving you all!" he yelled back.

"Are you insane! Open the door!"

Talk about a woman's scorn, he thought. "I came to save my brother, and that's what I'm going to do!"

"You are going to get killed!"

"Maybe."

The door rattled as if a rabid dog was tied to the knob. "Open the door!"

He couldn't bear listening to her. Maxine's tone was so frantic. It broke his heart. But he'd come for his brother. So, he turned from the door and began walking down the hallway.

Overhead, those bulbs blazed. He felt their heat on his head. Yet, he shivered as sweat dripped down his face.

What's the plan, Seth.

He wished he knew.

CHAPTER 9

"Jesus, help me now!" Maxine screamed like a banshee.

Unlike before when she's uttered that statement, the door remained closed.

She shrieked. Pounding on the door, bruising her hands. But she didn't care. All that mattered was getting to Seth. *I can't lose you again!*

She felt Jasmine's hand on her shoulder. "It appears that it's God's will for this door to remain shut."

She turned on the woman in a rage, slapping her hand away. "What do you mean? Why in the world would it be God's will to keep my husband a prisoner in there with that psycho-killer brother of his?"

"I don't know," Jasmine confessed. "All I know is, God's in charge. He always has been and he always will be."

"Amen," Pete chimed in.

"Are you all crazy!" Maxine couldn't believe it. "He risked his life to save yours. And now, we're just going to leave him there to die?"

She glared at them with rage and frustration. "What's wrong with you?"

Pete spoke soothingly. "Listen, I screwed up recently. I thought seeing my wife again was an answer to prayer. But it turned out to be a big mistake.

"Deep down, I knew it was wrong to want Beth back. She's with the Lord now. She can't come back. But I decided that what I wanted was more important than God's will. I made my own rules and told Him to follow them.

"And look what that got me," he said holding up a wounded hand. "So, if it's God's will for that door to remain shut. Then it will remain shut. Nobody can change it."

"That doesn't mean we just give up!" she said with anger.

"No!" Jasmine shouted back. "We never give up! We try to do God's will, but we never give up!"

Maxine pleaded with her eyes. *I can't lose him. Not now that I'm starting to know the real Seth!*

She started pulling on the door with renewed strength. "Maybe God will change his mind! He's a merciful God! He opened this door before, or have you forgotten!" She glared at Jacobson.

Jacobson averted his stare. "I've been shown recently to trust in God. Beyond that, I don't know much."

Jasmine brought Maxine into a hug and Maxine let her. "You hear that? Trust in God. He's in charge and He'll take care of his children."

Maxine broke down, sobbing uncontrollably. *I hate this!*

Worst of all, was the fact that they were right. She had to let go. She had to give it to the Lord.

Despite that knowledge, she cried harder.

***

The unmistakable sound of the door closing came to him as he progressed down the hallway. *Oh no! they're getting away again!*

Don't give up! the Spirits urged him. *You must not fail us again!*

The Spirits surrounded him as he went along. The light of the bulbs was diluted to a dirty gray. Their emerald-green eyes pierced the dimness, glaring.

Memories of pain permeated his thoughts. *I must not fail*, he agreed. *I will not fail.*

When attacked by his brother, the hit to his head left him lethargic. Now though, adrenaline and fear drove him onward, almost as fast as normal. *I cannot fail!*

Their shadows grew darker still. Now, the light barely reached him from above. The greenness of their eyes pierced the darkness, showing their fury – displaying their rage.

He gripped the Glock so that his hand trembled.

Yes, they said caressing his gun-wielding hand. *Use your rage to your advantage. Your brother deserves punishment for his rebellion against us – against you!*

Jason replied in thought. *He will suffer for his crimes.*

Only use restraint, they added. *Don't kill him. Use the gun for intimidation, not for killing him. Remember, he's the key to the prophecy.*

He ran as if in a tunnel. Ahead, the light of the hallway was brilliant. Here, he was in near-total darkness. The only light came from those green eyes, those glaring eyes.

Part of him wanted to escape the darkness. But, no matter how hard he ran, he knew there was no escaping it. He was of the Kinship. He was slave to the Spirits. There could be no escape. His only hope was to bring his brother into it, to make him part of it – to fulfill the prophecy.

That's just what I'll do.

***

Seth hoped the lock on that door would hold. He needed those he cared about to stay out of harm's way.

It's down to you and me brother, he thought as he walked down the hallway.

He tried walking confidently, but inside panic was erupting. It was all he could do to keep it under wraps. *I've got to stay in control.*

It helped that there was no choice. He couldn't run away from this. Running away from the Kinship is like running from an aggressive dog, it'll only chase you harder if your run.

It's time to face my past. Whether he lived or died, it would end here – today. *I'm tired of hiding. I'm tired of running. I'm ready to move on.*

He heard footsteps echoing to him from down the hallway. *Alright brother, let's see what you've got!*

***

The fog pushed in on the group huddled outside the door. Maxine no longer pounded on it.

She wept bitterly. "I can't lose him again!"

The others gathered around her, placing their hands on her. They bowed their heads as Maxine fell to her knees in the center of the circle.

Pete began to pray. "Jesus, you are God. All power is yours. Please give Maxine comfort now. Open her eyes to see your greatness in this situation.

"Also, protect your servant, Seth. Grant him strength when it's needed to defeat this enemy that dares come against your church."

The fog seemed to lessen immediately around them as they prayed.

"Give us all your strength and comfort," Pete continued. "Most of all, let your will be done."

And they all said, "Amen."

***

Ahead, Jason heard footsteps. Somebody was still here. He held the gun tighter, ready to confront whichever of them hadn't left. *I'll fill them with lead.*

Not if it's your brother, The Spirits shouted in his brain. *You shall not kill him, or the prophecy cannot be fulfilled.*

Jason didn't reply.

***

Seth rounded a curve in the hallway and came face-to-face with Jason. Behind him, darkness.

Seth beheld the darkness and a shiver escaped. He knew these shadows. "You'll not drag me down again," he shouted at them. "Not like you did in the river!"

They tried to reply, but Seth didn't allow them into his mind. They would not infiltrate his thoughts. Not this time.

Jason shouted. "If you won't listen to them, listen to me. They say, you are right that it won't be like last time. This time no mercy will be given, unless you join your brother."

Seth smiled. "I can't do that."

Jason raised his gun and took aim. "Then, you will die!"

***

Do not kill him! The Spirits shrieked in Jason's head.

Jason shook his head. *He's determined not to join me. What good is he to us?*

We have ways to convince him!

Jason scoffed. *You couldn't convince him two years ago. You haven't succeeded in convincing him now, even under the pain of losing those he cares about.*

He looked at Seth. The man trembled with fear. He'd give one last chance – one last opportunity to fulfill the prophecy. "Join me or die. This is your last chance."

"Jason, please…"

"I'm done playing games!"

Don't shoot him! We need the prophecy fulfilled.

There it was, finally. The Spirits needed the prophecy fulfilled for their own needs. They didn't care about him. They didn't care about the Kinship – just themselves. *We have enough power without the prophecy.*

Don't be a fool!

"Seth, join me or die!"

Seth dropped his hands to his side in resignation. "I can't join you, not under any circumstance."

Jason pulled the trigger.

***

The group jolted in unison. They all knew what the sound was – *gunfire.*

Maxine began crying once more.

***

Jason screamed as the gun fired. He fell to his knees. The bullet missed, blowing away a bulb and driving a tunnel into the ceiling.

Seth stood there, dazed and confused.

Jason continued to scream.

***

How dare you! The Spirits shrieked in Jason's head.

The instant he pulled the trigger, they pounced and his aim went awol. The pain was excruciating. He immediately regretted his brief surge of courage – his failed attempt to show them he could lead.

Now, as the pain crumbled him to his knees, he realized how futile his actions had been. There was no place for him here. He wasn't High Priest. He was truly a slave.

Forgive me! he begged them. *I was wrong to take charge as I did.*

Forgiveness? They screamed in his mind. *Forgiveness is not in our thinking.*

***

Seth didn't know what to do. His brother fell from his knees to the ground, writhing like a wounded snake.

The gun fell from his hand and landed on the floor. Seth took a step toward it, but the darkness of the demons hid it from view.

He looked up at them. They glared down with emerald eyes full of malice. And all the while, Jason screamed in obvious pain.

In the chaos, Seth felt weak. They broke his barriers down, and he heard them speaking.

Hello, prodigal son.

Seth's skin erupted in gooseflesh as they spoke in his mind.

We're glad you decided to return. Their collective voice along with Jason's shrieks, made the situation unbearable.

Seth gritted his teeth and took a step away.

There is no escaping. Haven't you discovered that yet, you stupid pig?

Seth said a prayer they couldn't hear and then spoke. "Release my brother."

We would, but he doesn't want to leave. Plus, we own him.

"You're hurting him!"

The Spirits just laughed as they loomed larger, blocking out more of the light.

"You don't own me!" but his voice betrayed his confidence. "Now stop!"

You are very demanding for just a common mortal. What will you give us in exchange for your demands?

That question hit Seth like a punch to the gut. He knew what they wanted, but also knew the dangers of bartering with demons.

He looked down at Jason. His brother's eyes had rolled back. Only the vein-webbed whites showed. Foam was dripping from his mouth and puddling on the floor.

What is your brother worth? Can we strike a deal?

"I will unite with my brother," Seth said quickly, so quickly that he barely had time to consider what he'd said. "I will fulfill the prophecy."

Do not toy with us mortal man.

Seth said nothing.

We accept your proposal.

And with that, Jason quit screaming.

Seth ran to him. The shadows allowed it.

Jason appeared deceased. The puddle of foam from his mouth smelled like death. His eyes remained rolled back.

Seth looked closer and listened for any sign of life.

Jason gasped and unrolled his eyes. Trembling, he whispered "Why did you come back?"

"You're my brother," Seth answered.

Jason shook his head. "You shouldn't have come back."

It is time to complete the barter. It is time to fulfill the prophecy.

"You should have run when you had the chance," Jason hissed.

"I couldn't just leave you behind."

Jason unsheathed his knife. "You know what must be done."

Seth nodded.

"The prophecy requires blood sacrifice."

"I know."

Above them, the demons rose. Their green eyes shone like emeralds gleaming in the gloom created by their bodies. The light from the ceiling barely penetrated to the floor.

"You shouldn't have come," Jason said as he sliced his own palm, drawing a flow of blood.

The demons above grew still, watching with great anticipation.

Jason grabbed Seth's hand and raised the knife. The air itself felt heavy with the scene, saturated with its significance.

"There's something you should know brother," Seth said as the knife drew nearer.

"What's that?"

"The blood's already been spilled. The sacrifice has already been made on a cross."

With that, he grabbed Jason's wrist and wrenched it so the knife fell to the ground. Above them, the demon's darkness became darker than that of a cloudy night.

"What have you done?" Jason gasped.

"Saved your life!"

Seth shivered. The air dropped by at least ten degrees. The emerald eyes pierced the deep darkness, filled with rage.

"Run!" he shouted as he helped Jason to his feet.

They ran down the hallway, toward that exit.

And the demons followed close on their heels.

***

Out in the fog, Pete began to sob as Jasmine put her arm around him. *What's this about,* she wondered.

"I will be resigning my position as pastor if I make it through this," he said between sobs.

"Nonsense," she answered.

"I can no longer lead this church. I am too weak and I've given in to temptation."

"Hush now," Jasmine said. It broke her heart to hear him say such things. "Pastors are no different than the rest of us. You just fell into a pit created by lies of the Devil."

"Exactly, and that's why I am not fit to lead Zion's Hill."

"Aren't you sorry for what you did?"

"Of course." He sounded hurt that she would ask such a question.

"If you're repentant, then God's promise is to forgive. Isn't that correct?"

He stayed silent.

"Come now, Pastor, this is what you've been preaching since day one. Now answer the question. If you do something wrong, and then repent to God, then doesn't God forgive?"

He nodded reluctantly.

"And when God forgives, then it's as if the sin never occurred from His perspective. Isn't that what the Bible teaches?"

He sighed. "It is."

"Isn't it written that God throws those sins as far away from Him as the East is from the West?"

"Yes, but..."

"Well, if you've done something that God's erased that completely, then who am I to argue?"

"But it shows such weakness."

Jasmine nodded. "But through such trials of weakness, the Christian's faith grows stronger."

She gave him a quick hug. "Now I don't want to hear another word about resignations. You are our pastor, and that's how it shall remain."

"But I..."

"We don't have time to bicker. We need to find a way into this place and help if we can."

Pete nodded and dried his tears away with the sleeve of his shirt.

Jasmine began to walk the perimeter of the building and the rest followed. She didn't have much hope that they'd find another way inside, but looking for one would take Pete's mind off of what he'd done.

And that's what he needed more than anything else at that moment.

***

The members of Zion's Hill (minus those at the Kinship's compound) gathered in the church's lobby. All of them prayed in earnest.

Earlier, they discovered Jasmine, Jacobson, Pete, Maxine, and Seth were missing. Some wandered into the fog searching for them, but soon returned.

Out there, they felt the emptiness in the fog – a deep loneliness. For those that endured for more than a minute, hopelessness engulfed them. All of them returned crying, or screaming or shaking with fear.

The effects were temporary, wearing off within minutes. So, they relied on God, speaking to him in prayer, lifting up those missing and asking for God's mercy and protection.

It was all they could do.

***

Except for Jason, all the Kinship stayed in their quarters. They all heard the gunfire resonating from down the hallway. But, not one of them investigated because of Jason's orders to stay in their rooms.

Instead, they crawled into the furthest corners of their quarters, hiding under beds and desks and tables.

Terror overpowered them, inexplicable terror. Some with guns took what they thought was the best option.

But of course, suicide never fixes anything.

***

Jason's head spun. His plan was so far off course that nothing could drag it back in line.

Why did I hesitate? He should have drawn blood faster. *Why did I hesitate!*

He knew why. *You came back for me. Why did you come back for me?* he thought as he ran down that hallway.

Why?

He also had no clue as to why he ran from the Spirits. From observation, he knew this was a very stupid decision.

I failed.

That's why he ran. The Spirits made it clear they'd accept no more failure from him. But, that's just what he'd done.

Why did I hesitate?

That hesitation was pricey. It would cost him one life – his own.

Something popped over his head and glass showered down. One of the bulbs had burst. Its flash was like the single pulse of a strobe light.

Another pop, then another, and another. They blew fast, sounding like an automatic weapon. Each bursting bulb made the hallway darker.

He glanced back. The Spirits were advancing. Their green eyes pulsating brighter with every bursting bulb.

They said nothing to him. They didn't need to. He knew his goose was cooked.

Something ripped and drywall dust fell like snow. The wire connecting the bulbs were being pulled from the ceiling. The staples which held it pinged like bullets upon him.

He shielded his eyes, successfully keeping the staples out of them. The dust though burned them.

I'm dead meat, he said to himself, knowing the Spirits could not be outrun.

Yet, he kept running as if he had a chance. The air was suddenly very cold. His breath came in visible bursts.

It was so cold that the fire sprinklers burst. Sleet rained down, hitting him, feeling not like water, but like slivers of glass.

Ahead, the exit door came into view. Seth was almost there, his hand reaching for the handle.

Chunks of ceiling fell now, landing on his head and shattering into smaller bits. Above him, the Spirits were pulling down the ceiling.

Chunks of drywall landed in the newly formed puddles. Also, sizzling sections of electrical wire segmented with broken-bulb sockets, dangled by what staples remained. It hung precariously near to the puddles, swaying only inches from its surface.

The last bulbs burst and generator-ran emergency lights flickered on. The red emergency lighting cast everything in a hellish hue.

Jason pulled on the door as Seth worked the barrel lock near the floor. "Hurry!" he shouted.

"It's stuck!" Seth answered.

Above them, the Spirits glared. *Looks like our priest has had a change of heart.*

He pushed Seth aside and tried working the lock, but his fingers were numb with cold. The brass lock was slippery and cold – so cold that a coating of ice covered it, freezing the bar in place.

"Help!" Seth screamed. He pounded on the door as Jason tried to break the ice on the lock.

Above, the Spirits laughed and laughed.

"Why did you come back for me?" Jason yelled to his brother.

"Because I love you, and Jesus loves you."

Jason pulled hard, but that lock would not disengage. He turned to face the Spirits just as the wiring completely fell free from the ceiling.

The live wire and exposed light sockets hit the puddles, creating an instant steam cloud.

Jason saw a bright flash as pain radiated from his core to the tips of his toes and fingers. His body went rigid.

For the first time ever, he prayed in his mind to a god he'd never prayed to before. *Jesus, if what my brother says is true, then please save me.*

"Jesus save me!" He shrieked as the current surged through is body, lighting him up like a Christmas tree.

Then all went dark.

***

They came full circle. Maxine's hope fell. There was no other entrance besides the battered steel door. She tried it once more. It was still locked.

Through the door's bullet holes, a red glow beamed. She tried to peak through the holes, but they were all at angles and revealed nothing.

Who builds a building this size and only puts in one door? Nothing about the last 24 hours made sense – not a single thing. *And that included Seth's stupidity.*

Why did you go back for a brother like that? It made no sense.

She started pulling on the door with all she had. "Help me!"

No one helped. "You can try, but it'll only open if it's God's will."

She knew it was true. Still, hearing it made her want to punch somebody in the face.

She glared at Jasmine. She clenched her fists. *No. It wouldn't do any good to hit her.*

She returned to the door, pulling while pushing against the warehouse wall with her feet. But nothing changed. The door remained shut.

Jasmine put her hand on Maxine's back. Her touch, meant to be reassuring, only frustrated Maxine further.

"So, what then?" Maxine shouted. "Are we supposed to just give up?"

Jasmine shook her head.

"What then?"

And with that, Jasmine led them in more prayer.

This sucks, Maxine thought.

Still, she joined in.

***

The pain ceased. Jason was no longer being electrocuted.

He was flying through darkness. In the distance, he saw a speck of light. It appeared far away, but growing steadily nearer. He was gliding toward it, not under his own power.

He existed in a tunnel of sorts. And he wasn't alone.

"Hello, brother."

Jason turned. Seth was floating beside him. He could just barely make out his silhouette in the glow of that distant light. With every second though, he became more visible as they approached it.

"Are we dead?" the thought occurred to him.

"I'm not sure," Seth casually replied. "I've been here before, but I don't know if we're alive or dead."

"What does that mean?"

Seth just shrugged.

Most of him was content. However, a small seed of fear existed. As they floated nearer to the light, that fear began to increase. "Where are we going?"

"I don't know."

Jason's fear bordered on terror. "I thought you said you've been here before."

"Yes."

"But you don't know where we're going?"

"Last time was last time."

Jason was in no mood for riddles. "Where did you go last time?"

"Just wait and see."

In the glow of that ever-nearing light, he could tell his brother was smiling, and it frustrated him. *This isn't a joke.*

The approaching light made him fearful. He tried paddling away as if he were in water. But this seemed to be a frictionless environment.

He tried grabbing onto the sides of the tunnel. But they were beyond reach.

"Jason," Seth said through his grin. "It's pointless to resist."

They moved quicker now, the light growing brighter and larger by the moment. The tunnel ended and Jason found himself soaring through a great expanse. In the distance was a throne, and the one who sat upon it defied description.

He neared the throne, stopping directly in front of it.

The light came from the one seated on the throne. It blazed from him like bolts of lightning.

Jason knelt. The one upon it – that indescribable one, was a king. Kneeling felt compulsory.

While kneeling, the fear inside grew almost to the point of insanity. Terrified was the proper word here.

Yet, he didn't try to run. *Where could I go?*

The light illuminated everything. There was nowhere to hide.

The one on the throne was more than a king. He didn't know how he knew this. He just did. The king was also a judge, and Jason was a guilty man.

His terror nearly overflowing. It was about to undo him.

Just then, calmness took over. Someone was putting their hand on his shoulder.

He looked up, expecting to see Seth, but it wasn't Seth. If his brother was near, he wouldn't have known it. The one touching him drew all his focus.

He had long hair, a white beard, and was dressed all in white. In his hand, he held a shepherd's crook.

The light from the one on the throne reflected off this shepherd. Yet, his light was just as bright. Or maybe the light was coming from this one as much as from the other. Jason couldn't tell which it was.

The shepherd pulled Jason away from the throne, not forcefully, but with care. And he was glad.

Being in front of that judge, bearing so much guilt, it was too much. Here though, in the presence of this shepherd, he felt peace.

"Behold." The voice of the shepherd was powerful and gentle simultaneously. "What do you see?"

The shepherd pointed with his crook and Jason looked into the distance, beyond the great expanse. "I see darkness." He looked away because that darkness disturbed him.

"Take a closer look."

He was guided closer to the darkness by the shepherd, and as he neared it, his discomfort grew. "Please, I don't want to get any closer."

Jason found himself on the edge of a very high cliff. He looked down and saw that the chasm was deep – so deep in fact that he could not perceive its bottom.

On the other side of the chasm was where the darkness existed. It rose tall and black, but stayed on its side.

Something moved within the darkness. He didn't like watching that movement. It disturbed him.

He suddenly realized what they were. *The Spirits!*

From the far side of the chasm, they didn't look as big and bad as they did in Cain's old quarters. One of the shadows moved to the very edge of the chasm. Jason saw its green eyes glaring. "This one belongs to me!" Its voice sounded like thunder.

Jason cringed at that voice. It sounded like the Spirits, but more powerful.

The figure took greater form, now far larger than in Cain's quarters – an imposing monolith to match that thunderous voice. "This one belongs to me!" it shouted again.

It stood on the very edge of the precipice. Only the chasm separated them.

Jason wanted to flee. Memories of pain and torture and time in the inner room flooded his mind.

Then the shepherd stroked his shoulder, and Jason felt a peace that surpasses understanding come over him.

The dark figure beat his chest as he shouted. "He is mine!"

"You are in no position to make demands, Lucifer." The shepherd's voice was calm and confident, yet powerful in its own way.

"This one is mine," Lucifer reiterated, a little quieter than before. "You took the other one, but surely this one is mine."

As Lucifer spoke, he reached a pitch-black limb as far across the abyss as possible. Fortunately for Jason, the chasm was wide, and he remained beyond the grasp of that claw. The shepherd made no act of retaliation, but simply stood there, straight and strong. His hand remained on Jason's shoulder and his shepherd's crook was planted firmly upon the ground.

Lucifer snorted. "This one surely belongs to me." Lucifer's voice came almost as a whine. "Do you dispute it? Can you disprove it? Was he not my high priest, puppet leader of my servants who operate the stronghold in my city?"

"Enough!" The shepherd's voice sounded like a crack of thunder and Lucifer took a small step back, retracting his clawing reach as if it'd been slapped away. "None of these sins are being held against him. He called on MY name and all who call on the name of the Lord shall be saved!"

Other spirits, black as the deepest night, emerged from the darkness and joined Lucifer. Their show of solidarity seemed to rekindle Lucifer's confidence and he rose to an unprecedented height, a giant among giants.

The Spirits he knew were here. Plus, there were more, many more – a whole army of them.

Jason saw them now for what they were, not benevolent beings, not friendly spirits. These were demons.

"This one is mine!" The shepherd boomed loud enough to shake the ground. "He has been purchased with my blood!"

Lucifer stumbled as the ground shook. In those green eyes, a rage flamed.

"It is finished," The shepherd uttered.

The force of those words shoved Lucifer and the other demons back into the darkness. The darkness still existed, but it was far off, barely visible. The ensuing silence was absolute.

For a time, Jason soaked in the quiet. His mind was clear. For the first time in ages, the demons were absent from his thoughts. *Such peace.*

Jason glanced up at the shepherd. That's when he noticed the scars – his wrists, his feet, his brow – so many scars. They were deep but healed – old scars.

The shepherd smiled. "What do you see?" His voice changed. It no longer hinted of anger as when addressing Lucifer.

"Scars."

"It's good you perceive them. Do you want to know more about them?"

"Yes," Jason answered truthfully.

The shepherd's smile grew. "So did your brother. When Seth noticed my scars, I told him to go to Zion's Hill to learn the meaning of them."

Jason suddenly realized he hadn't seen Seth since they were flying through the tunnel. "Where is my brother?"

The shepherd ignored Jason's question. "Just as I told Seth, so too, I tell you that Zion's Hill will teach you the meaning of my scars."

"Where is Seth?" Jason persisted.

"He is not here. You must go back. You must learn about the sacrifice that my scars represent. To know about my scars is to know about me."

Jason did not want to go back and the shepherd must have known this, for he said, "It's not your time. Go back. Learn of me."

Jason was torn. He wanted to stay, but he also wanted to obey, he felt compelled to obey. The conflict brought tears to his eyes. He looked away.

"Look at me, little one," he heard the shepherd say.

Jason looked, and the shepherd wiped away his tears using the sleeve of his cloak. The cloak smelled like fresh linen.

"You will come back some day. Then you can stay. In fact, I have a place already prepared for you."

"You do?"

The shepherd nodded. "If it were not so, I would tell you. Now though, you must go back."

And with that, Jason felt himself begin to drift away. The shepherd stood tall, holding his shepherd's crook like a royal scepter.

"What is your name?" Jason called out.

"Why do you ask my name child? You know me. You called me by name when the live wires struck you down."

Jason let that sink in.

"You know who I am. Have faith in me and you will live."

"Jesus?" Jason managed to ask.

The shepherd didn't confirm or deny that name. He didn't need to, because Jason knew that's who it was. *Jesus.*

"Go to your brother. He needs you."

Jason blinked once and the light from the one on the throne was only a speck in the distance. He blinked again and was back in the tunnel.

He looked around. "Seth!"

But he was alone.

***

Jasmine prayed for all of them, but mostly for Pastor Pete. She realized now he was the third one referenced in her prophecy, the one at Zion's Hill that Satan asked to sift like wheat.

But that was all behind them now. *Pete repented,* she prayed. *Let him understand he is 100% forgiven. Let him feel no guilt. Let him feel no shame. Let him know his sins are forgotten. He's washed, white as snow.*

The truth was, Pete was no different that herself, or anyone else for that matter. *We all fall short of God's expectation,* she said to herself. *But Jesus didn't die for nothing. He sacrificed himself so we could receive forgiveness.*

Praise God!

***

Jason gasped and sat up. The first thing he noticed was the red light, which tinted everything the color of blood. All the bare bulbs were broken, and the puddled floor was littered with glass, pieces of ceiling, staples, and exposed lengths of electrical wiring.

The wet wiring no longer sizzled. The circuit was shorted out.

Somewhere unseen, an emergency generator hummed. The crimson emergency lighting it powered was harsh and disturbing.

He shivered and shook the water from his clothes and hair, but it was a pointless effort. The sprinklers were still raining down. The hallway was submerged in an inch or two of water.

Seth lay next to him, against the exit door. He wasn't moving.

***

The fog crowded in once more, thicker than ever. Jasmine hated it because its origins were less than Godly.

She continued praying. She didn't know what else to do.

But her prayers became labored. The fog pressed on her, trying to cloud her thoughts – trying to disrupt her efforts.

"No!" she shouted at it.

Everyone else looked at her. "Keep praying!" she yelled. "Whatever happens, don't stop praying. There is power in prayer. It's all we can do now!"

She doubled her efforts and the fog backed away just a bit.

***

Jason shook Seth.

No response.

Seth was whiter than a sheet. His eyes were partially closed. Drool dripped from his chin. As far as Jason could tell, he wasn't breathing. He placed his fingers along Seth's carotid artery. *No pulse.*

It looks like your brother has abandoned you, he heard the demons say.

Jason grabbed Seth by the shoulders and shook him. No response.

It looks like you're the only one left, the demons taunted.

Hearing them in his head created a surge of terror within him. He turned and faced the shadows, shaking like a leaf.

The demons emerged from the shadows, towering over him, pushing against what remained of the hallway's ceiling. Jason's heart sank.

"Wake up!" he shouted.

But Seth didn't move.

The Spirits taunted him. *Wake up. Save me. Please...*

Jason had trouble creating coherent thoughts. Plus, he hadn't practiced CPR since high school, and then only on a practice manikin. Regardless, he started in on Seth.

The demons spoke. *If your brother dies, then the prophecy will remain unfulfilled.*

He wasn't sure if he was doing it right or wrong – he couldn't remember. He alternated between chest compressions and clearing the airway and blowing into Seth's lungs.

And if the prophecy remains unfulfilled, then you are of no use to us.

He looked up. They surrounded him. The deepness of their darkness blocked out much of the blood-red light. Any residual light that did manage to filter through was sickly and thin.

"Seth! Wake up! Please, wake up!"

***

Maxine sat on the ground, leaning against the door – praying. That's when she heard shouting. "Seth! Wake up! Please, wake up!"

Seth? Seth!

She tried the door. It was still locked.

"Seth!" She pounded the door in a frenzy, breaking nails and bruising knuckles.

Someone grabbed her from behind, wrapping strong arms around her, pinning her limbs to her side.

She clawed at whoever held her. They were pulling her away from the door. *Away from Seth!*

Her hands were red with the other's blood. She kept on clawing, but nothing changed.

Jasmine was in front of her now. She grabbed Maxine, one hand on each cheek. "Look at me, Maxine," she yelled. "You're only hurting yourself. That door isn't opening until whatever is holding it lets go."

Maxine went limp, sobbing. The one holding her let go. She turned toward him. It was Pete. His arms were streaked red.

She picked his flesh from under her remaining nails. "I'm sorry."

He smiled. "I forgive you."

And that was that.

***

The demons hissed in Jason's mind. *Your brother is dead,* they uttered with great relish.

He felt the pressure of them. They pushed down on him as he mourned the loss of his brother.

He looked down at Seth as he sat with him on the floor. He cradled his brother's head in his lap. Already, the body was growing cold.

My brother is dead.

It no longer mattered that the prophecy would go unfulfilled. It no longer mattered that the demons had no use for him any longer. It didn't even matter that they would likely torture him to death.

Nothing mattered now because he finally knew the truth. *Jesus is my Lord and Savior.* That's all that mattered.

"Why did you come back for me?" he moaned "You shouldn't have come back!" he shouted at Seth's body. "I'm not worth it. I'm not worth anything."

Very true, the demons chided. *You are truly worthless.*

He collapsed beside his brother, crying bitterly. *I'm so sorry. This is all my fault.* The weight of those thoughts had the strength of a steel trap.

You are a complete disappointment to us, the demons shouted at him as they pushed into his personal space.

"I'm so sorry," Jason blubbered.

The demons laughed. *We accept results, not apologies.*

"I wasn't apologizing to you," Jason looked at them, enraged.
Such insolence! they screamed.

Jason was done fearing his demons. He took his stand. "I am apologizing to my brother, and to my Shepherd, Jesus Christ!"

Don't speak that name! the demons shrieked.

They skittered back to the shadows of the hallway, the corners where the red emergency lights shone dimmest. Their green eyes emblazoned with hatred. *Don't ever speak that name!*

Jason stood up. His legs wobbled, lost integrity and he leaned against the door, but he stood against them nonetheless. "I will follow you no longer! I follow the God of my brother. I follow Jesus!"

In the silence of that moment, Jason heard a cough. It came from near his feet.

He looked down in disbelief. Seth gasped, coughed again and inhaled a lung full of air.

Then Seth opened his eyes. It was a miracle.

***

All was still in the lobby of Zion's Hill. The congregation was deep in silent prayer. Outside, the fog swirled angrily, but none inside the church noticed. They all had their eyes closed and heads bowed.

Then something strange happened. They all opened their eyes at the exact same time. They all heard the voice, "I follow Jesus!" and knew something important had happened.

***

Outside the warehouse, Amanda and the others stood still as stone. "Did you hear that?" The others nodded. "Did you hear that?" she said again.

"Yes," Pete answered.

I follow Jesus. Those words had power.

In that moment, the fog began to thin.

***

Every member of the Kinship quaked in fear. Despite being alone in their rooms, the voice was heard. "I follow Jesus!"

They all knew the voice. It was their High Priest. *Such blasphemy!*

That name was torture. Still, a few wondered if it was time to change sides. *Would the gods of Zion's Hill allow it?*

For most of the Kinship though, they lived lives that excluded mercy and assumed their enemies lived by that same code. They started fashioning their bedsheets into ropes and then searched their quarters for sturdy ceiling supports.

***

Seth opened his eyes and sat up. The red light hurt his eyes. He squinted against it.

At first his thoughts were hazy. *Why am I all wet? Why does my head hurt? Why does my body hurt?*

The minute he saw Jason standing beside him, he scooted away in fear. But then he remembered…

You saw the Shepherd. I was distraught because I wasn't permitted to go with you, but only viewed the expanse from a distance.

Seth had a visitor while he'd waited for Jason in the tunnel. "Do not be afraid," the angel said. "This is not your time to enter the great expanse and approach the judgement throne where the glory of God shines forever and ever."

He wanted to ask the angel so many things. But his tongue was tied in its presence.

The angel said, "Mercy has been given to your brother. He will be given the same choice you were given."

Seth remembered bowing to the angel in worship and receiving a quick rebuke. "Do not worship me," the angel said. "I am only a servant just as you are. Worship God alone."

With those words, the angel vanished, and Seth woke up in the hallway beside his brother.

Jason appeared fearful, standing there shaking. Back in the hallway's corners where the red light was dimmest, something moved – a shadow, or a shadow of a shadow. *The Kinship's demons!*

They stared out from the shadows, their green eyes glowing with rage.

"You're alive?" Jason shouted. "Thank God, you're alive!"

"Barely," Seth answered, his voice barely audible.

"You're alive!" Jason said again. "I can't believe the CPR worked."

Seth spoke quietly, rubbing his temples to ease his pain. "CPR? You saved me?"

Jason smiled. "Of course. You're my brother."

Jason reached down and helped Seth to his feet. He stood like a newborn fawn, using the doorway at his back for support. "Why are the demons hiding?" Seth inquired. "Why don't they attack us?"

"I think they're afraid."

The shadows shifted angrily at that accusation.

Seth took one step and moaned with pain. His nerves were fried. "We can barely stand. What could they possibly be afraid of?"

"They're afraid of us. And they're afraid of the prophecy." Jason glared at them as they shifted and flowed along the corners of the hallway.

Seth grew wary. "I told you before, and I'll say it again: I will never join you."

Jason smiled. "The prophecy, like all of the demons' lies, holds a bit of truth. I'm not asking you to join me. The prophecy never says you have to join me, but only that we join each other. I am joining with you."

With those words, it clicked. Seth understood.

Jason announced in a loud voice, "Like you Seth, I follow Jesus!"

A blinding light filled the hallway. It overpowered the red light. It overcame the shadows in the corners. It purified everything.

For a brief moment, Seth thought he heard shrieking. Then only silence – deep silence.

***

Outside, the door to the warehouse blew open so hard it ripped free from its hinges. A hurricane wind followed it out of the hallway, howling like – well, like demons. With the wind, came a blindingly white light, brighter than a spotlight aimed point-blank at one's face.

Pete ducked just in time, avoiding the flying door by inches. He turned and watched it sail away through the fog as if it were made of paper mâché. Somewhere, hidden by the mist, it clattered to the ground. By the time he turned back, the light was already fading.

Those with him all stared into the hallway with dazed looks and dropped jaws. The silence was absolute.

As the white light faded, it was replaced by a red glow. The red was much duller than the previous white, and less easy on the eyes.

Pete recognized it immediately as emergency lighting. *The electrical system must have malfunctioned at some point.*

With the white light gone, so did the silence. He heard birds. They were singing their morning tune. He turned to look.

The fog was no more. The sun was rising.

"Look!" Jacobson shouted. He pointed into the hallway.

"Be careful!" Jasmine yelled. And they all took a step away.

Something moved in the dimness of that red-lit hallway. And it was coming toward them. *What now?* Was Pete's only thought.

The shadow-thing crept toward the open doorway. Without a door to close, there was no way to keep whatever it was inside.

The thing approached the entrance slowly, leaning against the side of the hallway – slithering along its wall.

"Seth?" Maxine mumbled and then screamed, "Seth!"

She ran into the hallway. Pete knew this was unwise. *It could be a trick!*

A moment later, Maxine emerged. She had two beaten up brothers around her arms.

"It's a miracle!" Jasmine exclaimed. "Thank you, sweet Jesus, Thank you!"

Jacobson and Amanda ran to them and began to help. In one strange mass, they all stumbled into the morning light.

"We need to get you to a doctor," Jasmine said.

Indeed, they were worse for wear. Yet, both the brothers had smiles stretching across their faces.

"The demons are gone for good," one of the twins said.

Praise Jesus, was all Pete could think.

EPILOGUE

Inside the warehouse were dead bodies – all of them victims of suicide (with the exception of Cain's body, who died at Jacobson's hand). These were those that regretted their allegiance, but could not fathom the idea that a forgiving God was waiting for them if they only repented and put their trust in Him.

On the brighter side, some of the Kinship did not kill themselves, but came to believe. They eventually joined Zion's Hill or other churches. These were those who came to understand that Jesus can wash away all wrongs no matter how deep or how awful those wrongs were.

As for Pete, he did offer his resignation, but Zion's Hill would not accept it. They contended that they were no better than he was. Any one of them could have fallen prey to such powerful temptation. The congregation's only requirement was that Pete repentant, know he was forgiven, and promise to continue in his position as pastor of Zion's Hill.

Amanda went into rehab, got clean, and spent her time rebuilding a relationship with her two sons. She also joined Zion's Hill and was baptized in the name of the Father, Son, and Holy Spirit.

Jason renounced his past. He understood now that there's no such thing as good spirits. There's only God and his angels vs. Lucifer and his demons. All other perceptions are only deceptions of a sly enemy.

Jacobson also went into treatment for addiction. He now spends his days helping others get off the streets. He preaches the gospel boldly, at every opportunity, and on every street corner.

Jasmine, despite her age, didn't take much of a break after the warehouse incident. She organized prayer marches and entered neighborhoods housing enemy strongholds. And through her efforts, many of those bastions of the enemy came crashing down and many more souls came to know salvation.

Maxine and Seth grew even happier in their marriage. They had children. They had each other. They had God.

They had everything they needed.

ABOUT THE AUTHOR

Shawn Brink (writing under Shawn D. Brink and Shawn David Brink) resides in Eastern Nebraska, U.S.A., and is represented by Liverman Literary Agency. He's building a following with a growing list of novels (mainly speculative fiction), as well as shorter works published in various publications and anthologies.

Check out his website to learn more:
https://shawnbrinkauthor.wordpress.com/.

Also, Shawn posts (formerly Tweets) at @shawnbrinkauth2.

***

Milton Keynes UK
Ingram Content Group UK Ltd.
UKHW031324181124
451360UK00017B/1846